FIRST SKIRMISH

Without warning, Chloe found herself in Edmund's arms, being kissed with considerable skill.

Still her tone stayed cool as she declared, "Since it is inconceivable that you have formed an uncontrollable passion for me in so short a span of time, I can only conclude that this is your customary conduct toward any female stupid enough to be private with you. Be assured that I shall take care not to repeat my error."

Edmund's crestfallen face reassured Chloe that she could keep this gallant in check. But her feelings of safety lasted but a little while . . .

. . . until she met Edmund's elder brother, Ivor, Earl of Montrose, and sensed that her struggle to preserve her virtue had only just begun. . . .

DOROTHY MACK is a native New Englander, born in Rhode Island and educated at Brown and Harvard universities. While living in Massachusetts with her husband and four young sons, she began to combine a longtime interest in English history with her desire to write, and emerged as an author of Regency romances. The family now resides in northern Virginia, where Dorothy continues to pursue both interests.

The Courtship of Chloe

by

Dorothy Mack

A SIGNET BOOK

SIGNET
Published by the Penguin Group
Penguin Books USA Inc., 375 Hudson Street,
New York, New York, 10014, U.S.A.
Penguin Books Ltd, 27 Wrights Lane, London W8 5TZ, England
Penguin Books Australia Ltd, Ringwood, Victoria, Australia
Penguin Books Canada Ltd, 10 Alcorn Avenue, Toronto, Ontario, Canada M4V 3B2
Penguin Books (N.Z.) Ltd, 182-190 Wairau Road,
Auckland 10, New Zealand

Penguin Books Ltd, Registered Offices:
Harmondsworth, Middlesex, England

First published by Signet, an imprint of New American Library,
a division of Penguin Books USA Inc.

First Printing, September, 1992

10 9 8 7 6 5 4 3 2 1

Chapter One

"LEAVING TOMORROW! But you have been at Applewood scarcely a sennight!"

The words rang with protest, matching the dismay in Lady Montrose's deep blue eyes, but this flattering reluctance to part with her guest apparently cut little ice with the woman sitting across the tea table from her hostess. Lady Dalrymple did indeed pause in her intention to raise a delicate porcelain cup to her lips, but there was no softening of her resolute expression.

"I have been here for twelve days to be precise, Elvira, and I warned you at the outset of my visit that I must leave by the seventeenth in order to allow ample time to reach Lavering Manor before Millicent expects to be confined."

"Oh, but first babies are notoriously dilatory in arriving. I am persuaded you may safely remain here another week or even a fortnight and still be present at the birth."

"Not being gifted with your medical intuition, I fear I shall have to rely on the information provided by the doctor in this case to govern my travel plans," Lady Dalrymple countered.

The dryness of her reply was not lost upon her sister, whose eyes flickered briefly, but Lady Montrose was not one to abandon a design without exhausting every possible avenue to its achievement. "Millicent is a sensible girl," she said persuasively, "not one to go to pieces should her mother not be at her *accouchement*. She would not begrudge me your company for a little longer."

"Millicent may not, but I have every intention of being on the spot when my first grandchild is ushered into the world. What is behind this sudden passion for my society, anyway, when you have managed very nicely without it for nearly thirty years?"

Recognizing the finality in her sister's argument, Lady Montrose allowed her mouth to fall into a discontented droop for a moment before she summoned up a martyred sigh. "I had counted on your assistance with the planning of Mary's party next month," she admitted.

Lady Dalrymple stared at her sister across the rim of her teacup with one eyebrow elevated above the other. "Since when has one of society's most indefatigable hostesses required the assistance of a country stay-at-home to plan a party?" she asked in honest amazement. "Let Mary help with the details. It is her party, after all."

This practical suggestion evidently did not recommend itself to the countess, whose mouth tightened into a thin line before she sighed again and spread her open hands in a gesture that seemed to express an uncharacteristic helplessness. "The wretched girl refuses to lift a finger to help," she said. "She has removed herself mentally from all the planning for the pre-wedding festivities. You cannot have failed to observe her sulks in the time you have been here."

Lady Dalrymple, who had been sitting upright, put her empty cup down on the railed tea table and sat back in her chair, her face thoughtful. "Certainly I have noticed that Mary has not been in spirits while I have been at Applewood," she acknowledged, selecting her words with care, "but that might have been a natural result of the separation from her fiancé since your return from London." Alert dark eyes asked the question that delicacy forbade her lips from forming.

Lady Montrose made a small shrugging motion with one shapely shoulder. "It would be idle to pretend that this is a match made in heaven, but then, not the most doting parent could claim that Mary was one of last Season's successes. I am aware that she does not possess her sister's beauty, but she is well-looking enough, and I saw to it that she made the most of her physical assets. Her eyes are not a brilliant blue but they are large and well opened, and her hair, though an undistinguished beige color, grows quite prettily into a natural wave. I put her in the hands of the best hairdresser in London and oversaw every detail of her wardrobe personally. There was nothing to fault in her appearance, but would the chit make the slightest push to attach any of the men who approached her initially? Not she! I swear to you, Augusta, one would have t hought her dull-witted, so inert and insipid did she contrive to appear, with never a word to say for herself in company. Despite the sizable portion her father settled on her and the generous sum Ivor made available to rig her out in a manner befitting her station, Thrale's was the only offer she received.''

''And so you compelled her to accept Lord Thrale?''

''Nothing of the kind,'' snapped the countess, bristling at this accusation. ''There was no hint of coercion. It is true that she was inclined to refuse at first on the grounds that she was not in love with Lord Thralle, but I pointed out that ''falling in love,'' as it is vulgarly termed, is an emotional phenomenon that is indulged in almost exclusively by the lower orders of society—at least insofar as it applies to choosing a marriage partner. In any case, the sort of attachment a young girl hopes to feel for her husband cannot possibly exist before marriage, as I have told her repeatedly. It would be different if Mary had taken Thrale in irremediable dislike, but she allowed that she had nothing against the young man personally. She agreed that there was nothing in his character or manners that would mitigate against his becoming a most satisfactory husband and conceded that she had not known him long enough to develop any of the more tender feelings toward him. Finally, she concurred that the fact that she is a year older than most of the other girls this Season, owing to her father's untimely death last year just before her scheduled come-out, would put her at an even greater disadvantage next year. It was entirely her own decision to accept Thrale's offer, but it would appear now that she may be having second thoughts and encouraging romantic regrets about not having contracted a so-called 'love match.' Her sister did that, and look where it got *her*. If there is any creature on earth more disposed to act against its own best interest than a young girl with her head stuffed full of romantic notions, I am sure I do not know what it may be.''

Lady Dalrymple had been listening with complete concentration to her sister's version of Mary's betrothal. Familiar from old with Elvira's unfailing habit of representing all situations in the light that reflected best on her own actions, she could envision the amount of unrelenting pressure that must have been brought to bear on the girl, but to appear to sympathize too openly with her niece would be to produce a deepening of Elvira's sense of ill-usage and result in no benefit to Mary.

"Have you questioned Mary about her mopishness?" she asked, keeping the inquiry carefully neutral.

"You may be sure I have done no such thing," the countess replied smartly. "It is so long ago now that you may not remember, but before Patricia succumbed to that disastrous piece of folly ten years ago"—which description Lady Dalrymple had no difficulty in recognizing as alluding to her elder niece's marriage—"she was all but formally engaged to Lord Cathcart, which would have been a brilliant match. She too seemed to fall suddenly into a sustained fit of the dismals, and when I tried to get to the bottom of it, she confessed that she had fallen in love with that impossible Frenchman and begged her father and me to refuse Cathcart. Nothing we could say to her about Emile Robert's lack of fortune or family could budge her from her decision to have him. When I remember the tears and hysterics"—Lady Montrose shuddered delicately—"before we finally recognized that she was so dazzled by a handsome face as to be beyond the reach of reason! We were forced to take her away from town, but as you know, it was too late to save the situation."

"She eloped with her Frenchman and caused a minor scandal," Lady Dalrymple finished for her. "That is ancient history. We were speaking of Mary, not Patricia. The girls are very different in temperament."

"It is true that Mary does not possess Patricia's willfulness and volatility. She has always been a placid, biddable girl, which is precisely why I mistrust this present moodiness of hers. One would think that the disastrous results of her sister's rebellion would keep her from contemplating any similar rashness, but one never knows with young girls, so I have resolved not to dignify her sulks with the least notice."

"As far as past history is concerned, I would term Patricia's case tragic rather than disastrous. Who could foresee that Emile Roberts would die so young? That the marriage itself was a success I could see from their brief visit to me two years ago."

"How can you say this?" Lady Montrose turned astonished eyes on her sister's face. "Always scraping and striving to put a good face on things all these years, but in the end he left her nearly penniless. If she had married Cathcart she would be a marchioness and the mistress of one of the finest estates in the country today instead of being reduced to living off her brother's charity."

"I do not believe Patricia ever regretted her choice, Elvira, and Ivor is more than willing to shelter his sister and his niece permanently at Applewood."

Lady Montrose gave a dismissing wave of one white hand. "As to that, Patricia is still young enough to marry again once she has done with this excessive parade of grief. I have one or two ideas in that direction for the future."

"She loved her husband deeply, Elvira, and he was taken from her. Naturally she grieves. It is less than a year since it happened." A shade of protest colored Lady Dalrymple's quiet words, but her sister brushed this aside.

"Do you call it natural to shut herself away in her room for days on end, refusing even to come down to meals? Is it natural to refuse to see old friends when they come to call, or to dash out of the room in tears at the merest mention of that man's name or an inadvertent reference to the past, or even to the future? I can only term such unbridled grief excessive after ten months. And she is ruining her looks!"

"I must agree that Patricia does not look at all well these days, apart from her 'looks.' Her color is bad, she is far too thin, and obviously lives on her nerves. Can you not encourage her to return to her music? I remember how devoted she was to the piano before her marriage. It would do her good to find a release. And she seems to take no interest in Emilie at all. My heart breaks for that poor child."

"Unfortunately our old nurse died last year, but the child is well looked after by a woman Ivor found in the village," said the countess, dismissing her grandchild to return to her daughter. "Patricia refuses to take an interest in anything. I have repeatedly asked her to play for us after dinner, but she turns that vacant stare on me and says she cannot. I tried to enlist her aid in planning Mary's party, but she burst into tears and hid away in her room for two days. Even Ivor can get nothing out of her but monosyllables these days, and you know they were closer than most brothers and sisters growing up. I am at my wits' end, and with Mary's wedding coming closer—well, you see why I am so distressed at your leaving this soon.''

"Yes . . ." Lady Dalrymple replied, drawing the word out slowly. "I believe you do need someone to help you at Applewood. Order some more tea, Elvira, and let me think for a moment.''

Lady Montrose complied with this request. As Hawkins, the butler, cleared away the used tea things, her hopeful gaze never left her sister's face. Lady Dalrymple sat perfectly still in her chair, her left elbow resting on the arm of the chair, her chin cupped in her hand, and a frown of concentration gathered on her brow.

Waiting anxiously for the result of this weighty cogitation, Lady Montrose could not help but note the considerable amount of gray in the knot of hair showing beneath Augusta's ruffled muslin cap and the matronly proportions of her form, encased in folds of stiff purple cotton. No one would ever take them for sisters, she reflected with simple satisfaction, aware of her own slim elegance in a soft gown of periwinkle-blue silk, nor could the sharpest eye discern that she was actually the elder by more than two years. Augusta had really let herself go to seed, buried alive in the wilds of Yorkshire, and by her own choice. Even when they were girls she had displayed very little interest in fashion or personal adornment, declaring blithely that since her sole claim to beauty lay in the size and brilliance of her dark eyes and the luxurious thickness of her long lashes, which needed no enhancement, she might as well forget about fashions and beauty creams. She eschewed the attentions of hairdressers for the most part and settled for comfortable clothes in which to enjoy whatever pleasures came her way. As far as Lady Montrose could tell from intermittent and sporadic contacts with her sister since her marriage, Augusta had never deviated from this early position, remaining unperturbed and unfettered by the demands of changing fashion over the years. Despite her plainness, she had captured the heart of a previously resistant and very eligible peer during her first season and had happily turned her back on London society for the next twenty-five years, emerging from her hermitage only when it was time to launch her only daughter. Millicent too, though no beauty, had sailed successfully through her come-out, achieving a desirable alliance within a month of her first appearance at Almack's. Really, the unmerited good fortune of some people passed all understanding—not that she begrudged her sister or her niece theirs, of course.

When Hawkins returned to the small drawing room bringing fresh tea, Lady Dalrymple's abstracted expression cleared and she focused her remarkably fine eyes on her sister's expectant face. "Since you are resolved on this big party and the girls are not disposed to be helpful, you are going to require a temporary social secretary, as it were, someone to run your errands and help with the invitations and such. Is there anyone in the village whose services you could hire for a few weeks?"

The countess looked a reproof at her sister's indiscreet tongue in the presence of a servant and waited until Hawkins had left the room before she replied. "Well, there is that Bateman woman who has been complaining that she misses her youngest daughter, but she writes a wretched hand and her tongue is hinged at both ends. She would drive me to distraction within a sennight, apart from the fear of having our affairs discussed all over the village."

"Could one of the younger women or girls in the neighborhood spare you a few hours a day for a while?"

"I won't have any giddy young misses in my house while Ned is here," Lady Montrose said sharply. "My plans for him do not include an alliance with any of the local families."

"Or Ivor either, I presume?"

Lady Montrose delivered herself of a ladylike snort halfway between amusement and exasperation. "Ivor, I fear, is immune to feminine charms, at least to those embodied in women of his own class, which is an additional reason to steer Ned into a good match."

"Heavens, Elvira, Ivor is not yet thirty! Is that not a bit early to write him off as a confirmed misogynist?"

"Perhaps, but you have been here long enough to discern the cold nature beneath his surface charm and impeccable manners. It is my belief that he dislikes women," his mother

stated coolly. "But we were not speaking of Ivor but my
problems in the next few weeks," she reminded her gaping
sister. "I hoped for a moment that you had come up with a
solution."

"Well, I think perhaps I have," Lady Dalrymple replied,
readjusting her mental focus once more. "If you would not
object to paying her coach fare, I believe I might persuade my
godchild, Chloe Norris, to come and act as your right arm for
the interim. Being a doctor's daughter, she is a very sensible
and practical young woman and she seems to have a knack for
getting things accomplished. She is very well educated and
writes a beautiful hand. She has been her father's hostess,
medical assistant, and housekeeper since her mother died, but
Reggie, her father, has found a locum to take his place while
he goes up to Scotland for the grouse hunting this year. I was
planning to stop on my way to Lavering Manor and take Chloe
with me just for a change of scene, but matters really do seem
to be getting into a coil here. I think you will find Chloe a
godsend."

Lady Montrose had heard her sister out in silence, frowning
a little at the catalog of her unknown Miss Norris's virtues, and
now she said, "I take it your goddaughter is a *plain* young
woman, Augusta?"

Lady Dalrymple looked surprised. "Why, no. I think her
quite attractive in a subtle fashion. Chloe may not be instantly
eye-catching, but her looks grow on one the longer one knows
her."

"The point is, I don't wish them to grow on Ned," came
the tart rejoinder. "I told you, Augusta, I won't have a good-
looking young woman around the house making eyes at my
sons."

"Oh, that won't be a problem. Did I forget to mention that
Chloe is betrothed?"

Lady Montrose, her expression considering, began to pour
out the fresh tea.

No one would take them for sisters, Lady Dalrymple conceded
with wry acceptance as her eyes followed the graceful
movements of Elvira's smooth, long-fingered white hands
around the tea tray. She glanced down at the prominent blue

veins in her own blunt-fingered hands with their short nails and sighed inwardly. Feature for feature, Elvira had certainly gotten the better of the distribution of physical characteristics handed down in the family. She it was who had inherited their mother's golden hair and sapphire eyes as well as their father's narrow straight nose, while her own fine brown eyes were scarcely a compensation for limp mouse-colored hair and a broad, *retroussé* nose. In build too, Elvira had emerged the decided winner with her tall, slender yet feminine figure. Short and squat was the combination that sprang to mind to describe her own stature in her late forties, though she had been delicately built as a girl. Ah well, at least she had kept her husband contented for more than a quarter of a century, which must count for something. She simply did not possess Elvira's heroic self-discipline and grim determination to hold back the ravages of time. She picked up her cup and reached for another biscuit.

Two days later Lady Dalrymple was again sipping tea, this time in the sunny small parlor in the modest villa belonging to Dr. Reginald Norris. The doctor was her sole companion at the moment, for a domestic crisis had taken her goddaughter to the nether regions a few moments before, leaving her to pour out. Noting the speculative gleam in the doctor's eyes as he accepted his cup, she chided herself for being too voluble and promptly took a gulp of tea. It was too hot and she sputtered a bit.

Dr. Norris leaned over and nudged the milk jug closer to her hand before sitting back at his ease once more. "You seem rather eager to consign my daughter to a term of domestic servitude, Augusta," he observed. "I thought Chloe mentioned after your last letter arrived that you had invited her to accompany you to Lavering Manor. My memory must be failing me."

"Wretch! You know it isn't," she confessed, trying to decide how much to confide in the man who had married her dearest friend in the teeth of fierce parental objection and taken her away from the world into which she had been born in order to share his life of constant service to his small community. Until the day she died Helen Norris had never voiced a single regret over

14   *Dorothy Mack*

her decision to eschew her former life with its multitude of diversions and unceasing round of social exchange. Lady Dalrymple had always respected the tall, broad-shouldered man with the riveting strength of purpose shining out of him, and over the years she had come to know and appreciate not just his erudition and capacity for hard work but the vast understanding and tolerance for all mankind that was revealed in the quiet humor that was intrinsic to his nature. They had not met often, but she could not recall ever seeing him at a loss in any situation. Such strength and competence must be a great comfort to all whose lives he touched. She raised her eyes to see a hint of amusement lurking in his steady gaze now as he waited for her to explain herself.

"Reggie, how do you feel about Chloe's betrothal?"

"I wondered if that situation had any bearing on this sudden shift of yours," he replied. "Frankly, it has gone on too long for me to be sanguine about it any longer, though I have said nothing to Chloe on the subject."

"Five years does seem rather . . . protracted."

"Ridiculous is what it is at this point. She was only eighteen when she accepted Bertram Otley. He seemed a solid, decent young man, and I had no legitimate objections at the time, especially since his ship was sailing shortly and there would be time to discover if she had any second thoughts about contracting to marry a man whom she had known for only a few weeks and one whose career would mean long absences from home."

"How did they meet?"

"Otley came to visit some relatives in the district. She met him at their home. There was really no one suitable in our small circle here, and with her mother in failing health Chloe had refused your kind offer to bring her out with Millicent. She seemed very taken with young Otley at the time, but he went off and she became deeply involved in caring for Helen during her last illness. The young people had not gotten around to actually setting a date for their marriage when Helen died. After her mourning period was over Chloe continued to postpone the wedding, I believe out of concern for my welfare, for a considerable time, and I am ashamed to say that I was selfish enough to accept the sacrifice for too long. For the last couple of years, though, it has been my impression that it is Otley who is dragging his feet. His letters have grown fewer and farther apart over the years, and she has only seen him twice since Helen's death. Whatever they felt for each other once must have worn iself out by now through lack of nourishment. The arrangement, I venture to say, is no more than a habit at this point. It is a thoroughly unsatisfactory situation.''

"I had reached more or less the same conclusion myself— oh, not from anything Chloe has said,'' Lady Dalrymple explained when the doctor's thick brows ascended, ''but from what she didn't say. She barely mentions her fiancé's existence in the letters we have exchanged in the last few years. Millicent says the same. She is not getting any younger, Reggie. Life is passing her by.''

"I know this and I am most criminally at fault for not bringing matters to a head before now,'' agreed Dr. Norris, his rather austere features somewhat more drawn than usual.

"I had Chloe's interests more in the front of my mind than my sister's when I proposed that she lend that hapless household the benefit of her practical talents for a few weeks,'' Lady Dalrymple went on, aware that she had her listener's rapt attention by now. ''It will be good for her to have a complete change of scene, to go among strangers. It will stimulate her mental faculties,'' she improvised in an attempt to add as many incentives as it might take to secure the doctor's permission.

"Chloe is not accustomed to associating with the aristocracy in general, Augusta, and I must tell you that I am not keen on her going to Applewood in the nebulous role of some kind of upper servant, a position in which she is likely to be patronized.''

"It is understood that she is a lady. Naturally she will dine with the family. There will be many visitors and guests during this period, and she will help to entertain them almost as another daughter of the family.''

"Please do not mistake that I could ever undervalue my lovely daughter, Augusta, but you are beside the bridge if you are expecting that some gallant sprig of the nobility will come galloping up to your sister's home and sweep Chloe off her feet and into a splendid marriage. And if through some kind of arcane feminine sorcery this remote possibility should actually seem to be coming to fruition, I must remind you that my daughter considers herself promised to Captain Otley.''

''Yes, of course. In which case, there will be absolutely no harm done and Chloe will have had an interesting new experience. All experience is to be valued, do you not agree?''

''I do indeed.'' Dr. Norris's expression matched hers in bland innocence except for a telltale gleam of amusement in his dark eyes which she prudently chose to ignore.

''You do indeed what, Papa?''

This pert question accompanied the entrance into the room of the subject of their discussion, thus effectively bringing it to an end.

''I do welcome a break in my reading about this time of day,'' Dr. Norris replied, smiling up at his daughter as she placed a hand on his shoulder before slipping past him to seat herself beside her godmother on the sofa.

''I talked myself dry restoring peace in the kitchen and am perishing for my tea,'' Chloe declared gaily, accepting the cup Lady Dalrymple had prepared for her.

Her eyes roving over the bright face of her goddaughter, Lady Dalrymple was glad that she had not tried to deceive her sister about Chloe's attractions. When the young woman's face flashed into that all-over smile, her quiet good looks were elevated into startling beauty. At least Elvira could never accuse Chloe of flaunting her attributes. Her quite remarkable hair was always worn neatly coiled and affixed to the back of her head, and the plain dark dress she was wearing was a prime example of her typical attire whenever her godmother had seen her in the last few years. When Millicent had taken her friend to task for neglecting her appearance after her betrothal, she reported that Chloe had claimed that her frequent occupation as her father's asistant demanded dark practical clothing.

As Chloe made an amusing tale of the recent domestic dispute, Lady Dalrymple listened with only half an ear while she racked her brain trying to think of some way to ensure that her goddaughter should have at least one pretty dress to wear at Applewood. There was no time to have anything made up before she set off even if she could persuade Chloe to accept a gift, which was doubtful when her birthday was months away. If there were an abigail or dressmaker from whom she could obtain the girl's measurements she could have something made and sent on to Applewood later, but such was not the case. Lady Dalrymple had reluctantly conceded the impossibility of enhancing Chloe's appearance during her stay with Elvira's family when it came to her in a flash that Millicent and Chloe were nearly of a size. She would wait until she got to Lavering Manor and enlist her daughter's assistance in providing her goddaughter with at least one ravishing gown for the festivities scheduled to take place at the Montrose estate.

This much resolved in her own mind, Lady Dalrymple turned her attention, not for the first time, to the situation at Applewood, debating with herself how much or little to tell Chloe about the complexities in the relationships obtaining in her sister's family. Her first impulse had been to prepare the girl for the undercurrents so she would not blunder in her dealings with the various temperaments with which she would be dwelling temporarily. The carriage ride to the pretty village where the Norrises lived had provided hours in which to reconsider this impulse, however, and she'd almost decided to let her goddaughter arrive at Applewood without the burden of preconceived ideas about the people she would meet, as if she were indeed a totally disinterested person coming among strangers to do a specific job of work. If Chloe's influence on the unhappy souls at Applewood was to be beneficial at all, let it happen naturally. This tentative decision had not been reached without a few qualms on Chloe's behalf at leaving her so unprepared for crosscurrents, but she quashed them firmly. When the young woman had asked in all innocence about the family to whom she would be lending her services as a social secretary, Lady Dalrymple had done no more than list the inhabitants and their familial relationship to her sister, keeping open the option of elaborating on her description before she departed for Lavering Manor. Now as she watched her goddaughter smilingly parry some teasing remark from her father, the affection between them readily apparent, Lady Dalrymple concluded for good or ill that she would let matters

stand. She would trust to Chloe's balanced and generous nature
and her sunny sanity to guide her safely through the upcoming
ordeal.

"Yes, thank you, my dear, I believe I will have another slice
of that delicious plum cake," she said, beaming at her young
hostess.

Chapter Two

MISS CHLOE NORRIS sat in her corner of the stagecoach staring fixedly out of the window. The landscape through which they were passing was not of a scenic splendor to warrant such dedication, but this was the only alternative to allowing herself to be used as an arbiter in the hearty argument being conducted by the other two passengers remaining in the stage, a garrulous mother and daughter traveling together to visit relatives outside of Woodbridge. Miss Norris had learned their destination and a great deal of extraneous detail about their lives and circumstances in the interval since they had boarded at Ipswich, and by now would have found herself arbitrating their quarrel willy-nilly had she not recognized the direction matters were taking in time to employ this last desperate ruse of complete absorption in the scenery. Actually, she admitted with rueful self-knowledge, there existed a third alternative, but she could never bring herself to be deliberately rude or snubbing to well-meaning persons who imposed unconsciously on others. This basic accomplishment seemed to be inherent in the makeup of the fine ladies with whom she had come into contact over the years and was one that would always keep her from being numbered in that category. An unnecessary distinction, to be sure, she added hastily, as her erratic thoughts kept pace with the turning wheels. Her modest circumstances and manner of living were sufficient to preclude her inclusion in any such rarefied group despite a long line of genteel antecedents on both sides of the family.

And therein lay the rub, the small kernel of concern that kept Miss Norris from looking forward to her stay at Applewood with comfortable complacence. It would not have occurred to her to refuse her godmother's request to lend her temporary help to the latter's beleaguered sister, but as the coach rumbled along at its plebian pace, steadily decreasing the distance between her quiet life of assisting her father in his service to

the community that entailed only limited contacts with the landed
gentry, and the gilded world of the aristocracy as personified
in Lady Montrose's family, she experienced a passing qualm
as to how she would fit into the Keeson household. It was to
be expected that the Keesons would find her manners and
outlook unworldly. Except for occasional visits to her
godmother's estate in Yorkshire and one brief sojourn in London
with Millicent and her husband, she had never traveled more
than a few miles from home until today. Nor was she possessed
of any of those drawing-room accomplishments considered
indispensable to a young lady of quality. She neither sang nor
played upon the harp or pianoforte. She had no skill at painting
or sketching and had never had sufficient time or inclination
to pursue any of the various decorative activities such as
découpage or shell work with which ladies of leisure occupied
themselves when such things were in fashion. Like most women
of her class she was proficient with her needle, but even in this
area she was more apt to be engaged in practical household
mendings and makings than in one of the more artistic forms
of stitchery, though she was glad she'd had the foresight to bring
along a piece of embroidery to keep by her to work while among
the Keesons. It would be unnecessary for anyone at Applewood
to know that she had been engaged on the same piece of
fancywork for upward of four years. At the very least it would
serve as a shield or invisible cloak behind which to efface herself
during those moments when her presence might be suddenly
intrusive or awkward in the family circle.

Her eyes indifferent, though still fixed on the flattish terrain
through which they were passing, Miss Norris continued with
her mental inventory, which had been rather lowering to her
self-esteem up to this point. On the positive side, it must be
considered an asset that she was not deficient in conversational
ability. At least, she was able to hold her own among her father's
old Cambridge cronies with whom he kept in contact. Of course,
the sort of conversation that flowed among seeking intellects
of this order and that obtaining in society drawing rooms was
probably vastly different, so she'd best qualify that boast. Miss
Norris stirred uneasily. So far the results of this self-examination
had been to call into question the wisdom of acceding to her

godmother's request that she lend her assistance to her sister's family. It would actually be simpler if no tenuous social connection existed between herself and the Keesons—if the too-solid Lady Dalrymple could ever be described as tenuous, she added with a flash of secret amusement. Better to be paid for doing a job and relegated to the company of the upper servants than to teeter awkwardly on the edge of the family's life, neither guest nor servant.

As the argument swirling around her in the stuffy carriage escalated in vocal violence, Miss Norris administered a meta-phorical kick to her cowardly qualms and sat up straighter. Since she could not change the situation she would simply make the best of it for the few weeks involved. Her fears would probably prove groundless. After all, Lady Montrose was her dear godmama's own sister, and no one could be more considerate than Lady Dalrymple at putting a stranger at ease. In any case, her questionable value as an amusing and entertaining guest was totally irrelevant. It was her practical help that was desired, and she was confident that she would find ways to be useful to Lady Montrose. How glad she was that she had not revealed any of these stupid misgivings to her father when he had brought her to Newmarket to put her on the stage before leaving for his shooting party in Scotland. Not for the world would she dim his pleasure in anticipating this rare break in his working schedule. He had not had a real holiday since her mother's death almost four years ago. She could count on the fingers of one hand the times he had been away from his patients, no more than a night or two in Cambridge with one or another of his old friends. The occasions were few and widely spread despite her routine urgings that he required more leisure to restore his strength. She suspected he was constrained from accepting more frequent invitations out of a natural though misplaced concern for her solitary state during his absence, but he could not be brought to admit this so that she might argue away any of his fears for her safety or comfort.

Chloe's lips curved gently as she pictured her father's face when he had taken leave of her this morning. His cheerful mien had been assumed, she was well aware, to mask the slight disquiet he had not permitted himself to articulate once she had indicated her desire to accommodate Lady Dalrymple in this matter. The understanding between them was very strong, and he had always fostered and respected her independence of mind from earliest childhood. She could not recall a single instance when he had interfered with her considered decision, even if in his greater wisdom he thought the decision one she might later regret. She had learned eventually that willingness to accept the consequences of one's independent actions was a surer sign of maturity than the making of the decision. Her father's unspoken concern for her well-being would always be a source of comfort, and the mere contemplation of it boosted her uneven spirits today. Naturally he would have preferred her to accompany Lady Dalrymple to Lavering Manor, where she would be made royally welcome, and indeed she was sorry not to be sharing the wonderful occasion of the birth of a child with her dearest friend. She had sensed that her godmother felt she could be of real assistance to Lady Montrose, however, and this was an opportunity to reciprocate a little for a lifetime of kindness from Lady Dalrymple. There would be other visits with Millicent's family. Much as she enjoyed being with Millicent and her agreeable spouse, she had to battle through a period of lowered spirits when she returned home to her quiet existence. She *thought* she could say in all honesty that it was not envy that produced this malaise. She did not begrudge her friend one iota of her happiness, but could not deny a sinking feeling that her own future seemed still as far from her grasp as ever. Most of the time she was quite content with her busy life in her childhood home, but a spell of witnessing Millicent's domestic bliss never failed to unsettle her.

It had been over five months since Bertram's last letter. As always his detailed descriptions of the ports at which his ships called made fascinating reading. She had put it in the carved sandalwood box he had brought back to her from Indonesia during the first year of their betrothal. She kept all his letters in that box. There was quite a pile of them by now; the shallow box was nearly filled. Last year she'd had to replace the satin ribbon that bound the letters, it had been retied so often that it had worn and raveled. The new ribbon was still in prime condition. She was rereading Bertram's letters less often these days, perhaps because there was less comfort to be found in the most recent ones. It had been a long time since there had been any sentiments of a gratifying nature to her personally except for a rather routine declaration that he missed her. These days the lyrical passages were reserved for descriptions of foreign places. In the last letter he had not even mentioned when he expected to be back in England again, let alone referred to their marriage. They had not met in two years. Their last planned meeting nearly a year ago had not taken place because Bertram had been given his own ship quite unexpectedly when its captain had died suddenly. He had sailed off again within days of reaching England's shores. Her disappointment at that misfortune had been much more acute than she had been prepared to admit even to her father.

The sweet curve to Miss Norris's mouth had vanished by the time she realized that the coach was approaching what promised to be a town of some size. This would be Woodbridge, where she was being met for the final leg of her journey. Her interest quickened as they rumbled past attractive dwellings, built of red brick for the most part, into the center of the town, which was older, judging from a glimpse of Tudor buildings. Her impressions that Woodbridge was a prosperous town suffered no eclipse as she descended rather stiffly from the coach and looked about her, eagerness replacing the qualms that had rendered the journey somewhat nerve-racking. This was going to be a splendid adventure. Hopefully she would have the opportunity to see something of the countryside while she was in East Anglia.

There were a number of persons milling about in the inn yard, most of them employees going about their various jobs. A noisy group of a half-dozen or so persons of all ages rushing toward her gave Miss Norris pause for a startled second until she comprehended that they were all members of one family come to welcome her fellow passengers, who were bidding her a friendly farewell before being swept into a communal embrace accompanied by many exclamations uttered in a broad Suffolk dialect that was all but incomprehensible to a stranger. Catching the guard's eye as he retrieved her large valise, she pointed to the wall of the inn and followed him, excusing herself with

smiles and gestures as she made her way out of the middle of
the extended family gathering to stand apart while she took her
bearings. Having tipped the accommodating guard, she glanced
around the bustling inn yard looking for some sort of conveyance
that would have been sent from Applewood to fetch her.

A carrier's heavy wagon had just come into the yard, but the
only other vehicle in sight at the moment was an elegant sports
phaeton following in the carrier's wake. Miss Norris was not
unduly concerned to find no one waiting for her. Lady
Dalrymple had sent off a letter to Lady Montrose announcing
her goddaughter's expected time of arrival, but any number of
unforeseen eventualities might account for the seeming mixup.
Or perhaps the stage was a bit early today.

Miss Norris had just sensibly decided that she would wait for
an hour or so before she inquired about hiring a vehicle to
convey her to Applewood when the phaeton pulled up in front
of her. Its driver, a young man whose fashionable dress was
a fitting complement to his dashing carriage, leaned toward her
with a smile.

"Would you be Miss Chloe Norris, ma'am?"

"Why, yes. Are you from Applewood?"

"That's right. Edmund Keeson very much at your service,
Miss Norris. Is that all your baggage, the one valise?"

"Yes, that is it."

As Mr. Keeson turned away from her for a moment to issue
an order to one of the ostlers to tie the valise onto the back of
the carriage, Miss Norris seized the opportunity to compose
her features into an arrangement suitably pleasant to the
occasion. She could only hope that her face hadn't mirrored
her astonishment of being met not by a polite servant but by
a son of the house, and one, moreover, whose spectacular good
looks were guaranteed to set any young lady's pulses flutter-
ing. Apollo, the sun god, must have made just such a first
impression on unwary females as this mortal counterpart. Like
Apollo, Mr. Edmund Keeson possessed a head full of golden
curls, though his were worn in the carefully careless windswept
fashion of the day, as she had seen when he doffed his hat on
identifying himself to her. No Olympian's eyes could be any
bluer or more brilliant than Mr. Keeson's, and his profile was

divinely designed to adorn the most precious coin of the realm. Something in his expression when he had smiled at her told Miss Norris that like the deity he resembled, Mr. Keeson was complacently aware of the effect his appearance produced on the female of the species.

She was treated to the beneficence of another dazzling smile as Mr. Keeson reached down a gloved hand to assist her in climbing into the carriage. She wondered if she detected a hint of speculation in the smiling regard he directed at her as she landed on the seat beside him.

"Well, well," he said softly, his eyes roving appreciatively over her features. "This visit has distinct possibilities after all, despite the Puritan garb. Now, don't poker up, there's a good girl," he added hastily, as Miss Norris stiffened and drew back slightly. "I beg your pardon. I'm afraid I have a deplorable habit of speaking my thoughts without censoring them. You'll get used to it in time. I hope you won't hold it against me?"

"Of course not, Mr. Keeson," she replied, not proof against the charm of his beseeching manner, little though she believed in his avowal of penitence. "But," she went on soberly, "if you have been expecting a fashion plate to come among you, I fear I shall be a sore disappointment to everyone at Applewood."

"Miss Norris, I believe I can promise that you will not be a disappointment to anyone," Mr. Keeson said promptly.

Miss Norris wondered a little at the deliberate rather than forceful impression left by this comforting remark, bringing into question whether her reassurance was indeed the principal motive behind it. She decided it was time to take an interest in her surroundings and wrenched her fascinated gaze away from her companion.

They came barreling out of the inn yard and she had to grab the edge of the seat to steady herself when they swerved suddenly to avoid another carriage going past the entrance. It would seem that speech was not the only area in which Mr. Keeson was impetuous. Fortunately for Miss Norris's peace of mind, they overtook no other vehicle before her driver got his mettlesome pair under control, and she was able to expel a long breath and relax her grip on the seat while she looked around her. Woodbridge was a clean, attractive town from what she had seen so far, and she made a comment to this effect.

"That's about all you can say for it," her companion replied. "There is not much doing here, though the King's Head on your right has a handsome room for assemblies upstairs."

Miss Norris swiveled her head to get a longer look at the corbels carved as faces that distinguished the lovely old Tudor building as they sped past.

When they had left the central part of the town behind, Mr. Keeson looked over at his passenger again. "I say, I hope you are not going to get chilled riding in this open carriage?"

"Not at all. It is such a beautiful early fall day that I was longing to be out in the fresh air after a few hours cooped up in a stagecoach. This feels simply marvelous." Miss Norris took a deep breath and smiled widely at her escort out of the sheer joy of living. She regretted her own impetuosity the next instant when Mr. Keeson's handsome features took on an additional warmth and she felt his thigh press against hers as they took a corner more sharply than was strictly necessary.

"I expected to be met by your coachman or one of the grooms today," she said, inviting his reaction by giving a questioning inflection to her statement.

"Sawyer, my brother's head groom, was about to set off for Woodbridge in one of the big carriages, but I was anxious to give my bays a little exercise, so I told him I'd fetch you instead," Mr. Keeson replied with another of his charming smiles. "I trust you are suitably grateful to avoid another hour in a stuffy old bone shaker?"

"Oh, I am," she said, willing to gratify his vanity while she kept to herself her unflattering opinion of his driving ability. "Are we near the sea?" she asked, looking about her with exaggerated interest to evade his flirtatious gaze.

"We're about five miles from the coast. Applewood is much closer, though you can only see the water from the highest point of the estate. The land is nearly flat hereabouts. As you can see, it is unimpressive from a scenic point of view. This part of Suffolk is naturally nearly treeless except for what has been planted. It's predominantly grazing land. The soil is too light and sandy to produce much. In fact, the area between here and the coast is called The Sandlings, which will give you some idea of the terrain.''

"The air is delicious, though." Miss Norris turned her face to the sun with no thought to protecting her complexion.

"I'd like to hear your description of the air around these parts in January," Mr. Keeson said, minus his ready smile for once. "It comes straight down from the Arctic Circle and can freeze the breath in your lungs."

"Perhaps it is fortunate then that I shall only be here for a few weeks."

"If you prove really helpful to Mama, she will not wish to lose your services so quickly. You may find yourself sampling our severe winter after all.''

Miss Norris laughed gaily. "You are strangely determined to subject me to the rigors of inclement weather, Mr. Keeson, and on such a lovely day too. It would be impossible, of course; my father will be back home in Cambridgeshire next month. But I shall do my best to assist your mother with all the preparations for your sister's wedding while I am here.''

"Anything might happen between now and next month," Mr. Keeson declared with what Miss Norris could only term a wicked grin. She asked him a question about the landscape through which they were driving to keep him away from personalities for the remainder of the ride to Applewood. It was crystal clear that the younger son of the house was a determined flirt, and no doubt a successful one too with that handsome face and wheedling smile as weapons at his disposal. She judged him to be her senior by a year or two despite his boyish manner. Lady Dalrymple had told her almost nothing about her sister's family, but she assumed that Lady Mary was about eighteen or nineteen, since she had made her come-out this past Season. Lord Montrose would obviously be older than his brother, and there was also a widowed sister with a child living at Applewood if she remembered correctly.

Miss Norris was still speculating on the Keeson family members in her mind when the phaeton turned in between brick gateposts. They had been on Montrose land for some little time. She had admired the serene pastoral picture made by a flock of fat sheep grazing in an extensive meadow and been told that they belonged to the earl. Now she saw they were in well-tended parkland with lovely trees and large shrubs scattered through it. She thought she caught the scent of apples briefly, though the orchard that presumably gave its name to the estate was not yet visible.

"If you do not object to walking up to the house from the stables I should like to turn the bays over to my groom first," Mr. Keeson said. "Someone will bring your bag up later and I'll show you the rose garden that is Applewood's pride. It is mostly my father's creation, but Ivor has continued to add new varieties since he inherited."

Miss Norris having no objection to this pleasant detour, they turned toward the stables. A few minutes later she found herself in a magnificent rose garden more extensive than any she had been privileged to visit. A large oval lawn was framed with hundreds of bushes representing dozens of varieties at first glance. A gravel path surrounded the beds and a brick wall covered with espaliered fruit trees faced her at the other end. Low hedges separated the garden from decorative terraces that descended gradually from the slight eminence where the house was positioned. In the distance she could glimpse water sparkling in the late afternoon sunshine—a stream, she thought.

"This is indeed marvelous, Mr. Keeson, and it smells heavenly." Miss Norris allowed her gaze to return from the distant vista to rove around the plantings once more, then said on a note of uncertainty. "Why, I have just noticed something rather curious. Are there no white roses? Every other shade imaginable seems to be well represented."

Mr. Keeson gave a delighted laugh. "I wondered if you would spot the omission. You'd be surprised how many people do not even notice. Come with me through the opening in the wall and all shall be explained."

Mystified, she allowed herself to be led through the arched openings in the brick wall ahead and immediately stopped short in sheer enchantment. They were in a small area, not enclosed but visually secluded by trees and sheltering bushes carefully placed to offer privacy and peaceful contemplation of the perfect setting. Here all the flowers were white. The sunny area in the center was filled with creamy roses intermingled with nonflowering but still green peony bushes. A few late daisies peeked coyly out in sunny spots while white flowering shrubs flourished within the shady embrace of tree branches offering their protection. There were little yellow-centered white corn marigolds and graceful double white soapwort and tuberose blossoms among other blooms she could not identify. As her eyes were feasting on the setting she became aware of the tinkle and splash of falling water in the silence and soon located the source, a charming little bronze dolphin fountain near an inviting wrought iron settee large enough for two.

Miss Norris turned shining eyes on her escort, who had remained silent while she looked her fill. She said simply, "It's beautiful, Mr. Keeson, an idyllic spot. Thank you for showing it to me."

He smiled and took a step closer, diminishing the space between them to mere inches. "I thought you would like it, and it is a spot well-suited to collecting a tangible expression of your appreciation for my escort services today."

Before the still-bemused young woman could deploy any elusive maneuvers she found herself wrapped in her guide's arms, being thoroughly kissed. She rallied quickly, however, and freed herself with a sudden mighty shove against her attacker's chest that rocked him backward. She had to discipline a smile at his astonishment as she put a safe distance between them. With that face he must be unused to having his advances repulsed. His expression was now a bit wary as she faced him, her bonnet askew but her composure still intact. Her voice too was dispassionate, though every syllable was a distinct entity.

"Since it is inconceivable that you could have formed an uncontrollable passion for me in the span of one brief hour, Mr. Keeson, I can only conclude that this is your customary style of conduct toward any female stupid enough to be private with you. You may be assured that I shall take care not to repeat my error during my stay at Applewood. Now, may be go inside?"

The tall man in the shrubbery watching this *tableau vivant* unbeknown to the participants allowed the muscles in his jaw to relax, softening the grim expression that had dwelt there since he had come unexpectedly upon what had appeared at first to be a lovers' tryst between Ned and some strange girl. Evidently the self-possessed young woman calmly resettling her hat at the proper angle was Miss Norris, his aunt's goddaughter, come to assist his mother with her social preparations. That was a masterly setdown she had just delivered. Was it possible that a female possessing the uncommon attribute incongruously called "common sense" was actually about to enter the portals of Applewood as a temporary resident? If true, it was indeed a noteworthy occasion.

Impelled by a sudden wish to be present when his mother met the young woman she had imported to serve as an unpaid slavey, Ivor Keeson, third earl of Montrose, tossed his cigar aside and made his way silently and swiftly through the shrubbery on a course to intercept his chastened brother and his mother's guest before they should enter the house.

Chapter Three

"HALLO, NED. Hold that door, will you?"

The words were addressed to his brother's back, but Lord Montrose had his eyes fixed on the woman about to enter the house through the garden entrance. He had only been able to see a line of cheek under a bonnet from his vantage point in the shrubbery.

Both turned at the sound of his voice, and he beheld a slender young woman a bit above middle height, wearing a pelisse of sheer brown wool and a plain brown velvet bonnet, neither of which could boast of being in the current mode. Her eyes, large, dark, and full of intelligence, flashed past him to the path from which he had emerged before returning to his face, and he could almost see her wondering whether or not the scene with his brother might have been observed. He knew his own face would give nothing away and noted with interest that no trace of a blush marred the creamy smoothness of the lady's complexion as she returned his gaze with perfect composure.

Ned, untroubled by any fears that his breach of decorum might be known, had replied to his brother's hail with a smile. "Well met, Ivor. I was about to bring our guest in to Mama. I have been showing her the rose garden. Miss Norris, may I present my brother?"

"How do you do, Lord Montrose?"

The earl accepted the gloved hand offered him and matched the lady's polite little smile with one of his own. "I am delighted to welcome you to Applewood, Miss Norris, and would like to express our gratitude at the outset for your generous offer of assistance to my mother. We shall do our best to make your stay here comfortable and, I hope, enjoyable."

"You are most kind, sir."

"Lord, yes," Ned chimed in. "We shall have to ensure that it does not become a case of 'all work and no play.' "

31

"Thank you," murmured Miss Norris, giving him a thoughtful look that caused him to shift his gaze to his brother.

"I assume Mama is in the blue saloon at this hour, Ivor?"

"I believe so. If you will come this way, Miss Norris."

Mr. Keeson carried on a lighthearted monologue to enliven the few minutes it took to walk from the garden entrance through to a small reception room at the front of the house. During this period Miss Norris limited her contribution to producing encouraging looks when he glanced her way. Lord Montrose too remained silent, assuming an abstracted air to cloak his covert study of the rather puzzling young woman who had come among them. His first impression of her physical presence was that she was quite good-looking in an unspectacular fashion, her best feature being a pair of big, beautiful brown eyes. Walking a half pace behind her, he cast a knowledgeable eye over her all-brown costume. Though of good-quality fabric and well-fitting, it could only be described as dull to the point of dowdiness. This self-effacing modesty was not extended to her manner, however, which, though far from forward, struck him as perfectly self-assured. She was looking about her now with frank interest in her surroundings. So far he had seen no sign of shyness or timidity in her reaction to Ned or himself. He was looking forward to the upcoming meeting with his mother with uncommon interest.

The door to the blue saloon was open. At the moment the sole occupant was his mother, who was seated on the sofa leafing through a periodical. She looked up as the three came through the entrance almost simultaneously, and the earl saw her eyes go directly to Miss Norris.

"Mama, here is our guest just arrived. May I present Miss Norris, Aunt Augusta's goddaughter?"

The earl sent his voice ahead into the little silence that had fallen when Ned's flow of chat had ceased. He couldn't tell from his position at her side if Miss Norris had seen the flash of dismay that had appeared in his mother's eyes at first sight of her guest.

The countess was equal to the occasion, recovering almost instantaneously. She remained seated but cast down the periodical. "How sweet of you to come all this way to help me, Miss Norris. I am so very grateful.'' Her famous smile appeared and she extended both hands in a pretty gesture of welcome that compelled Miss Norris to go to her hostess with her own hands out to accept the gesture. This Miss Norris did, saying warmly, ''It is my pleasure, ma'am. Pray excuse me for staring like a looby, but I simply cannot accept that you are the mother of these great gentlemen. You are too young surely.''

The frank disbelief in the young woman's face and voice was better than an elixir of flattery. Lady Montrose gave a delicious trill of gratified laughter and patted her guest's hands before releasing them. ''But I am afraid you must accept it, my dear child. Of course, I was very young when I married, but I assure you I am indeed the parent of these great hulking creatures. It is of no use to deny it when people are forever telling me that Ned favors me strongly in features and coloring.''

''Yes, I can see the resemblance,'' Miss Norris agreed, looking from one to the other.

''My good fortune,'' Mr. Keeson said with a grin, dropping a light kiss on his mother's cheek as he came past her to stand by a chair at right angles to the sofa.

Lady Montrose patted the place beside her invitingly and smiled at Miss Norris, who first obeyed the implicit command in Lord Montrose's suggestion that she might like to remove her pelisse. He helped her off with that garment before his brother could reach her, noting that the nondescript dress beneath was of the same dark brown hue in a heavy cotton. His mother, he saw, was conducting her own discreet survey of her guest while this action was going on.

''Ring the bell, Ivor, please,'' the countess said as Miss Norris took the indicated place on the sofa. ''I told Hawkins we would wait tea until Miss Norris arrived. Did you have a tiresome journey, my dear? I despise traveling and am overset by even the shortest trip.''

''I rather enjoyed it,'' Miss Norris said cheerfully. ''The scenery was all new to me, you see, and by the time I was beginning to feel the jouncing a bit, we were very nearly in Woodbridge.''

''I trust Sawyer was waiting there with the carriage,'' her hostess said on a questioning note.

"Actually, ma'am, it was Mr. Keeson who kindly met me in Woodbridge with his phaeton," Miss Norris replied with a smiling nod in that gentleman's direction.

"Ned drove you here?" The countess's eyes winged to her son's smiling face, then returned to her guest, who had blinked at the sharpness of the question. "I am so sorry that you should have been subjected to a drive in that ramshackle and unsafe vehicle of my son's after enduring hours in a horrid stage-coach."

"You wound me deeply, Mama," Mr. Keeson murmured, a wicked gleam in his deep blue eyes. "My phaeton is all the crack, the latest model."

"Oh, I found it delightful, I assure you, ma'am. One can see so much more from an open carriage. It was very kind of Mr. Keeson."

Lady Montrose's intent regard never left her guest's face during this earnest speech until the entrance of the butler called her attention away. When he had departed to carry out his orders, her ladyship turned once more to the young woman sitting composedly beside her. "That is an unusual ring you are wearing, Miss Norris. Is it a token of your betrothal?"

"Why, yes, ma'am. My fiancé thought I would like the jade stone in this intricate setting and indeed I do." With a complete lack of self-consciousness, she held out her hand for the countess's closer inspection, adding impulsively, "I hope you will like to call me Chloe as my godmother does, my lady."

"It is indeed a handsome ring," the countess said with a sweet smile. "Pray accept my good wishes for your happiness."

"You didn't tell me you were engaged to be married," Mr. Keeson said on a note of accusation.

"Well, really, Ned, why should you expect Miss Norris to go about making such personal announcements to perfect strangers, you foolish boy?"

His mother's tone of playful reprimand was well done and earned Lord Montrose's silent admiration. Less admirable was her tacit rebuff of Miss Norris's offer of her given name. Hopefully, this might have passed over their guest's head in the wake of the quick exchange with Ned. Her expression was now serene but less spontaneous perhaps. At least the small mystery of his mother's voluntary acceptance of an attractive young woman in their midst was now cleared up. Miss Norris's betrothed status had been her entrée to Applewood.

"Where are the girls?" he asked.

"Mary will be here shortly. I sent her up to change out of that dreadfully dowdy gray gown she seems to live in these days. Patricia begs to be excused from tea. She is having one of her bad days."

The butler reentered the saloon at that moment accompanied by a stout maidservant carrying a tray with an enticing array of small cakes and bread and butter. The next few moments were given over to the ritual of serving tea with its accompaniments. Miss Norris had worked up an appetite during her hours of traveling and did not need urging to partake willingly of the delicacies offered. She did not allow the fact that her hostess refused all sustenance except tea to weigh against satisfying her hunger and accepted a second slice of fruit cake pressed on her by Lord Montrose, though a hint of amusement lurking behind his bland expression caused her to straighten her spine an extra degree as she did so.

Miss Norris was on her second cup of tea when a too-slender young girl slipped into the room. Her mother spotted her as she was about to take the chair beside her elder brother.

"Here you are at last, Mary. Come and meet Miss Norris, who is going to help with the arrangements for your dance."

The girl obeyed, rising to meet the newcomer halfway between the chair and sofa. "How do you do?" she said politely.

"I am happy to meet you, Lady Mary. May I offer my felicitations on your upcoming marriage?"

Miss Norris's friendly smile was not returned. "Thank you," the girl replied in a voice as colorless as her face. She turned away to go back to her chair.

"I fear my daughter is always painfully shy with strangers initially," Lady Montrose said into the little silence that developed as Miss Norris took her place on the sofa once more. "Will you have more tea, Miss Norris?"

"Thank you, no, but it was delicious. I had not realized how thirsty traveling can make one."

Lord Montrose agreed that this had often been his experience and recounted an amusing little incident to illustrate the point while Lady Montrose prepared her daughter's tea. Shortly thereafter she suggested that their guest might like to see her room and settle in before it was time to dress for dinner.

"One of the maids will unpack for you, of course, and I am persuaded you will like to rest a bit before dinner."

"Thank you, ma'am, I confess I should like to put off this hat, but it is unnecessary to bother any of the maids. I can unpack my things in no time."

"It is no bother for them to do the work they are paid for," replied the countess, which seemed to settle that point. Miss Norris closed her lips and subsided, grateful that, once again, Lord Montrose relieved the slight strain with an inconsequential but timely comment.

The housekeeper arrived a few moments later and Miss Norris left with her, thankful to be done with the first difficult meeting with so many strangers. As she accompanied the pleasant-faced housekeeper to her room on the first floor she chided herself mentally for her choice of words. "Difficult" was much too strong. There had been awkward moments, of course. This was probably inevitable when a complete stranger came to live closely with a family, but everyone had tried to be welcoming with the possible exception of Lady Mary, the person closest to her in age and circumstances. Shyness could be a terrible affliction, though. It was undoubtedly a painful chore for the quiet girl to meet new people. Hopefully, they would become friends in time. She must not seem to rush the poor girl.

The bedchamber assigned to Miss Norris was charming. If the room where she had had tea was the "blue saloon," this must be the "green bedroom," she decided, glancing around with pleasure as Mrs. Meggs, the housekeeper, expressed the hope that she would be comfortable in her new surroundings.

"Oh, I shall, Mrs. Meggs. It is a lovely room. I am going to enjoy staying here. Thank you for preparing it so nicely. The flowers on the little table are beautiful."

When the housekeeper, visibly gratified by the young woman's appreciation, had withdrawn after hanging up the brown pelisse in a huge armoire, Miss Norris lost no time in removing the heavy bonnet that had taken on all the qualities of an instrument of torture after nearly eight hours. Having dropped it on the bed, she stood in the center of the room running massaging fingers over her scalp to the utter destruction of the neatly coiled arrangement in which she had confined her unruly tresses. Her eyes made a slow circuit of the generously proportioned apartment and found nothing that would alter her favorable first impression.

It was a corner room as evidenced by large, green-velvet-draped windows in two walls. Drawn by curiosity about her location in the house, for she had as yet formed no true picture of its dimensions, having come upon it from the stables and the garden side, she walked over to one of the windows and pulled back the curtain. She looked down on rather dense shrubbery at close quarters to what must be a wing at the back of the house. Beyond were extensive lawns and fields sloping down to a stream in the distance, very likely the water she had barely glimpsed from the rose garden. To the far right a few spreading low trees indicated the edge of an orchard, a guess she confirmed when she looked out the other window. On this side stretched a vast orchard. She could discern the military precision in which the rows of fruit trees had been planted. On an impulse she unlocked the window and raised the sash, instantly bringing the scent of apples into the room. She breathed in deeply. *Comfort me with apples.* The biblical phrase came into her mind unbidden, and she shook her head at her own silliness in thinking she might need conforting.

Miss Norris turned her back on the view outside her windows to make herself familiar with the interior of her apartment. The fine furnishings were chiefly of mahogany except for the delicate satinwood table under one of the windows that was inlaid with a gleaming mother-of-pearl border. She slid a finger lightly over its smooth surface as she admired the many-hued blossoms arranged in a vase of celadon porcelain with gilt ears. The walls of the room were painted the same pale green, while the background of the floral carpet was the deeper leaf-green of the velvet draperies. Thanks to the large windows and the white ceiling and woodwork, the room seemed bright and serene at the same time. A green and white pastoral-print fabric covered the bed and curtained the windows, but only a sheer netted lace formed a canopy over the tall carved posts. The lack of bed draperies might mean that the room was blessedly free of drafts. The house did not seem to be of a great age and the windows appeared strong and weather tight. The well-padded bench at the dressing table and an inviting small wing chair near the fireplace spoke further of a thoughtful concern for the comfort of the room's occupant.

Miss Norris retrieved her bonnet from the middle of the bed and crossed to the tall armoire with a beautiful triangular pediment containing a shell design. Her valise had been unpacked, its contents neatly put away. Her wardrobe did not make much of a show, she acknowledged ruefully, fingering her dinner gowns, two plain black dresses dating from her mourning period for her mother, and a newer but scarcely less somber costume of heavy brown silk. Frowning, she closed the armoire again and walked over to stare into the mirror on the dressing table. Ignoring the wildly disordered hair, she ran an assessing eye over her brown dress. Though having no pretensions to *à la modalité,* there was nothing actually wrong with it. It fit her well and was comfortable and—she might as well admit it—drab. Thirty seconds in Lady Montrose's company had been sufficient to make her feel like a little brown wren beside a gorgeous bird of paradise. Lady Mary too, though not spectacularly handsome like her mother, had been very fashionably attired in a soft muslin dress of cerulean blue.

Her hand went to her head to smooth back the loosened strands of hair as she continued to stare at her image as if she had never seen it before. How had things come to such a pass? She had had pretty clothes in abundance in her youth. Her mother had delighted in designing and making her gowns and hats. She had given away her colored clothes to various of her father's needy patients after her mother's death, and somehow since then she had tended to postpone thinking about or planning additions to her wardrobe until such additions were absolute necessities. At that point she merely ordered garments that were duplicates of those they replaced. Had her eyes been closed these last few years that she had not noticed that she was drifting into a premature and very drab spinsterhood? A half hour among the aristocracy had indeed opened her eyes, but there was precious little she could do to improve the situation at present. Since this was the case, she might just as well put the matter out of her mind.

By the time a maid appeared to conduct her to the room where the family gathered before dinner, Miss Norris had spent twice as long at her toilette as usual, without, however, achieving the satisfaction of knowing her appearance went any way past neat and appropriate. She had decided on a gown of black silk. It had long sleeves, which were not much worn at night except by elderly ladies, but at least the low round neckline gave her the opportunity to wear her mother's pearls. They were very fine pearls and glowed against her skin. She had brushed her hair furiously before twisting it into a great coil at the back of her head. The countess's complexion had been subtly enhanced by powder and rouge this afternoon, but her father disapproved of cosmetics so she owned none. She was dabbing a drop of the perfume her godmother had brought her on her throat and wrists when the maid appeared. After one quick check in the glass she hastily grabbed a handkerchief, which she tucked into her sleeve as she crossed to the door.

The room where she was ushered, again on the ground floor, was larger than the blue saloon and beautifully appointed. Here too the white ceiling and woodwork contributed to an overall effect that was bright and attractive. A light palette had been chosen for fabrics and wallpaper to complement the beautiful carpet that featured pale pink, gold, and blue designs against an ivory-colored background. Lady Mary was there with her brothers and, as Miss Norris had anticipated, was exquisitely gowned in primrose silk with knots of ribbon of a deeper yellow adorning the short puffed sleeves of this creation. The gentlemen were elegant in black and white evening dress, or rather, Mr. Keeson looked elegant. Nothing could tone down the impression of solid strength that emanated from the earl, who was considerably taller and broader through the shoulders than his brother. Reminding herself that she had no one to blame but herself for her drabness, Miss Norris raised her chin a trifle and entered the room, unhappily aware of three assessing pairs of eyes as she did so.

"Goodness," Lady Mary exclaimed, "your hair is a quite extraordinary color."

"Yes, but I promise you I am quite resigned to it by now."

"Resigned?"

"Oh, yes. In my youth I was used to rail at a malign fate that had refused to grant me either my father's shining black hair or my mother's lovely golden color, until my father took me roundly to task for my conceit."

"Conceit?" echoed Lady Mary, looking puzzled.

Miss Norris nodded. "Papa told me only an enormously exaggerated idea of my own importance in Nature's scheme of things could produce that childish ranting against a demonstrably impartial agency such as Fate."

"Did your mother also subscribe to this salutary philosophy?" Lord Montrose asked.

Miss Norris's lips curved into a tender smile for her own memories. Her eyes were focused on the past as she said softly, "Mother promised me that the glaring red would darken in time and become less conspicuous."

"Well, she was half right," Mr. Keeson put in with a laugh. "It has darkened to an absolutely gorgeous shade, but no one could call in inconspicuous. Why do you hide its glory in that tiresome bun?"

"I fear it is too curly and unruly to do anything else, Mr. Keeson," Miss Norris said, looking a bit taken aback.

"I warned you this afternoon that I always spoke my thoughts," that gentleman replied, reading hers from her face.

"It's past time you acquired a little conduct, Ned," Lord Montrose said sharply. "Will you have a glass of sherry, Miss Norris?"

"Thank you." She accepted the glass he was offering. She didn't care much for sherry but was grateful once again for the earl's tact and good manners.

Lady Montrose completed Miss Norris's rescue by entering the room at that moment, resplendent in a shimmering silk gown of a peacock blue that changed color as she moved with consummate grace and assurance. Her guest gazed at her in open admiration. The countess must have been a diamond of the first water in her youth. Indeed, if she'd come across her today without knowing of her grown family, she'd have set her age around five-and-thirty.

Lady Montrose greeted her guest with a smile and inquired into the comfort of her accommodations. Miss Norris was detailing the delights of her apartment when another woman entered the room and drew all eyes to her person.

"Tricia, my dear, come and meet our guest," Lord Montrose said, placing his sister's hand on his arm and steering her toward Miss Norris.

At the moment, that young lady was thinking that if Lady Montrose could be likened to Aglaia, the Grace of Splendor, then her elder daughter was the personification of Melpomene, the Tragic Muse. Wraith thin and deathly pale in her widow's black, she radiated a tragic beauty that was not quite of this world. Tall like her mother, she seemed to drift weightless, almost incorporeal, across the room. Lady Patricia had inherited her mother's sapphire-blue eyes and pale gold hair, and her features were beautiful. Lifeless perfection was the description that came to mind, Miss Norris decided, when she had been greeted in a low voice devoid of the least spark of animation.

Dinner went very smoothly and it was not until several hours later when Miss Norris was disposing herself for sleep between linen sheets smelling of lavender and reviewing her first day at Applewood that she realized that this was almost entirely due to Lady Montrose's superb social sense. The light conversation that danced over a number of topics had been launched, navigated, and controlled by the countess, ably abetted by the earl. She recalled in some surprise that neither of the daughters of the family had volunteered a single remark, speaking only when directly addressed. For the most part, the countess seemed to speak for them, saying with a light laugh, "Mary will not agree with me that such is really true in London," or "Of course, Patricia will say I am too strict in my notions of propriety," thus leaving the impression that those mentioned were participating in the discussion when in fact they were not even attending, or so it seemed at times to a stranger. Mr. Keeson had been disposed to flirt with his mother's guest but had been thwarted at every turn by his vigilant parent, though with a great deal of subtlety so that most of the evening had

elapsed before she herself had become aware of this minor
chord. She had been amused then and secretly relieved that she
was not obliged to deal with his brashness, at least not in front
of his mother.

They had returned to the lovely drawing room after dinner.
Lady Montrose had asked her elder daughter to play for them
on the beautiful japanned pianoforte, stressing that she was
persuaded their guest would like to hear some music. Miss
Norris had innocently added her voice to that of her hostess
out of courtesy and interest and had been appalled at the scene
this precipitated. Lady Patricia had turned even paler, if that
were possible, and begun to tremble. Haunted, beseeching eyes
had fixed on Miss Norris.

"Oh, no, please, I could not! You must excuse me, my head
aches so. I am so sorry." She had lurched to her feet before
this breathless speech was finished and had run from the room
in a stumbling fashion, her hands pressing against her temples.

Miss Norris had turned a dismayed face to her hostess. "I
. . . I am so very sorry to have distressed Lady Patricia. I
. . . I never meant . . ."

"You could not know that my sister has refused to play the
piano since her husband died," Lord Montrose had said soothingly. Later she recalled the slight stress on the "you" and
wondered at its significance.

At the time, Lady Montrose had apologized for her daughter's
loss of control. "I regret to say that Patricia has been
exceedingly slow to recover from her loss. I had hoped the
request of a guest might stir her to put aside her melancholy
in order to give pleasure to someone else, but it seems I was
mistaken. Will you play for us, Miss Norris?"

"I am sorry, but I have no accomplishments at all, my lady."

"Thank the Lord," Mr. Keeson had intoned with a fervor
that curved her own lips upward and brought a tiny frown to
his mother's smooth brow before she said playfully:

"Mind your manners, Ned. In any case, that is a very
sweeping statement, Miss Norris, and one that is surely not
meant to be taken literally. I promise you that we do not require
professional competence in order to enjoy a performance. You
are being too modest."

"But I am afraid it is the literal truth, ma'am," she had replied, determined not to sail under false colors. "I cannot sing a note or play the simplest piece of music through to the end without a dozen mistakes. Nor do I sketch or paint. I am terribly sorry to be such a disappointing guest." She had glanced around apologetically and discovered that Lord Montrose was staring at her with an intent expression as if trying to fathom the truth or falsity of her claims—or lack of claims—while his brother was frankly amused. She thought she detected a trace of sympathy in Lady Mary's face before the girl's eyes returned to her folded hands in her lap.

It had been an uncomfortable few moments, and she squirmed a little in bed later, remembering her sense of dismay, but fortunately Lady Montrose had not appeared at all disappointed that her guest possessed no drawing-room accomplishments and had said so in no uncertain terms. "We did not invite you here to be a performing monkey, my child," she had said firmly, and had brought the incident to a close by requesting Lady Mary to favor them with some piano music.

"Yes, Mama," the girl said and rose obediently to take her place at the instrument.

At that point Mr. Keeson recollected that he had to check on the swelling in the knee of his favorite hunter, and Lord Montrose excused himself to finish reading an article that he needed to discuss with his farm manager the next morning. The three women had finished the evening together with the countess putting delicate questions to her guest about her life as a physician's daughter while Lady Mary played all the right notes of several musical compositions in an uninspired fashion until the tea tray was brought in. There had been no opportunity for conversation between herself and Lady Mary up till then, and when the girl had joined them she had had almost nothing to say by the time the countess suggested they retire.

Given the events of the past few hours, Miss Norris was in the process of cautioning herself not to expect a rapid advance in friendship with the colorless young girl whose wedding plans she was here to assist with when she fell soundly asleep in her comfortable bed.

Chapter Four

MISS CHLOE NORRIS sat on the wrought-iron bench in the all-white garden and gazed about her with unfailing pleasure. In the sennight she had been at Applewood this beautiful spot had become her favorite retreat. The oval rose garden presented a dazzling feast for the senses and a day never passed without a short visit there. She had not yet begun to learn the names of the exotic varieties represented, something she was determined to do before she returned home. After strolling through it, though, she always headed for this secluded corner of Eden, which was a never-ending delight. There was a sense of intimacy in this spot, as if she belonged there. Except for the time spent in her bedchamber she had probably logged more hours on this settee than in any other location at Applewood. Sometimes she brought a book with her, but more often than not the pages went unread as she sat merely listening to the gentle splash of the fountain and the various twitterings of the bird population while she breathed in the scented air. Her eyes lazily examined the floral offerings but just as often gazed inward as she allowed her thoughts to wander at will.

There was a book of Latin poetry beside her at the moment, but she had not yet opened it as she went over the events of her stay at Applewood. It had been an enjoyable week for the most part, full of little satisfaction, but not without its minor frustrations too. The house itself was beautiful and comfortable, so well run by an efficient staff that one was mostly unaware of the intricate apparatus required to keep a large establishment functioning smoothly. It was certainly delightful to be treated as a pampered guest for a time with no responsibility for household arrangements. Cleaning went on unobtrusively here at Applewood and delicious meals appeared at regular intervals. Even the weather had obliged with a succession of warm, sunny days.

Though she felt as if she were on holiday, she had already been of some service to Lady Montrose, which was a source of quiet satisfaction. After conferring with her hostess, she had spent three mornings writing out the invitations for a ball the earl was giving in honor of his sister shortly before her October wedding. It was to be a large party but by no means the only social event scheduled at Applewood over the next few weeks. There was the wedding itself, of course, and before that a series of shooting parties. She had been unaware that the great landholders in this part of the country had begun stocking their estates with pheasants in the latter years of the eighteenth century and that many shoots were held in the area each autumn. This would be a new experience for her. Not that she expected to shoot herself. Though she had often shot at targets with her father, the thought of actually killing a bird turned her squeamish. She had no intention of mentioning this, especially in view of the damning fact that she was perfectly willing to dine on the pheasants shot by less squeamish souls. She had no desire to expose her hypocrisy for the delectation of any needle-tongued wits among the company.

Soon there would be a general turning out of the house to ready unused apartments for the guests who would stay at Applewood for some of the festivities. At that juncture there would be ways in which she could make herself useful, but at the moment she felt rather like a fraud. When she had said as much to the countess, begging for something to do, that lady had given her musical laugh, patted her hand, and told her kindly to enjoy herself while she was here. The problem was, she had to admit, that she had never mastered the art of enjoying herself doing absolutely nothing. Coming upon the housekeeper freshening up the flower arrangements in the drawing room one day, she had asked if she might take that chore off the busy woman's hands.

Mrs. Meggs had looked doubtful. "Oh, but you are a guest, Miss Norris. Her ladyship would not like it. It would not be seemly."

"A guest with too much idle time on her hands, Mrs. Meggs. Her ladyship directed me to enjoy myself at Applewood," she had persisted in wheedling tones, "and I will enjoy doing the flowers, especially when I know how very busy you must be these days.''

She had finally persuaded the housekeeper to turn that pleasant chore over to her. It took up an hour or two of her day and was intrinsically rewarding. She had become friends with Mrs. Meggs, who had spared the time to show her all over the lovely house.

The odd fact was that she was more advanced in friendship with the housekeeper than with any of the family, and therein lay the source of her frustration. From her limited observation, the only time the whole Keeson family was together was at dinner, and not always then. During the time she had been a resident at Applewood, Lady Patricia had only dined with the family on three occasions. Mr. Keeson had been away dining with friends more often than not, and the earl generally excused himself after dinner on the plea of work. She knew from his mother that he was overseeing the last of the apple harvesting and was busy about the estate all day. He and Mr. Keeson evidently had breakfast earlier than the hour she came down in the morning. Neither the countess nor Lady Patricia partook of a morning meal, and Miss Norris had no idea when Lady Mary appeared in the breakfast parlor. If she did, it was never while she herself ate in solitary splendor, waited upon by a correct Hawkins who replied to her tentative overtures with discouraging brevity. Prior to her arrival she had anticipated that she would see more of Lady Mary than anyone else. For one thing, they were closest in age, and it was the girl's approaching marriage and the extra work the arrangements entailed that were responsible for her own presence at Applewood. She saw the girl at lunch and generally later in the afternoon when the countess always presided over tea, but after a sennight she had no idea what Lady Mary did with her time, which was really quite odd when one thought about it.

The countess invariably retired to her rooms after lunch. She would leave the table on some playful remark directing them to enjoy themselves. If Miss Norris detected an assumption that they would seek this hypothetical enjoyment in each other's company, it was soon clear that Lady Mary read no such assumption into the words, for she always excused herself shortly after her mother left the room. In the beginning Chloe had made excuses for this antisocial behavior, citing the girl's shyness in explanation. Lately, however, she had come to the conclusion that Lady Mary was not so much shy as sullen. A smile would have given prettiness to the girl's fine pale features, but so far she had not been privileged to witness what must be a rare phenomenon.

As she sat with her eyes directed at the dolphin fountain, Miss Norris's mind was filled with speculation, not for the first time, about the puzzling young girl and her grudging—that was the only word for it—civility. The only spontaneous remark Lady Mary had so far uttered in her hearing was that abrupt comment on her hair color the first evening, and that had been more or less surprised out of her. She did her mother's bidding with mechanical obedience but never expressed a single thought or opinion of her own. Shyness could not account for this behavior. Chloe was forced to the conclusion that, unless she had always been a difficult personality, the girl was deeply unhappy about something. The next logical conclusion, lacking evidence to the contrary, was that this unhappiness was somehow related to her upcoming marriage. One would have thought that a newly engaged girl would be bubbling over with happiness. Miss Norris reasoned that even if this were not a true love match, a normal girl would still be caught up in the excitement of wedding plans. That this was far from the case was proved by Lady Mary's refusal to respond to the tentative openings she had given her to talk about her fiancé or her wedding. She had never obtained more than a curt reply, scarcely more than a monosyllable, to any overture. Even if Lady Mary had taken her mother's guest in dislike—and Chloe was not so insecure as to fear there was something about herself that roused a general sense of aversion in others—the younger girl might have tried to find some common ground with someone who was also betrothed and living in close proximity. Unless her own betrothal was the source of her unhappiness. That could account for her avoidance of another engaged female.

Having carried her unsupported speculations this far, Chloe confessed herself stymied. It was barely conceivable that a busy man like the earl or an insensible one, as she suspected Mr.

Keeson of being, might not notice that his sister was deep in
the dismals, but what kept the girl's mother from getting to the
bottom of the matter? Nothing in Lady Montrose's manner
indicated the slightest awareness of anything amiss with her
younger daughter. The question then became whether this
nonawareness was due to a natural insensitivity or was a
deliberate policy, and if the latter, why? Why did Lady Mary
not bring her problem to her mother, or had she already done
so and been dismissed without satisfaction or sympathy? It
disturbed Chloe to have to think poorly of her hostess, but she
could not prevent herself from speculating on the curious
situation at Applewood.

Lady Montrose was kindness itself to her guest, solicitous
of her comfort and quick to express appreciation for Chloe's
efforts on her behalf so far. She saw more of the countess than
any other member of the family and had certainly had more
conversation with her. Lady Montrose had begun to use her
given name within a day or two and seemed to welcome her
company. Gazing unseeingly at the hypnotic fall of water in
the fountain, she mentally reviewed some of the talks she had
had with her hostess. A frown puckered her brow as the
realization dawned that her frequent interactions with the
countess were of the most trifling and insubstantial nature. Lady
Montrose was a master in the art of light conversation; she never
allowed a significant silence to develop in her presence. This
talent, although that word seemed a poor choice, served to
prevent any underlying problems within the family to surface.
Chloe paused here. It was natural enough to wish to conceal
cracks in a family's solidarity from outsiders, but, as her
thoughts marched on, even allowing for this natural tendency,
there remained the question of why the countess seemed
determined not to recognize the unhappy state of her
younger daughter, for something was radically amiss with
Lady Mary. Chloe's heart went out to the girl, but there
was no way she could force her confidence. This had to
be freely given, and there was scant likelihood of that
at present. Lady Mary took care not to be alone in her
company.

Miss Norris's state of troubled abstraction was abruptly ended by the sound of a childish voice coming close to the little garden she had come to think of as her private retreat.

"Où es-tu, petit chat? Je ne ferai pas du mal à toi. Viens ici!"

As a startled Chloe looked for the owner of the breathless little voice, a striped cat streaked past her and leapt on the trunk of one of the spreading trees beyond the fountain. She watched it climb to safety before turning to face the child who had come running into the garden through the arched opening in the wall to stop precipitously at sight of the woman on the wrought-iron settee.

"If you are looking for a tiger-striped kitten, it is up in that tree," she said with a smile. Since the child had spoken in French, she automatically replied in that language.

The little girl's pale countenance took on a look of radiant pleasure. "How wonderful that you speak French," she said quickly. "No one has talked to me in French since my father died. My mother always speaks to me in English and 'Toinette did not wish to come out to the country when we came to live at Applewood."

"Who is 'Toinette?' " Miss Norris inquired.

"She was my nursemaid when Papa was alive, but now Addie looks after me, and she speaks only a strange sort of English. Everyone else here speaks only English too, and I do so miss speaking French to Papa."

"If you would like it, you may speak French with me," Chloe offered casually, continuing in that tongue as she tried to disguise the pity that took possession of her as she contemplated the little girl.

She should have been a beautiful child with her huge green-gray eyes and masses of curling red-gold hair that looked like spun silk. Instead she was a pathetic little figure, so white and wan that her features looked crowded and pinched in her delicate heart-shaped face. Her arms were no more than thin little sticks and her neck and shoulders did not appear solid enough to support the weight of her head with all that hair. The color that had given her face a momentary animation on hearing herself

addressed in French receded all too quickly until she reminded
Chloe of a little ghost.

"I would indeed like it if you were to speak French with me,
ma'am. You are most kind," the child replied with a quaint
formality.

"I learned my French from books and have had very little
chance to practice conversing in it, so I shall probably make
some terrible mistakes. I hope you will be patient with me and
correct my errors."

"It will be my pleasure, ma'am, but I am afraid I do not know
who you are."

Chloe held out her hand and stated her name. The child
solemnly took the offered fingers and dipped a little curtsy as
she did so. "My name is Emilie Roberts, Mademoiselle Norris.
It is spelled the French way because I was named after my papa,
who was Emile."

"Why have we not met before, Emilie? I have been visiting
at Applewood for a sennight, and this is the first time I have
seen you."

"Today is the first time I have been allowed outdoors in two
weeks. I have been ill with a feverish cold and I was not
permitted to visit *Maman* because her constitution is not strong
and I must not give her my cold."

"How tiresome to be laid up with a cold when the weather
has been so beautiful. If I had known I would have visited you.
My father is a doctor and I visit all his patients and rarely ever
catch a cold. Were you horribly bored in the nursery by
yourself?"

"Yes, a little, but Uncle Ivor came to see me every day. He
is not afraid of catching colds because he has the constitution
of an ox," the little girl parroted, still with that air of formality.
"He brought me books with lovely paintings in them, and the
cook sent me barley soup and sweetmeats to help me get well."

Naturally Miss Norris could not probe to discover whether
any of the other members of the child's family had paid visits
during her enforced stay in the nursery, but there was a sense
of aloneness about the little figure that tugged at her heart.

"Shall I help you get your pet out of the tree?" She made

the suggestion in the hope of seeing some animation return to the wan little face.

"Oh, the kitten is not mine. Cats make *Grand'mère* sneeze, so I am not allowed to have one in the house. He lives in the stables."

Miss Norris bit her tongue to prevent it from voicing the opinion that in a house the size of Applewood there could surely be found an out-of-the-way corner to shelter one small cat for the sake of this forlorn child. As the Keesons' guest it was not her business to question her hosts' household arrangements. "Well, then, the kitten must be taught that he is your *outside* pet at least. I do not believe he is too old to tame," she said briskly, directing an experienced eye at the ball of fluff watching them steadily from the safety of a tree limb just out of the woman's reach. He cocked his head at her efforts to entice him into her outstretched hands, then yawned and proceeded to wash a paw as she dropped her arms to her sides again with a laugh.

"I believe that furry rogue is mocking me," she said to the watching child, who was imploring *"petit chat"* to descend into her arms in a timid voice that had no visible effect on the busy little beast.

"Perhaps he doesn't like me anymore," Emilie said disconsolately. "Before I got sick he sometimes allowed me to pick him up and pet him, but today he ran away from me."

"He has simply forgotten you in the interval. He is very young yet, you see, and cats are excessively independent creatures. You must bring him some tidbits from the kitchen each day if you wish to make friends with him, and, of course, you cannot keep calling him 'little cat.' He needs a proper name so that presently he will come when you call him."

"A name?" the child asked doubtfully. "What sort of name would he like?"

"More to the point, what name should you like to give him?"

"I?" The big green-gray eyes widened in sudden excitement. "May I really name him?"

"If he is to be your pet, it is your duty to give him a name," Miss Norris assured the little girl. "What shall it be?"

"Well, I saw a picture of a tiger in one of Uncle Ivor's books. The little cat is not the right color, of course, but he looks rather like a small tiger, and a tiger is a very noble animal, do you not agree?"

Emilie was looking anxiously for Miss Norris's approval as she prattled on in her father's tongue. "Tigre," the woman repeated, nodding her head consideringly. "Yes, that is a very fitting and noble name for him. You are hereby and henceforth christened Tigre," she intoned, scooping some water from the fountain into her cupped palm and flicking it up at the kitten with the fingers of the other hand as she did so.

It would have been too much to expect an English stable cat to be impressed with his noble French name, but at least Tigre accepted his baptism with good grace, merely whisking the few drops of water from his whiskers with the paw he had been so industriously cleaning throughout the brief ceremony.

Emilie laughed. It was a rather tentative sound, as if she'd almost forgotten how to produce it, but it was undoubtedly a genuine laugh. Miss Norris added her own voice to swell the sound. "He may be small, but your Tigre has all the dignity of his jungle cousin, Emilie."

"Isn't he sweet? I wish he would let me pick him up."

"He knows he's safe from interference while he does his grooming up there. Perhaps if you take him a tasty morsel of meat or fish tomorrow, he will reward you. Meanwhile, I believe I would like to explore the grounds of Applewood a little if you would be so kind as to act as my guide?"

The child eagerly assented, and the pair strolled out of the white garden toward the orchard.

Like every corner of Applewood she had seen so far, the orchard was lovely and the trees beautifully maintained. Here and there a tree considerably smaller than its neighbors gave evidence of a policy of replacement. A few apples were rotting on the ground where they had fallen, and an occasional crimson glow could be seen up in the highest branches, but the trees had been stripped of their bounty for this season. Relieved of their delicious burden, their branches reached wide to the blue sky above in new freedom.

Speaking little, the woman and child wove their way through

the rows of trees to the highest point, where Emilie had promised a more comprehensive view of the house than Miss Norris had seen on her solitary perambulations to date. She had learned that the lovely red brick structure with its large white-painted sash windows regularly spaced in the main facade was less than thirty-five years old, having been built by the grandfather of the present earl when his heir came of age. The first earl had never lived at Applewood personally. Lady Montrose had mentioned that she had come to the house as a bride and had been given carte blanche to decorate the interior to her taste. The second earl was primarily responsible for the beautiful grounds that so enhanced the graceful structure. Obviously the present earl was extending his father's work, for Chloe could see a new section of young trees from the low hill where Emilie led her. The extent of the orchards amazed her. She had not previously realized what a large operation fruit-growing must be at Applewood. No wonder Lord Montrose was personally involved with this aspect of his estate on a daily basis during harvest season.

As if the random thought had conjured up the person, Lord Montrose appeared from another part of the orchard as Emilie and Miss Norris headed back toward the gardens. The child spotted his tall figure first and called out to him.

"Uncle Ivor!"

The man in dirt-encrusted top boots and leather breeches halted his swift progress and put out a hand to stop the headlong dash of the child, who was about to cast herself into his arms. "Not now, my pet. I've been working in the fields and I'm filthy."

"You're hurt, Uncle Ivor. You're bleeding!"

"It's nothing, Emilie. I got scratched by thorns while clearing some hedges, that's all."

Miss Norris, having come up at her normal pace, put a comforting arm around the shoulders of the child, who was trembling in sympathetic distress, and ran an assessing eye over the earl's face, which was indeed bleeding from several scratches. "His lordship is telling you the truth, Emilie," she said calmly. "The cuts will seem much less worrisome when they are cleaned. But what is wrong with your eye, sir?" she asked in a different tone as he continued to blink one bloodshot orb rapidly.

"Just some grit in it. My man will remove it. If you will excuse me, ladies . . . ."

"No, don't rub it. Stay," ordered Miss Norris, laying a hand on the arm he raised toward his face as he turned away. "At this time of day it might take you some time to locate your man, and this eye should be attended to without delay. If you will come into the white garden, sir, I'll remove the grit for you."

"No, really, Miss Norris, I could not permit you to perform such a distasteful chore. I'm dirty from head to toe and no fit company for ladies at present."

"Nonsense, sir," Miss Norris replied, taking him by the arm and directing his reluctant steps toward the garden. "I am not suggesting you should put in an appearance in the drawing room in your present condition, but that eye needs attention and, most opportunely, Emilie and I are right at hand."

"Emilie must not—" the earl began, but his unwanted attendant pushed him down onto the settee with a firm hand and turned to the anxiously hovering child.

"If you will soak my handkerchief in the fountain pool, my dear, I'll have that grit out of your uncle's eye in a trice. Don't wring it out," she added as the little girl dashed to obey the request.

"I fear I shall get you rather wet, sir," she said apologetically as she tilted his chin to the desired angle and proceeded to squeeze the water into his eye, "but it's helpful to flood the area completely. Do you have a clean handkerchief with you?"

"I did this morning," replied her patient dryly, exhibiting a dirty rag that he pulled from an inner pocket of his coat.

"Then mine will have to do, though it would go quicker with two."

"My handkerchief is clean, Miss Norris," Emilie put in quickly.

"Capital, my pet." Miss Norris turned an approving smile on the eager child. "If you will just continue to wet these in turn, we'll have the dirt out of your uncle's eye in no time."

Except for one soft exhortation to her unwilling patient to

"try to keep your eye open and your head still, sir," Miss Norris accomplished her mission in silence with deft fingers and an air of complete concentration. The little girl ran between pool and settee with the sopping white squares, her anxious eyes returning to her uncle's immobilized face each time she approached.

"I believe it is all out now, sir, and the scratches are quite clean," Miss Norris said a few moments later, raising her head from where it had been positioned a foot above the earl's back-tilted head during the cleaning process. "Blink your eye a few times. Do you feel the presence of any foreign matter in there?"

"No," said the earl after performing the directed actions. As she stepped back, he got to his feet and looked down into the serene brown eyes that had been close above his for the last few minutes. "Thank you very much, Miss Norris," he said quietly, holding out his hand. She put hers into it unselfconsciously, but her smiling gaze slid immediately to the little girl at her side. "Emilie deserves half the credit, sir, for her efforts. I think you would make a very capable doctor's daughter, Emilie. You kept your head and did what was necessary, both essential qualities for the daughter of a doctor."

The earl swooped to kiss his niece's soft cheek as he seconded Miss Norris's praise. There was a quizzical light in his gray eyes as he straightened and addly slyly, "I fear Emilie may yet be lacking one essential quality of a doctor's daughter. She isn't bossy enough."

"I'm not bossy," Miss Norris denied quickly, but her lips twitched at the corners as the earl's eyes continued to challenge hers. "Well, perhaps I am a *little* bossy," she admitted with a throaty chuckle.

"I think Miss Norris is perfectly wonderful!" Emilie spoke up in a tone so decided that it seemed to surprise her as much as her auditors, who both glanced at her.

The earl swept an arm around his niece's shoulder, hugging her to his side briefly, dirt or no dirt. "I quite agree with you, my pet. Miss Norris is perfectly wonderful . . . and a little bossy too," he added with a mock solemnity that made the child's gaze waver and seek that of the lady under discussion with a hint of entreaty.

"His lordship is teasing us both, Emilie, but we are going to prove ourselves above such crass conduct by ignoring the provocation," Miss Norris declared loftily, before adding, "Look, would you believe that your kitten is still sitting on the same branch of the tree after all this time?"

The child's attention was instantly diverted and she ran toward the tree, calling, *"Oh, petit Tigre, viens ici; viens à moi!"*

Since the conversation among the three had been conducted entirely in English to this point, Lord Montrose was understandably startled at the sudden spate of French, and he glanced to Miss Norris for enlightenment.

"Emilie misses speaking French with her father, so we have agreed to converse in that language between ourselvess," she explained, wondering a little at the penetrating stare the earl bent on her, though he said nothing. Neither of the adults found anything to say in the next few moments until the child, having failed to persuade the kitten into her arms, returned to them. Her disappointment was evident, but her face cleared presently as she explained to her uncle.

"Tigre forgot me while I was sick, but Miss Norris said if I bring him morsels of food every day he will soon learn that he is my pet, at least not in the house, of course, because of *Grand'mère's* sneezing, but outside."

"Yes, that should prove an efficacious method of securing his affections," the earl agreed. "It works equally well with the female of the species."

The words were lightly spoken, but there was something about the tone in which they were uttered that brought Miss Norris's chin up to a challenging angle. Mindful of the child's presence, she refused to be drawn on the subject, but the quick look she cast at the earl was eloquent of disagreement with this unflattering reference to her sex.

"It is getting near the hour for tea, Emilie. Your grandmother will be in the blue saloon by this time. Shall we go in together? I am persuaded your uncle would like to change out of his work clothes, and we are delaying him with our chatter."

Miss Norris extended a hand in invitation, and the little girl skipped over to her at once. The two females headed for the garden entrance, leaving the superior male being to follow at his pleasure.

Being still young and innocent, Emilie rather spoiled the effect of their dignified exit by glancing over her shoulder at the man standing stock still staring after them.

"I'll see you later, Uncle Ivor," she caroled, waving her free hand.

Chapter Five

AFTERWARD, looking back on her stay at Applewood, Chloe could point to her first meeting with Emilie and their subsequent ministrations to the earl as the beginning of her real involvement with the Keeson family. At the time, however, the incident possessed no unusual significance. She was conscious of a slight feeling of pique at the earl's seeming cynicism toward women as she walked with the child toward the blue saloon, but that was scarcely sufficient to mark the day as different from those that had preceded it.

Lady Montrose was alone when Miss Norris and Emilie entered. She smiled at both but said, "Emilie, my love, should you not be in the nursery? You still look quite peaked to me."

The child curtsied and replied earnestly, "I am feeling all better now, *Grand'mère.*" She remained by Chloe's side, taking a seat beside her on the settee.

Miss Norris smiled at her hostess. "I am persuaded you will concur, ma'am, that the best prescription for Emilie now is to spend hours outdoors to bring the roses back to her cheeks."

"As long as she does not overtax her strength," Lady Montrose replied. "Emilie is not a robust child, I fear. She gets her delicate constitution from her mother. Patricia is the only one of my children to inherit my susceptibility to infectious complaints, but at least I have never been prone to succumb to a *'crise de nerfs.'* Patricia has developed that regrettable tendency only since her unfortunate marriage."

Aware of the tension in the little girl at her side, Miss Norris said in cheerful accents, "My father is a great believer in the value of reasonable amounts of physical exertion and simple good food. He contends that such a regimen can strengthen and improve one's constitution over a period of time."

"No doubt Dr. Norris has helped to heal a great many people over the years, but one cannot fight one's nature, after all."

"No, but one can lend nature a helping hand," Chloe returned. "A few weeks in this beautiful crisp air will soon put Emilie to rights. Even today she conducted me all around the orchards with no signs of shortness of breath or fatigue."

"Yes, *Grand'mère,*" the child piped up, "I am not at all tired really."

"I am delighted to hear that, my child, but here is our tea tray. I expect that Addie is waiting for you in the nursery with your tea."

"But may I not stay to see *Maman*?" Emilie's bottom lip was quivering.

Chloe dug her fingernails into the flesh of her palms as she concentrated on holding her tongue. It was not her place to question Lady Montrose's decisions, especially after having just ventured to advance her father's theories in opposition to her hostess's opinion. To her great relief, a light rustle at the doorway at that fraught moment presaged the entrance of Lady Patricia. Emilie jumped to her feet and ran to her mother, throwing her arms about her waist.

"I am all better now, *Maman*. I cannot give you my cold."

Lady Patricia had been rocked nearly off her feet by her daughter's enthusiastic embrace. The countess spoke out in quick reprimand to the child, but Lady Patricia implored, "Don't scold her, Mama; she hasn't seen me in nearly a fortnight." She smiled at the clinging little girl. "You still look a bit peaky, darling. Come sit with me."

For the first time there was a sparkle of life in the young widow's lovely countenanace, and Miss Norris could picture how enchanting she must have been as a carefree girl making her come-out. She must have attracted men like shavings of iron to a magnet. Chloe rose from the settee and took a chair to allow mother and daughter to sit together. Lady Patricia gave her a sweet absent smile as she sank onto the settee's firm cushion, the temporary animation already leaving her. Lady Mary came in at that moment, creating a mild diversion as her mother eyed her gray gown with disfavor.

"I will never understand why you persist in wearing that old rag, Mary. One of these days I am going to order your maid to burn it."

"No, you will not!" Two spots of red flared in the girl's cheeks as she defied her mother, who blinked in surprise at the vehemence. Lady Mary apologized immediately for her intemperate reaction, but there was a stubborn set to her chin as she accepted her tea. "I won't wear it in your presence anymore, Mama, since the sight of it offends you, but I shall keep the dress."

They were on their second cup of tea when Lord Montrose entered the room. Miss Norris had spun out her reactions to the beauties of the grounds as long as she could, assisted once or twice by embellishments from Emilie. The two daughters of the house had sunk back into their usual uncommunicative silence almost immediately, and the countess had been less assiduous in maintaining the semblance of a conversation than was her wont. Her pique forgotten, Chloe greeted the earl's arrival with a relieved smile. She knew by the very faint twitch at the corner of his mouth that he had taken in the situation with his first sweeping glance about the room.

"Any more tea in that pot for a thirsty man, Mama?" he asked after issuing a general greeting.

"Of course, Ivor." Her glance narrowed as the earl approached the tea tray. "Good heavens, what has happened to your face? You look as though someone had clawed you."

"Something, not someone," he replied, reaching for a cup. "My people were hacking out some overgrown hedges today."

"And you were hacking along with them, obviously. You are just like your father. He could never leave the labor to the laborers either."

"My father knew the value of physical labor to a man. Apart from the satisfaction of using one's physical strength in a difficult task, it is a decided advantage to have one's men know that you can if necessary perform the same work demanded of them."

"Ah, but is it necessary?" his mother countered. "No one will ever convince me that your father did not weaken his health trying to outdo the men over a period of years. And for what purpose? The crucial element that is required for the efficient management of an estate is adequate supervision."

"This may be a point upon which men and women are

constitutionally unable to agree, Mama. All I am saying is that some participation is necessary to me, as it was necessary to my father.''

"Is it not rather similar to a good mistress knowing how to produce all the things required of her kitchen and stillroom?'' Miss Norris asked.

The earl looked at her with a faint smile that might have been agreement, but it was the countess who replied. "I would certainly concede the similarity in that it is equally *un*necessary in both cases. It is no more necessary for the mistress of a house to sink her elbows into the flour bin in order for the kitchen to produce good bread then for the owner of an estate personally to rip out hedges in order to get his land cleared. I believe I may assert without fear of contradiction that this house is an example of efficient management. All that is required of me is close supervision of the staff.''

The earl bowed to his mother. "You are justly renowned for the skill with which you manage the domestic machinery at Applewood, Mama. As I said, the owner's physical participation may be a point on which the sexes cannot agree. Perhaps it is merely a case of eccentric personal pride that motivates those owners and mistresses who occasionally like to demonstrate their capabilities in the actual performance of necessary labors.''

The last part of this speech was directed to Miss Norris, who returned his conspiratorial smile and kept to herself the traitorous opinion that the credit for the smooth running of this particular household belonged almost entirely to Mrs. Meggs. Presumably Lady Montrose had selected her capable and hardworking housekeeper and maintained a strong control through her, so she must be accorded the credit ultimately. Chloe kept her eyes discreetly lowered, resolved not to seem to disagree with her hostess again. She reminded herself that she did not have the freedom of a desired guest to speak her mind; she was here solely to serve the countess's interests.

As though to mock her politic resolution, the conversation switched back to the earl's injuries when the countess called attention to his reddened eye. "Did those beastly thorns gouge your eye, Ivor?''

"No, Mama, nothing like that. Some dirt got in my eye,

that's all. Now that it is out the redness will soon disappear.''

"Miss Norris got the grit out of Uncle Ivor's eye and I helped her,'' Emilie announced proudly.

"Miss Norris got it out!''

The countess modulated her voice, which had rung shrilly. "How extraordinary! How did this come about? Were you and Miss Norris clearing out hedges too, Emilie, and you just out of a sickroom?''

The attempt at playfulness in no way lessened Lady Montrose's determination to get to the bottom of the incident, Miss Norris could see as she hesitated. The question had been addressed to the child, but somehow she felt it was her own version of the situation the countess desired to hear.

The earl spoke up before either feminine participant could frame a reply. "Of course they were not near the hedges, Mama. I met Emilie and Miss Norris on my way back to the house to have the eye seen to, and Miss Norris skillfully got rid of the grit for me.''

"Indeed. How fortunate that Miss Norris was on the scene.''

Such was the effect of Lady Montrose's softly uttered words that Chloe felt compelled to add to the earl's minimal explanation. "Lord Montrose was going to seek out his valet, ma'am, but my father has impressed upon me the importance of swift action where the eyes are concerned. I am afraid I overbore his lordship's arguments and proceeded to flush out the dirt with the water from the dolphin fountain, as my father would have done.'' She turned to Lady Patricia with a smile and added, "You will be pleased to know that Emilie kept her head quite coolly and was of enormous help in speeding up the operation. It was she who performed the tiresome chore of repeatedly soaking our handkerchiefs under the fountain.''

"Did you really, darling? What a very competent daughter I have.'' Lady Patricia put her arm about the child's shoulders and squeezed her to her side briefly.

"It is to be hoped that Emilie does not suffer a recrudescence of her illness after getting herself soaked in the process. There are great patches of damp on her dress still,'' the countess pointed out.

"Oh, dear! You must instantly go to the nursery and change

to dry clothing, Emilie,'' Lady Patricia cried, swift alarm settling over her features.

"I am not wet, *Maman,* not my skin, I mean. Only my dress got wet, not even my petticoat—see, there is only a little damp down by the hem.''

"Nevertheless, I should like you to change into something else, dearest. We shall take no chances with your health.''

"Yes, *Maman.* Will you come with me to the nursery so Addie won't scold me for getting my clothes wet?''

"Not today, *chèrie.* I feel my headache coming back. Tell Addie I said you are not to be scolded.''

"Yes, *Maman.*'' Emilie sighed and rose reluctantly.

As the child dropped a curtsy to her grandmother, her uncle said, "Thank you again for your services today, my pet.''

"Pray accept my thanks too, Emilie, for your assistance.'' Chloe added her measure in an effort to lessen the little girl's disappointment at being banished to the nursery.

Lady Montrose took firm charge of the conversation when her granddaughter had quit the room. "What do you think of our little village, my dear?'' she asked Chloe. "Does it remind you of home?''

"I don't know, ma'am, I haven't seen it yet.''

"You haven't?'' Lady Montrose turned her deep blue gaze on her younger daughter. "I am astonished that you have not yet brought Chloe into the village, Mary.''

"We . . . we must not have walked in that direction, ma'am. Where is it?'' Chloe asked quickly, hoping to divert attention from the girl, whose normally pale cheeks were flying flags of color for the second time that afternoon.

"It's about a half-mile down the path that starts behind the stables.'' Lady Mary avoided her mother's eyes and addressed herself to Chloe. "We'll go tomorrow if you like.''

"That would be pleasant,'' Chloe replied, smiling at the girl.

Lord Montrose had been regarding his sister with a thoughtful expression. Now he said to their guest, "There is a fascinating shop run by two sisters, maiden ladies who had earned quite a local reputation for their baking prowess. You must sample their gingerbread.''

"I will.'' Chloe returned his smile, pleased to have avoided a scene, though she would have bet against the chance that the elusive Lady Mary would keep their tentative appointment.

This time she'd have lost her wager. The next day when Lady Montrose rose from the table after lunch with her usual vague hope that they would enjoy their afternoon, Chloe replied with her usual murmur of appreciation, but Lady Mary said clearly, "We are going to walk into the village, Mama. Do you have any comissions for us?"

"You might check again for that odd shade of blue embroidery silk that I have been unable to match."

Her daughter nodded. "Very well."

When the countess had closed the door behind her, Lady Mary met the other girl's carefully neutral gaze with a wry grimace. "I don't blame you for looking as though you expected me to vanish into a puff of smoke at any moment. I expect that's what you think I've been doing since your arrival at Applewood. Ivor gave me a rare trimming last night for being inhospitable— actually that is softening it," she added with disarming frankness. "What he really said was that I'd been an insufferable little beast lately and appallingly rude to a guest. I hope you'll believe that it wasn't a deliberate policy against you, Miss Norris. I'm afraid I've been preoccupied with my own . . . affairs lately. It really didn't occur to me that you were left on your own so much. Please forgive me, anyway."

"I gather your brother constrained you to make this handsome apology?"

"Yes," Lady Mary replied, flushing faintly at the other's mischievous smile, "But I wanted to anyway when it finally dawned on me yesterday that we were neglecting you badly. Ivor is always busy about the estate and poor Tricia is unconscious of what goes on around her these days, but I should have noticed that you were being left to your own devices too much had I not been so . . . so preoccupied myself."

"An *amende honorable*," Chloe said with another smile after an encouraging look had produced no expansion of the reason for Lady Mary's recent preoccupation. "We do not need to go to the village today, you know, if there is something you would rather be doing. I am certain I could find it myself if you would direct me."

"I can say with complete truth that there is nothing else I'd rather be doing this afternoon."

The words were lightly spoken but not lightly meant, Chloe guessed, hearing a note of bitterness underneath. She supposed no single activity had any more appeal than another to Lady Mary these days because, for some reason she did not propose to divulge, all activities were equally unattractive. That being the case, Chloe decided she might as well take advantage of the girl's services as a guide to widen her own acquaintance with the Suffolk area.

"Are my shoes sufficiently strong or should I change to half boots?" she asked, holding out her sandaled foot for the younger girl's inspection.

A half hour later the two young women were walking down the path that led to the nearest village. They had changed to firmer footwear and added shawls over their shoulders to compensate for the gusty little breeze that took some of the heat from the sun. Their conversation was confined to an exchange of questions and information about the area, but Chloe didn't mind that. After a period of feeling that her presence was an intrusion despite the civility with which she was treated, she was content to enjoy the impersonal companionship of Lady Mary, who had for the moment cast off her previous self-absorption and was setting out to be agreeable.

When they were barely out of sight of the stables Lady Mary pointed out a path that led to the home farm, though they couldn't see it from the lane. Their way led between fields and pasture land dotted with the occasional tree, but they did not come upon any signs of human habitation until they were nearly into the village, when they passed two timber and plaster cottages with thatched roofs. They stopped for a few moments near one of the cottages to watch two men renewing the outer layer of thatch, the "coat" that is applied over the thick inner "waistcoat" layer that is sewn right onto the roof rafters when the cottage is built. Though the men called down a greeting to the girls, they didn't pause in the work of setting in the hairpin-shaped spicks that affixed the new thatch to the old.

Presently the two young women came to the village itself, a straggle of cottages along a graveled road that ran at right

angles to their path, which ended in a cluster of buildings around
a solid-looking church built of local flint. Lady Mary pointed
out the manse, an L-shaped structure with a newer, larger
addition of red brick grafted onto the original flint-faced
building. Lovely old trees leaned over the fence that separated
the garden from the cemetery.

There were perhaps a score of buildings in all along the main
road, most of them cottages belonging to agricultural workers,
each with its attendant garden. They passed a smithy and entered
a shop that offered a wide variety of goods and sundries, though
its small stock of embroidery silks did not contain the shade
Lady Montrose sought. Chloe purchased a collar of point lace
with some idea of brightening up her brown gown and
exchanged a few civilities with Mr. Kett, the shopkeeper, when
her guide made them known to each other.

Emerging from Mr. Kett's shop, the women had to sidestep
quickly to avoid the headlong progress of a pair of village boys
racing past them with their cheeks stuffed full of some treat.
The tantalizing scents of cinnamon and baking bread wafted out
of the cottage from which the youngsters had erupted.

"Ummmmm," Chloe said appreciatively. "Something smells
delicious."

"This is the bakeshop of the Misses Bonifer."

"There isn't any sign"—Chloe glanced down the short,
flower-bordered path to the cottage door—"but with such
aromas as advertisement, I don't suppose a sign is necessary.
May we go inside? I'd like to sample that gingerbread your
brother recommended."

"Of course."

As they stepped over the threshold Chloe looked about her
with frank curiosity. She saw at once that the bakeshop was
also the home of its proprietors. It appeared to be a typical
cottage with one large front room. The door in the far wall
probably led to a "back-us" or unheated scullary. She knew
that a steep staircase behind the door near the fireplace would
lead into one of the two upstairs rooms, also unheated. Here
the staircase had been enclosed to provide much-needed
cupboard space downstairs. A large oak dresser against one wall
was crowded with dishes and pottery displayed on its upper

shelves. Cupboard doors concealed more storage space below. A fine yellow sand was sprinkled on the brick floor of the cottage, which was rather dimly lighted through its small latticed windows of leaded glass. Potted plants on the windowsills partially blocked the available light but lent a cheerful air to the dimness. A beautifully carved bread trough on splayed legs stood beside a small square table crammed with the necessary equipment and ingredients that went into the baking.

There was certainly no want of warmth in the main room, what with a steady fire going in the open hearth to provide heat for the baking oven in the brick wall beside it. A tall, stout woman with a round face was in the act of removing two long loaves from the oven, which she brought over to the rectangular table standing foresquare in front of the door. This table already held an appetizing array of the products of the sisters' labors.

Another woman bustled in from the scullery, drying her hands on her apron as she came. Equally stout and round-faced, she barely reached her sister's shoulders. Both ladies possessed an abundance of silvery curls showing beneath snowy muslin mobcaps, and the full cheeks of both were rosy from working in the heated room. Identical smiles of welcome adorned their faces as the girls approached the large table.

"Good afternoon, Miss Bonifer, Miss Agnes," Lady Mary said. "This is Miss Norris, who is visiting with us for a few weeks."

"How do, miss," said the smaller of the sisters, Miss Agnes, bobbing her head to the newcomer before turning a beaming smile on the other girl. "We heard talk of a young lady up at the house to help with all the wedding plans. When is the big day, Lady Mary?"

"The twenty-fourth of October," Lady Mary said shortly, and turned to stare at the dresser.

"Your baked goods look and smell simply wonderful, Miss Bonifer and Miss Agnes," Chloe said into the breach, glad to see the sisters' smiles revive in the wake of her enthusiasm. "Lord Montrose spoke of your fame as bakers, but my nose would have told me anyway. His lordship has commanded me to sample your gingerbread, but I don't see any here."

"Oi'm hully regretful, miss, but we only bakes gingerbread

on Monday, Wednesday, and Friday. Today it's cinnamon rolls. Here, do you have a chice o' that,'' said Miss Agnes, who seemed to do the talking for both, as her sister sliced a slab off one of the loaves on the table and held it out to the visitor. ''That rummian' cook up at the house has been atryin' to get that receipt from us for years, hasn't he, Meg?'' she finished with a chuckle that shook her several chins.

Miss Bonifer nodded and waited for Chloe's reaction as she nibbled at the warm cinnamon bread. The expectant expression on her broad face became a huge smile as the nibble became a near gobble.

''That is scrumptious, quite the best I've ever eaten,'' Chloe declared when she had swallowed and licked the last stray crumb from her fingertips. ''Be assured I shall come back to try your gingerbread one day soon. May I buy this roll to bring back with us for tea?''

Sensing a rising impatience to be gone in her companion, Chloe concluded her business with the friendly bakers with expressions of mutual satisfaction. As the girls went out into the crisp air, she carried Lady Mary's basket, turning to wave a farewell to Miss Agnes, who had escorted them to the door.

Though they had not reached the end of the village, Lady Mary turned back the way they had come. Chloe did not comment on this, merely saying into the continued silence, ''That was indeed a treat. Thank you for bringing me into the village today. I have enjoyed myself.''

''The Bonifer sisters are the biggest gossips in the neighborhood,'' Lady Mary muttered.

''Is there any village in England where gossip is not the main activity?'' Chloe asked lightly. ''Or in the world, for that matter?''

Lady Mary ignored this rhetorical question and they walked on in a silence Chloe did not attempt to break. She took advantage of the young girl's moody abstraction to make a covert study of her profile. For a brief period that afternoon, Lady Mary had been able to set aside her personal problems and take the trouble to do something for someone else. The accommodation was over and one did not have to look far for a reason. It had been the reference to her prospective wedding that had brought the girl's troubles storming back. There was a tightness about her mouth and an occasional muscle twitch in her cheek as she walked along the village street with downcast eyes. If anything had been needed to confirm her suspicions as to the underlying cause of Lady Mary's unhappiness, this reaction would have provided it. Knowing her companion was blind to anything happening in her vicinity at present, Chloe gave a quiet warning as they approached the church again.

"I believe that is Mr. Keeson ahead of us talking with someone in front of the manse."

"What?" Unfocused light-blue eyes turned her way, then followed the direction of Chloe's gaze. "Oh, that is Ellen Vessey, the pastor's daughter. Like every other female within a day's ride, she is enamored of Ned's handsome face. He flirts madly with all of them in turn, and gossip being what it is, they all know this, but it doesn't seem to make any difference to their determination to fix his interest. They are all sheep where Ned is concerned. At least Ellen is not so silly as most of the local girls. She has enough pride to conceal her smitten state from my conceited brother."

This gratutous information had been delivered in a rapid undertone as the girls neared the engrossed couple standing outside the gate leading to the front door of the manse. Mr. Keeson held the reins of a neat gray hack and Miss Vessey had a basket over one arm. She looked up when the other young women were within a dozen feet and produced a sweet smile of welcome.

"Hello, Mary. I was just telling Mr. Keeson that it has been over a fortnight since I have set eyes on you. I hope you did not fall victim to the wave of feverish colds that seems to be sweeping through the parish."

As Lady Mary disclaimed any illness and went on to present the Keesons' guest, Chloe decided that she liked the look of the minister's daughter. Though not an outstanding beauty, she had lovely hazel eyes set in an oval face whose creamy complexion would be coveted by many a less-favored young lady. An expressive low-pitched voice was an additional asset. Though she had looked a trifle self-conscious when her conversation with Mr. Keeson was first interrupted, Miss Vessey turned her full attention to making the stranger feel welcome, asking Chloe about her impressions of Suffolk and listening with grave attention to the responses. She smiled on spotting the loaf in the basket over Chloe's arm and indicated her own.

"I was on my way to the bakeshop to buy some of his favorite cinnamon bread for my father when Mr. Keeson rode by."

Lady Mary then asked about Mrs. Vessey's health. After Miss Vessey had assured her that her mother was gaining strength daily after a severe and persistent attack of bronchitis, she hesitated for a second before saying, "My father received a visit today from the squire. Mr. Trainor wished to share some good news with us. It seems that Mr. Thomas Trainor is expected home within the next few days." She explained for Chloe's benefit, "Mr. Thomas Trainor, the squire's son, has been away tending to his family's business interests in Bermuda for more than two years. As you may imagine, his parents and sisters are elated by these tidings and are happily making plans to celebrate his safe return to the family circle."

"Is that so?" Mr. Keeson said. "I saw the squire just two days ago and he never said a word about Tom coming home. By Jove, that is good news. Things will be looking up in this dead-and-alive place when old Tom arrives."

"I believe they just received word at the manor this morning. It was not expected for—Oh!" Miss Vessey broke off as two young lads engaged in juvenile horseplay came racing past them. Chloe just had time to identify them as the same two boys they had seen on the street earlier when one pushed the other, who fell sideways, knocking the basket off Miss Vessey's arm and startling Mr. Keeson's horse. The gray threw up his head and pawed the ground.

"Be off, you two clodpolls, before I give you a ding about the lug-hole," Mr. Keeson threatened the heedless boys as he quieted his horse, switching to a soothing tone as he addressed the beast.

Chloe picked up the fallen basket and returned it to Miss Vessey, who thanked her and made her adieux and apologies for leaving them. "Papa will be grievously disappointed if I am too late to buy his cinnamon bread," she said with a twinkle in her soft eyes. "I shall hope to see you again, Miss Norris. Good-bye, Mary . . . Mr. Keeson."

Lady Mary had not said a single word since Miss Vessey's announcement of the return of the squire's son. Chloe had not missed the color that had flared into her cheeks on hearing this news before the pastor's daughter had claimed her attention. The girl did not speak now but set her face toward the lane leading to Applewood and moved off as soon as her friend had walked away.

By the time Chloe and Mr. Keeson, leading his horse, caught up with Lady Mary, the color had faded from her face once again. There was a gleam of something that might have been excitement in her eyes, but when her brother demanded to know what was the mad rush, all she said was, "Mama will scold if we are late for tea."

Not another word did she utter during the course of the return walk, which she took at a pace that had Chloe stretching to keep up with her, a task made more difficult by Mr. Keeson, who seemed determined to carry on a lighthearted flirtation. Chloe was getting better at parrying his thrusts by now and thus had a little corner of her mind free to devote to the question of what there was about Mr. Thomas Trainor that caused his young neighbor to go into a distracted state, for she was convinced that it had been the introduction of his name that had had this curious effect on Lady Mary.

Chapter Six

WHEN THEY REACHED Applewood, Mr. Keeson stopped at the stables to see to his horse, Lady Mary slipped away without a word, and Chloe descended to the kitchens to leave her purchase from the village bakeshop. They met again in the blue saloon within the hour.

Lady Montrose, sitting in her usual place behind the tea table, brightened visibly at sight of her younger son, who had been off visiting friends for the past two days. He came over to kiss her scented cheek, complimenting her on her new cap with its pleated frill.

"I swear you don't look a day older than Tricia in that ravishing cap, Mama."

"Spare my blushes, flatterer. I hope I have not languished so long in the country that I no longer recognize Spanish coin when it is offered me," his mother protested, though with an indulgent smile about her lips.

"Mama, you cut me to the quick with such unjust accusations. If you require the opinion of a disinterested observer, I am persuaded Miss Norris will echo my sentiments."

"Gladly," Chloe replied with flattering promptness. "It is indeed a vastly becoming cap, ma'am, and makes your eyes look even more intensely blue than usual."

Mr. Keeson grinned across the tea table at the smiling young woman. "No one can doubt Miss Norris's veracity, and she has totally supported my contention. There, Mama, do you not feel ashamed for questioning your child's truthfulness?" His handsome face assumed a wounded look as he took the chair to his mother's right.

"I feel ashamed for raising a bare-faced rogue," Lady Montrose said lightly. "I can see I shall have to caution you against any but the most casual association with this scapegoat,

Chloe. Your father would not thank me for exposing your integrity to a corrupting influence.''

"Worse and worse," Mr. Keeson groaned. "That the woman who bore me could turn against me so cavalierly is a misfortune I could never have foreseen in my worst imaginings. Besides,'' he added, dropping the dramatic pose, "I am confident that Miss Norris's integrity would stand proof against the most evil influence in the world. And with that in mind, I am going to petition for the privilege of using her very delightful name.''

"Of . . . of course, Mr. Keeson, if you wish." Chloe was no less startled than Lady Montrose at the switch from theatrical nonsense to sincerity on her son's part. She could feel a slight betraying wave of heat rising from her throat at the unexpected tribute, so unlike his usual glib compliments, and she was hard-pressed to maintain her air of nonchalance, especially in the face of what she sensed was his mother's consternation at this turn of events. The sounds in the doorway that heralded Lord Montrose's arrival were as welcome as a choir of angels.

The earl's oddly light eyes took in his brother's look of satisfaction, the relieved smile of Miss Norris, and his mother's smooth mask of civility in one sweeping pass as he approached the tea table. He glanced down at the Limoges dish beside the tea tray. "Ah, unless my nose deceives me, this is the Miss Bonifers' cinnamon roll, second only to their gingerbread in my affections. May I assume from this evidence that you and Mary walked into the village today, Miss Norris?''

As Chloe nodded smilingly, Lord Montrose piled several slices of the bread onto a plate and accepted his tea from the countess. The two daughters of the family came in together and Chloe relaxed into her chair while they settled themselves into place. She never felt quite comfortable when Mr. Keeson directed his battery of charm at her under his mother's eye, though she was not the least bit embarrassed at dealing with his even more pointed advances at other times. Surely the countess should be well-enough acquainted with her son's proclivity for flirtation to discount its importance. She wished, not for the first time, that she could find some unexceptionable way to reassure the protective mother that she had no designs on her volatile son and was not about to have her head turned by his attentions. Short of issuing a blunt statement that she would be immune to his brand of charm even if she were not already betrothed, no acceptable method suggested itself. Supposing for the sake of argument that she could frame this sentiment in words not likely to be interpreted by a doting mother as an insult, tact and good manners were still ranged against such crass action. It seemed her only course was one of continued deliberate ignorance of any undercurrents, which had the built-in disadvantage of never allowing the air to be cleared between herself and her hostess. For a person who much preferred taking direct action to settle problems as they arose to a policy of doing nothing in the hope that time would resolve the issue, this could never be a wholly satisfactory decision.

Chloe sipped her tea slowly, hoping to be able to fade into the background today since Lady Montrose had both her sons present to assist her in keeping the conversatiaon from limping badly. She was staring down into her cup when her hostess's voice pierced her abstraction.

"You are looking very pensive, my dear Chloe, as if your thoughts were miles away. Perhaps they are," she continued archly. "Perhaps they have wafted far away over the seas."

"Not quite that far, my lady," Chloe riposted, having grasped the implication and not wishing to discuss her betrothal. "Only so far as Scotland, actually. I was wondering if my father is having a successful shoot."

The countess smiled in sweet sympathy. "It must be difficult to be separated from the persons who are most important to you."

"It is only for a few weeks, and I felt strongly that my father needed a good rest. He is so deeply involved with his patients that he almost never has any time to himself at home. I received a letter from him two days ago. He is thoroughly enjoying his visit with old friends." Chloe smiled widely at her hostesss and began to sip her tea again. Her satisfaction at her adroit handling of the delicate situation proved premature, however.

"I am so glad your mind is relieved of concern for your father at present, dear child. You have been so kind to lend us your assistance with plans for my daughter's wedding. I fear I have been quite remiss in not ascertaining whether your coming here was quite convenient in terms of your own wedding plans. I don't believe my sister mentioned when your marriage is to take place.''

Neatly boxed into a corner, Chloe accepted defeat and arranged her features to portray a carefree girl pleased with the interest of others in her future plans. ''Lady Dalrymple could not have told you that, ma'am, because she knew we would not be able to set a date until Captain Otley returns to England. Meanwhile I am very content to be here at Applewood where I hope I may be of real service to you.''

''I take it that your betrothal is of fairly recent date since you have not yet made wedding plans?''

''Why . . . no, ma'am. Actually we have been engaged for some little time, but circumstances have not been entirely propitious to date.''

''How long have you been engaged?''

The blunt question came from Lady Mary. Chloe glanced at the girl, struggling to keep her bright expression from slipping. She rejected her first impulse to declare that it was none of the girl's business, and said pleasantly, ''A bit under five years.''

''Five years!''

His sister's disbelieving exclamation was nearly drowned out by Mr. Keeson's drawling, ''Now, there is a stupid man!''

''If I take your meaning correctly, sir, you are assuming the delay in my marriage is due to some reluctance on the part of my fiancé?''

''Good lord, no! Furthest thing from my mind to insult you, Chloe. I just meant that if *I* were your fiancé there would be no long engagement—that is—''

''Cut your losses, Ned,'' Lord Montrose advised his maladroit brother before turning a charming smile on Chloe. ''You must think us a family of busybodies, Miss Norris. Please accept our joint apology for invading the privacy of a guest in our home.''

''Oh, no, you need not apologize . . . I should not dream . . . I mean . . .'' Chloe broke off her flustered response when she realized that the earl was not listening. He had turned away to address a question to his brother.

She picked up the cup she had set down with fingers that

trembled slightly, and took a sip of the cooling liquid to ease
her dry throat. She kept her eyes on her cup, battling to regain
her composure. Her mind was a seething mass of emotion, of
which the main component was anger. No, that was too strong;
annoyane or irritation was a better description of what she was
feeling, she assured herself, trying to slow her breathing down
to a normal rhythm again while she sought to make some sense
of her own reaction. Normally she was not a person of quick
temper, but a moment ago she had flown at poor Mr. Keeson,
who had most likely only sought to offer her a compliment. It
was even more disconcerting to have to acknowledge a strong
irritation at Bertram as the person responsible for placing her
in a position to be so publicly humiliated.

When Chloe had replayed the brief scene in her mind and
examined her behavior she was left with the lowering conclusion
that the person she should be most annoyed with was herself.
Everyone at home knew of her long engagement. Some had even
twitted her about it on occasion, and never had she reacted with
anger. Though she had slowly come to realize that her circumstances vis-à-vis her eventual marriage were no longer entirely
desirable, until she came to Applewood she had not experienced
any humiliation at her situation, which left the question: why
now? Obviously it was more than time that she stopped coasting
mindlessly along and applied herself to a serious consideration
of her future. A social hour in a home where she was a guest
was scarcely the time or place, though. She owed the company
her attention and civility.

In control of herself once more, Chloe raised her eyes from
the contents of her cup and attuned her ear to the conversation
going on around her. Evidently, Mr. Keeson had repeated the
news of the imminent return of the squire's son to his home.
The earl was stating his intention of calling at the manor when
the anticipated happy homecoming had taken place.

"Should you like to come with me, Mama?"

"No, I shall leave it to you to communicate our pleasure in
Mr. Thomas Trainor's safe return."

"You would not like the Keeson family to be thought
backward in any neighborly attention."

"I refuse to step foot over that threshold unless civility makes it unavoidable. This is largely a masculine affair, so it is perfectly understandable that the Keeson participation should also be male."

"You will of course write to the Trainors inviting Tom to Mary's ball."

"Yes," Lady Montrose agreed. "There is no escaping that."

"I should think not," Mr. Keeson said. "Mary and I have grown up with Tom and his sisters, after all. I don't see what you've got against the Trainors, Mama."

"I have nothing against the squire. He's a good enough sort of man with no ambitions to move in exalted circles. The creature he married is another matter, however."

"I think Mrs. Trainor is a very nice woman, always so pleasant and kind," Lady Mary put it with unwonted energy.

"Marcella Trainor is an underbred, encroaching individual with designs above her station, and those two daughters of hers are cast in her image. But none of this can possibly be of interest to Chloe, who is unacquainted with anyone in the vicinity."

Lady Montrose went on to speak of other things, and the subject of the neighbors did not surface again that day.

The next morning found the unbroken succession of lovely clear days at an end, at least temporarily. Eyeing the gathering mass of gray clouds on arising, Lord Montrose decided to take advantage of the promised inclemency to spend a few hours catching up with the arrears in his correspondence and farm accounts. Between harvesting and overseeing the preparations for the upcoming pheasant shooting he had been almost constantly out on the estate these past weeks. He might have managed to keep abreast of the accumulating mass of clerical tasks by working throughout every evening—indeed, that had been his standard plea to excuse himself from sitting around the drawing room after dinner—but he had done far more reading than working or writing; the growing piles of papers on his desk testified to that. His conscience did not greatly trouble him on this account. At this busy season there would be no time at all for reading if he did not steal it.

In any case he could not have stood to expose himself to a succession of family evenings of excruciating boredom without the resultant strain on his disposition becoming apparent. He was very fond of his sister Patricia, just a year younger, but their childhood affinity had ceased with her marriage a decade ago. Though he was desperately sorry about her unhappiness, his attempts to reach out to her since she and Emilie had returned to Applewood had been not spurned so much as not even noticed, which was infinitely more discouraging. Mary was more than ten years his junior, a gap too great to be bridged with a girl raised almost exclusively by her mother. Ned, though only five years younger, remained a closed book intellectually under the surface amiability that characterized his behavior, and since his father's death the earl's relations with his mother had stayed on a cool, dutiful level.

He let the window curtain fall back into place and with it any ruminations on his relationship with his remaining parent. There were things in everyone's life that could not be changed and must simply be endured with the best grace possible. Yes, he decided, today would be a good opportunity to work indoors.

As good as his word, the earl was sitting at the big desk in the library when the butler sought him out sometime after mid morning.

"Yes, Hawkins?"

"The ladies from the manor have called, sir, and Lady Montrose requests that you join her in the main drawing room if that should be convenient."

"I see. Thank you, Hawkins."

"Very good, sir."

His pen suspended over the sheet of paper on which he had been writing, Lord Montrose continued to stare at the door for a moment after the butler had closed it soundlessly. His strong-boned face wore its usual mask of civil indifference, but no one could have mistaken it for pleasure at the prospect of doing the pretty to a bunch of females. His chin rested on his left fist and his eyes came back to the pen he was slowly rolling between his thumb and first two fingers as he sat pondering. In the next second his glance chanced to fall on a leather-bound book reposing near the far corner of the desk. The rolling motions with the pen ceased and the straight line of his lips softened as a glint came into his eyes. He deposited the pen in its stand

and rose from the desk, running a smoothing hand over his dark hair as he did so.

A few moments later, Lord Montrose entered the drawing room with the quiet tread that was a bit surprising in a large man. Before anyone even looked up, his active intelligence had assimilated the situation. The squire's lady, a placid-faced woman with fine dark eyes, a nondescript nose, and a kind mouth, was seated on the sofa with her hostess. Occupying the settee were Miss Trainor—Jane, if memory served—and Miss Caroline Trainor, attractive girls both but with a tendency to giggle at unseasonable moments. They were flanked by Mary and Ned in armless chairs drawn up at right angles to the settee. Patricia was not present, but Miss Norris, with a piece of embroidery in her lap, was sitting at a little distance from the other young people.

"Mrs. Trainor, what a pleasant surprise," he said, sending his voice on ahead as he approached the sofa. "I don't need to ask how you are, for I can see that your good news has put a sparkle in your eyes."

Mrs. Trainor smiled delightedly as she shook hands with her host, revealing a row of gleaming white teeth and raising her ordinary good looks up a notch or two in his estimation. "I won't try to deny it," she replied on a chuckle. When the earl turned back to her after greeting the young ladies, who, predictably, were overcome with blushes and giggles, Mrs. Trainor went on, "Tom is due home tomorrow, and I must confess the girls and I cannot contain ourselves simply waiting around the house, as I explained to her ladyship when we arrived. We are planning a dinner party for the day after tomorrow so that Tom may meet all his old friends at once. It is late notice, I am aware, but I do hope you are free to come to us on Friday."

The earl glanced at his mother, cool and regal-looking, her lips curved in a small social smile. "I believe we are completely free that evening, ma'am, and will all be delighted to welcome Tom home again. It is very kind of you to include us, isn't that so, Mama?"

"Most kind," replied the countess, taking her cue smoothly. "We shall certainly be pleased to attend, although I cannot speak for my elder daughter, who has not yet begun to go out into society since her bereavement.''

''The poor thing.'' Mrs. Trainor shook her head in sympathy. ''I would not dream of persuading Lady Patricia, but please convey my compliments to her and assure her of our great pleasure if she should feel able to join us.''

Lady Montrose inclined her head at this, then went on to say, ''I must confess I would have expected that you would wish to have your son to yourselves for a time after such a long absence.''

If the squire's lady detected any implied censure in this remark she elected not to take offense, saying with another chuckle, ''Lord, ma'am, it is more likely that the girls and I will so smother Tom with attentions that he'll be desperate to get us off his neck and that grateful to see other people by Friday. It seems an age since we last had him home, though I must say to his credit that he has been a faithful correspondent. We've enjoyed hearing all about the island of Bermuda and the way the people live there with all that heat and burning sunshine. His last few letters have been full of longing for home, though. Not that he'll find everything exactly as it was when he left, of course. His sisters have grown up since he went off, and here is your Mary about to be married. I wrote to tell Tom of your betrothal, my dear, but I think he may not have received that letter because he never commented on it, and generally he will have something to say on the bits of local news we send off to him.''

The earl had remained standing near Mrs. Trainor as she addressed her rambling remarks first to his mother, then to his sister. Though his head was inclined politely toward their voluble neighbor, from the corner of his eye he had actually been watching Miss Norris's hands as they set neat stitches in her work. He had known they were capable hands, both gentle and skillful, since the day he'd gotten dirt in his eye, but he had not noticed before that they were exceptionally lovely also, beautifully formed with smooth tapering fingers and almond-shaped nails. As Mrs. Trainor ended her monologue, he saw Miss Norris's fingers cease their sewing motions and tighten around the needle. His eyes winged to her face, then followed her gaze to where his sister was sitting frozen into immobility, her eyes fixed on Mrs. Trainor with what he could only call painful intensity.

Hawkins entered the room at this juncture, carrying an enormous silver tray containing a coffeepot and attendant accoutrements. He was grateful for the timing of the interruption for it diverted attention from Mary, who wrenched her eyes away from Mrs. Trainor and stared blindly at the butler. He was puzzling over the significance, if any, of what he had witnessed when his mother's voice scattered his thoughts.

"You will stay and take coffee with us, Ivor?"

"I should have loved to, Mama, but the truth is that I came in here just now to borrow Miss Norris if she will be so kind as to lend me a hand—literally—for a half hour." Avoiding that young woman's startled look, he smiled blandly at his narrow-eyed parent. "I seem to have sprained my wrist slightly chopping out the hedges the other day, because I am finding it rather painful to write. There are one or two business letters that must be done today, so if you can spare Miss Norris . . . ?"

"Can't it wait until after lunch, Ivor? We have guests—" Lady Montrose began, only to be interrupted by Mrs. Trainor.

"Please do not regard that, Lady Montrose. We cannot stay long in any case and would be distressed to inconvenience his lordship by our unexpected call."

"You are most understanding, ma'am." The earl smiled at Mrs. Trainor with genuine liking.

"Naturally if your work is pressing, Ivor, and Miss Norris is willing to lend a hand, I have no objection," Lady Montrose said, making a virtue of necessity.

"I'll be happy to help, sir."

As Chloe folded away her sewing materials, Lady Montrose made one last effort. "At least let the poor girl have her coffee first, Ivor."

"That's all right, ma'am," Chloe said, rising to her feet. "I don't care for any coffee just now."

"I would not dream of depriving Miss Norris of her refreshment," the earl said, aghast at the implication that he could be so unfeeling. "Hawkins shall bring coffee to the library. Good-

bye until Friday evening, Mrs. Trainor . . . Miss Trainor . . .
Miss Caroline.''

Lord Montrose held open the door and stood back for Miss
Norris to precede him. She walked by his side perfectly
composed and saying nothing as they descended the main
staircase to the ground floor. He eyed her serene profile
obliquely and said, ''This is very good of you, Miss Norris.''

''Not at all, sir. I am happy to be able to help. I'm sorry about
your wrist.''

''My wrist? Oh, that . . . yes.''

She looked questioningly at him, but he was frowning at his
own thoughts. He turned abruptly and caught her eyes. ''What
was that business with Mary just now?''

Miss Norris blinked long lashes. ''I beg your pardon?''

''I saw you glance over at my sister when Mrs. Trainor
mentioned writing to her son about the engagement. Mary
looked—I don't know how to describe her expression except
to say she was obviously disturbed about something. Do you
know what?''

''I am not in Lady Mary's confidence, sir.'' The words were
perfectly polite and perfectly final.

The earl grunted and pushed open the door to the library.
Miss Norris stopped a few feet into the room and gazed about
the paneled walls while her companion walked around to the
far side of the mahogany desk. He was standing there watching
her when her eyes completed their circuit of the large room with
its galleried shelves along one long wall.

She colored faintly. ''I'm sorry, sir. I did not mean to waste
your time.'' She assumed a business-like air. ''Where would
you like me to work?''

He ignored her words. ''Why don't you sit here?'' he invited,
indicating one of a pair of green leather chairs facing the desk.

Obediently she sat down, but before he could do likewise,
she was on her feet again, looking behind her.

''What's the matter?''

''I'm afraid this chair is too low to allow me to write
comfortably at the desk,'' she explained. ''Is there a straight
chair I might use?''

''Never mind that for the moment. Sit here,'' he repeated.

She did so, looking an inquiry at him. He had picked up a pen and was rolling it between his fingers as he sat with both forearms resting against the edge of the desk, looking at his hands. Miss Norris allowed her gaze to wander over the cluttered desktop, past the open ledger book and two haphazard piles of papers, past the half-written sheet of paper in the center of the desk beneath his hands, to a neat stack of envelopes apparently ready for the post. Her eyes passed on, stopped, and returned to linger on this stack while a little pleat formed between her well-arched brows.

He was waiting for her when her regard shifted back to his face. "Yes, I wrote those letters earlier; there is nothing wrong with my wrist."

She waited, electing not to pose the obvious question, and he went on after a short pause. "I didn't wish to interrupt my work to do the social bit for an hour, nor did I wish to hurt anyone's feelings; thus the elaborate lie. Are you scandalized?"

She smiled faintly. "No, but you obviously don't require my services, so I had better leave you to your work." She made as if to rise.

"If you go back to the drawing room, it will either be assumed that your penmanship did not meet my exacting standards or that my conduct did not meet your exacting standards," he pointed out gently.

Miss Norris did not allow this particular Hobson's choice to faze her as she got out of the leather chair. "Then I shall head for my own room, thus giving rise to no speculations."

"But I would feel terrible to deprive you of your coffee," he said for the second time.

"You are very thoughtful, but I don't care for any, really, sir. Now I'll let you get on with your work."

"Wait," he said.

As she paused to look back over her shoulder, the earl reached for a leather-bound volume lying on the corner of his desk. "I believe this is your property," he said, holding it out to her.

Miss Norris came back to the desk with a smile. "I wondered what had happened to my book. Where did you find it, sir?"

"On the settee in the white garden the other day after you had attended to my eye. I apologize for not returning it earlier,

but I assumed it had come from this library until I went to return
it to the shelves this morning and discovered another copy
already there. Somehow I could not picture Ned selecting a book
of Latin poetry to read for pleasure. Since no one else at
Applewood can read Latin, that left you as the only possible
owner.''

As Miss Norris put out a hand to take her property, he laid
the book down in front of him and opened it at random, glancing
down the page as her arm fell back to her side. "Did your father
teach you Latin?''

"Actually it was my mother who instructed me. My father's
medical practice left him very little time for any other sustained
activity, though as I advanced he was always the final source
when I had trouble with a translation.''

"A physician and a scholar for a father and a bluestocking
for a mother," he said softly, allowing his glance to rove freely
over her flashing brown eyes, soft mouth, and flushed cheeks.
"No wonder you are unique.''

"I consider myself exceedingly blessed in my parents," she
declared through clenched teeth, for once jolted out of her
customary self-possession.

"So do I, my dear Miss Norris," he said to take the wind
out of her sails, "and what is more, I am excessively grateful
to them." He witnessed the sudden confusion in her eyes and
the descent of those luxuriant lashes with peculiar satisfaction
but went on without pause. "Tell me, does your father permit
you free access to everything in his library?''

"Well, most of his Greek books are beyond my limited
knowledge of that language, but if you mean does he censor
my reading, no, he does not," she finished, puzzlement giving
way to a challenging tilt to her chin as she returned his regard.

"Do you have a favorite poet among the ancients?" he asked
to surprise her yet again. He waved her back into the chair with
a minimal gesture and she sat down automatically as she
considered the question.

"I don't believe I could name one particular favorite. I enjoy
the *Aeneid* and some of Catullus's poetry. I have read Sappho's
works but only in Latin translations.''

"Are you familiar with the background of Catullus's poetry?''

"I know that it arose out of an adulterous love affair with a married woman of a singularly licentious nature, but a number of the poems are quite beautiful."

"Have you read Ovid's *Ars amatoria*?"

"Yes."

"And your opinion of this work?"

"Clever, amusing, thoroughly cynical."

"Your father did not perhaps see any danger in exposing a young girl to the writings of persons imbued with a far different moral code than that espoused by modern Christianity?"

"Should my father consider my intellect so feeble that I would be corrupted by the knowledge that Roman society of the period was morally corrupt?" she countered, not waiting for a response from the earl before continuing in the same measured fashion, "You perhaps do not take into account that my father is always there to interpret and explain and put things into a wider historical perspective for me. What better way for the young to learn than to be exposed to all that has gone before under the guidance of a wise teacher?"

"You are an advocate then of comparable education for both sexes?"

"Unequivocally." She flashed him a smiling challenge as she got to her feet. "But I must not hold up your work any longer, sir, after you perjured your soul in order to continue it." She reached out a hand for her book and gave him a superior little smile as he released it into her grasp. Halfway across the room she turned and said with a mischievous glint in soft brown eyes. "Perhaps if more females were allowed to read *Ars amatoria*, men would find it less easy to seduce them using the age-old techniques set forth in the poem. I have observed that there are certain definite similarities between today's Christian society and that of pagan Rome in the first century."

Lord Montrose did not immediately resume his writing when the door closed behind Miss Norris. A smile lingered in his eyes even after it had faded from his lips as he stared at the door, a picture of a vibrant young woman glowing with life still clear before him. Her garb might be nondescript, but that odd combination of creamy skin as a marvelous foil for dark red hair and deep brown eyes, which were not so dark that the pupils were not distinctly visible, compelled admiration. He had not realized until he listened to his own words how truly unique she was. He could not call to mind any young woman of his acquaintance, past or present, who was less concerned with the impression she made on others. All of Miss Norris's considerable faculties seemed to be available to deal objectively with the events going on around her rather than some portion of her mental energies being diverted to keeping some cherished internal vision of herself intact. He would not describe her as vivacious—that implied at least a minimal degree of putting oneself forward, something Miss Norris did not do—but hers was a lively and unconventional intelligence. He had enjoyed their sparring match just now and looked forward to exploring the complexities of her nature in greater detail.

A frown replaced the smile as he considered the practicalities of converting the desire into the deed. He was not so naive as to waste a hope that real conversation could flourish in any drawing room presided over by his mother with her undeviating determination to skim over life's surfaces, permitting nothing of real import to disturb her sybaritic pursuits. Nor, under his mother's smothering brand of chaperonage, could he expect to find opportunities for furthering his acquaintance with an attractive young woman who did not meet her exacting criteria for matrimonial eligibility—namely, descent from the first families of the kingdom. If he attempted to single out Miss Norris for private conversation in the midst of a family assembly, he would not be granted five minutes of her exclusive company before his mother aborted the encounter, using one or another of the proven tactics in her social arsenal to achieve this end.

Lord Montrose's mouth twisted wryly as he admitted that even with the fates temporarily aligned on his side this morning, he had not succeeded in charming Miss Norris into prolonging their recent tête-à-tête once she apprehended that he did not require secretarial assistance. There was no shyness or reticence in her manner; his impression was that she enjoyed a clash of ideas and might welcome a testing of her wits given the right setting, but there was nothing of the coquette about her. Not that he had any desire to flirt with her, of course. It was not a romantic curiosity but a desire to become better acquainted with the workings of her mind that Miss Norris aroused in him, though he certainly agreed with Ned that her fiancé was a stupid man not to have made sure of her before now. He chuckled silently as he recalled the scene at tea yesterday. Lord, hadn't she jumped down his brother's throat! She could not be all cool intellect, not if she were woman enough to resent an implication poor Ned had never intended. It was the only occasion on which Miss Norris had ever appeared less than completely collected and mistress of herself. Oddly, it made her seem more human.

The earl picked up his pen, his mood assuredly lighthearted considering the inherent difficulties to a successful persuit of his quest. He rather thought his mother was going to find eternal vigilance more wearing than she anticipated.

Chapter Seven

CHLOE WAS SMILING when she left the library. As she headed for the main staircase she heard a faint sound of tinkling china. That would be Hawkins toiling up the service stairs with the coffee Lord Montrose had ordered. Her smile broadened as she pictured the earl forced to come up with a reasonable explanation of his solitary state when the butler knew they had gone to the library together, but she took great care not to make a sound as she hurried past the main drawing room a moment later. *She* did not fancy having to come up with a similar explanation if the countess should chance to spot her.

Luck was with her and she met no one on the way to her room and a delicious privacy. No social duties awaited her until lunchtime. She hugged herself and fairly danced across the room to drop into the wing chair. As she caught a glimpse of her smiling face in the mirror when she passed the dressing table she realized that she had enjoyed the last ten minutes more than all the rest of her stay at Applewood. The surprise that followed on this errant thought withered the smile on her lips as she tried to make sense of this odd phenomenon.

Chloe did not consider herself to be a person overly inclined toward introspection. Indeed, her life was generally too full of small but pressing duties to allow much time for such personal indulgence. Since coming to Applewood, however, the opposite seemed true. For one thing, time hung rather heavily on her hands here. For another, her dealings with the various members of the Keeson family were—the word that forced its way into her consciousness to describe them was "unsatisfactory." At least there was enough mild disssatisfaction to make her root around in her mind for the cause or causes and seek to better understand the persons with whom she was associating in a deceptively close fashion. Deceptive was the *mot juste* because physical proximity in no way corresponded to mental affinity.

No blame attached to anyone for this state of affairs. They were all strangers and had not voluntarily chosen her for the role of friend; she had been more or less foisted on them by Lady Dalrymple. The same was true from her perspective, of course. It was to be hoped that they were all sufficiently civilized to rub along tolerably well together in this pattern of artificial closeness.

Having worked that out to her own understanding over a period of days, she must now revise her rationale somewhat. Sitting in the comfortable wing chair, her eyes resting on the book in her lap, Chloe made the surprising discovery that she did feel an affinity for one of the Keesons. The surprise was in the identity of this person. Her first impressions of the family would have led her to put the earl at the bottom of a list of prospective friends.

It wasn't that Lord Montrose had impressed her unfavorably; indeed, he was every inch the gentleman in bearing and manners without appearing the least stiff or above his company. She had quickly realized, often with a sense of personal gratitude, that he possessed his mother's social finesse in full measure. His timely intervention had smoothed over awkward moments on several occasions she could call to mind. No, the impediment she had considered a bar to friendship was the apparently impenetrable reserve that cloaked his feelings, if indeed he was subject to the normal range of human emotions. If aloof was too strong a word, at the very least there was an aura of separateness from the others on an emotional level.

When she reached this point of analysis, Chloe stopped short, struck all at once by the disconcerting intuition that all the Keesons seemed to be isolated one from the others in an emotional sense. With Mary and Patricia, however, she had had little hesitation in attributing this isolation to personal unhappiness, though she now wondered if misfortune had merely exaggerated a preexisting tendency. Ned, while not precisely disaffected, seemed shallow and self-absorbed, and Lady Montrose remained an enigma to her. She appeared to dote on Ned in a superficial way, but Chloe had sought in vain for small signs of true affection in her relations with her other children or Emilie. Pursuing this train of thought, she searched her memory for instances of positive filial feeling on the part of the countess's children. At one time or another her daughters had variously displayed impatience, disagreement, and reluctant deference toward their mother, but except for Ned's playful teasing, which might spring from affection, none of Lady Montrose's children ever showed her anything warmer than dutiful respect.

A little chill feathered down Chloe's spine. What a cold-natured family they were! And until this morning she would have flatly characterized the earl as the most distant of all. Even his looks set him apart. In a family of blue-eyed blonds, he alone had dark hair, though his eyes were the lightest of all, a pale gray that could take on the texture of dirty ice when he detected a lapse in courtesy. His manner toward his mother was invariably correct on all points. He never failed in any little attention to her comfort, listened politely to what she had to say, deferred to her in all household matters, and spoke to her with careful respect. Despite the flawless performance, Chloe suspected early on that his impeccable manner concealed, if not active dislike, at best a complete lack of filial affection that must be repellent to one who had found the family unit the source of all that was loving and positive in life. Though she had received at his hands the gracious consideration due the most desired of guests, her attitude to him had been colored by his perceived relationship with his mother. She had assumed that his flattering treatment of herself arose out of a sense of *noblesse oblige* and had no reference to her own personal qualities.

In the library just now she had seen real liking in those cool gray eyes and it had pleased her enormously, whereas Ned's extravagant compliments produced only mild irritation. The underlying reason was simply that the earl had discovered she had a questing mind that she was prepared to use, given the chance. His surprise probably meant he regarded her as a curiosity among females, but at least he hadn't dismissed her with condescension. It was not easy of achievement in present-day society, but her father and mother had proved that intellectual respect and companionship between the sexes was possible. It was heartening to know that one other intellect at Applewood was prepared to reach out to hers.

* * *

Chloe experienced a few qualms on going into the dining parlor for lunch. It was to be expected that Lady Montrose would mention her supposed stint as a secretary to the earl, and she was never comfortable when telling an untruth, even one clearly called for by the circumstances. She had worried unnecessarily, though. The earl, who never returned to the house for lunch on the days he was out on the estate, was present this afternoon. When the countess inquired if she had been able to complete the business letters that had been of such paramount concern, he came smoothly to her rescue.

"Everything that needed to be finished today is already written, thank you, Mama."

"You'd be well advised to give that wrist a chance to heal completely."

"I intend to."

Before Lord Montrose went back to cutting his meat—with the hand in question—he shifted his gaze from his mother to Chloe, who, before she dropped her eyes to the safety of her own plate, thought she detected the merest suggestion of a wink disturbing his grave countenance.

The early part of the afternoon was spent by Chloe in the undemanding company of young Emilie. After a morning cooped up indoors, she decided to take a brisk walk before the cloudburst that had been threatening all morning became a reality and prevented an outing. She met Emilie near the shrubbery behind the rose garden and was welcomed by the child as a companion. For the brief hour allotted them, Emilie showed Chloe her favorite places about the estate, including a lovely old willow tree by the stream whose spreading root system offered a secluded spot for daydreaming. Chattering away in rapid French that was often too fast for Chloe's unaccustomed ears, the little girl was much more animated than on their first encounter in the white garden. She was eager to confide all the pertinent details of her campaign to woo the affections of Tigre, the stable cat, to one who had conceived the grand strategy. She had enlisted the active cooperation of the cook, who supplied her with choice bits of meat or fish with which to court the wary kitten. Tigre had bitten her finger the first time she tried to pick him up but had then relented and allowed himself to be petted for a minute or two before squirming out of her arms.

Chloe and Emilie were sailing leaf boats in the stream when the first low rumble of thunder sounded in the distance. Too engrossed in their regatta to heed this advance warning, they were taken by surprise a few moments later by the first fat drops that plopped into the stream. Abandoning their game, they hiked up their skirts to the unladylike degree that permitted them to run freely and raced for the house. It was a quick-striking storm and overtook them in full spate before they had ascended the last terrace below the rose garden.

Lord Montrose, standing at the French doors in the library watching the rain fall in sheets, spotted the mismatched pair as they cut through the rose garden, running with hands clasped, their free hands holding up soaked skirts that revealed mud-spattered ankles and, in Miss Norris's case, an alluring length of shapely calf above. He had the doors opened in seconds as he raised his voice to a shout to attract their attention and divert them from their assumed goal of the garden entrance some seventy feet away.

"In here! Hurry!"

Miss Norris looked up, understanding his intention, but she called a breathless refusal. "We'll ruin the carpets!"

"Damn the carpets; get in here!" he roared, taking a step out into the rain as if to drag them inside.

The woman changed direction, pulling the child the last few feet to shelter. As they stumbled into the room panting, Lord Montrose swung the doors closed, shutting out about half the noise of the storm.

The gasping breaths of the two bedraggled figures streaming with water sounded loud in the sudden quiet. Chloe pulled strands of hair away from her eyes and watched dazedly as Lord Montrose took off his coat and wrapped it around his shivering niece. His words were a long time penetrating her hazy brain.

"Where were you that you could not find shelter before the storm broke?"

"D . . . down at the stream, sailing leaf boats."

"Are you mad, woman? And Emilie just out of a sick bed!" He paused in the act of sweeping the child into his arms long enough to issue a curt command. "Get yourself up to your room and into dry clothes. I'll send tea up to you after I've brought Emilie to the nursery. Don't just stand there; get moving," he added from the doorway before striding through it with his niece clasped tightly in his arms.

Chloe didn't respond as quickly as Lord Montrose would have desired. Racing through the pelting rain had required only those survival instincts built into the human machine. Once the machine stopped, it was taking a long time to get a message through from her brain to her limbs. She continued to pull sopping strands of hair back off her face while her steps took her slowly toward the door. She noted some mud and a trail of water on the Persian carpet with some dismay, but if his lordship could damn the carpets, she felt free to dismiss this concern from her conscience. Of more urgency was the need to avoid all human contact while she was in this deplorable condition.

Chloe took the service stairs and arrived in her room undeterred by servant or family member. She was shivering by that time, but a brisk rub with a towel before donning dry clothing had her feeling near normal by the time the promised tea arrived. The knock at the door sounded while she was trying to rub her long hair dry. The little maidservant who brought the tea tut-tutted and offered to complete the drying process. Chloe handed over the towel with sincere expressions of gratitude. Over the next few moments she sipped the revivifying beverage while the maid, who could not have been much more than sixteen, proceeded to brush and rewind her hair for her, a rare luxury that today must represent an undeserved reward for stupidity.

Revived physically by the hot tea and emotionally by the simple good nature and generosity of Tillie the maid, who had crooned with pleasure at being entrusted with the task of arranging such beautiful hair, Chloe was nearly her normal self once again when she knocked at the door to the nursery a half hour later. Nearly but not quite herself. One small corner of her mind was actively regretting the carelessness that had caused her to forfeit the budding friendship with the earl that had earlier distinguished this day from the ones that had preceded it. There was nothing she could do save own up to her mistake and try to live it down.

Thankfully, all seemed well in the nursery. She found Emilie warm and dry and sitting by the fire drinking hot milk. The child was disposed to regard their race before the storm in the light of a great adventure. Addie, the nursery attendant, proved to be a good-hearted sensible soul with the country woman's calm acceptance of adverse weather. She had followed those of Lord Montrose's zealous precautionary measures that seemed warranted, but had not compelled Emilie to get between the sheets for the remainder of the day as his lordship had strongly recommended.

"Oh, the little mawther's, a'doin'," she assured Miss Norris when that lady inquired anxiously after Emilie. "Come in and see for yersel'."

"That means I am getting along famously in Suffolk," Emilie interpreted from her position by the fire.

Chloe remained in the nursery playing jackstraws with Emilie and Addie for an hour, only leaving when it was drawing near the time for tea. She felt it was her responsibility to report that they had been caught in the rain to the child's mother herself before Lady Patricia learned of it from her brother. Her second tap on the door to the widow's apartment elicited a faint indistinguishable response that she took to be permission to enter.

Chloe's first impression was of heat and dimness as she stepped into an overfurnished sitting room. The blinds were drawn at the windows, leaving the room's lighting to various branches of candles and a much larger fire than one could wish at this time of year. Lady Patricia was lying on a chaise longue placed near the fireplace. For an instant Chloe thought there was another person in the room, and she had opened her mouth to apologize for interrupting when she realized that what she had taken for a man in the gloom was actually a tall stand holding a man's top hat and opera cloak, while a walking stick stood beneath in a rack. She returned her eyes to the chaise where Lady Patricia was lying with what looked like a stack of letters tied with a blue ribbon on the cushion beside her. Her hands held a sheet of paper she had lowered to her lap and her eyes were slow to focus on the intruder. Nor, when Chloe had completed her explanation cum apology, did she seem to grasp all the salient points at first.

"Has something happened to Emilie?" she whispered, a look of panic coming into her eyes.

Patiently, Chloe went back over the essentials, stressing the fact that she had just left Emilie well and happy. She suggested gently that Lady Patricia might wish to reassure herself of her daughter's condition by popping up to the nursery before tea.

At first Lady Patricia continued to stare blankly, but when Chloe let drop a casual mention of playing jackstraws with the child, who had bragged that her mama had the cleverest fingers of anybody and invariably beat all opponents, she had the pleasure of seeing a reminiscent little smile replace the young widow's vacant expression. "It's the years of musical training," Lady Patricia replied in an offhand explanation as she sat up and put her feet on the floor. "Thank you for telling me what happened, Miss Norris. I'll check on Emilie now."

"Shall I tell Lady Montrose you have gone to the nursery for tea?" Chloe asked, greatly daring but hopeful that the power of suggestion was still operating with the widow.

"Yes, thank you, Miss Norris."

Chloe effaced herself with a smile, thankful a moment later to be on the other side of the door where she no longer had to breathe overheated air heavy with the sickening smell of incense or burning pastilles that had assailed her nostrils in Lady Patricia's apartment. No wonder the widow generally looked ill if she kept herself constantly in that cloying atmosphere. If her father were here, he would have no hesitation in prescribing fresh air and healthy exercise for Lady Patricia as well as her child. Chloe's expression was somber as she headed for the blue saloon. No one could look at Lady Patricia without experiencing pity for her desolation along with a feeling of powerlessness to aid her in returning to life. Somewhere in the back of Chloe's mind a nearly unacknowledged little voice whispered that *she* could never so abandon herself to grief that she thus abandoned her child to the care of others. Addie was kind, the earl was affectionate, but Emilie needed more of her mother than a five-minute meeting, always in that incensed shrine Chloe had just left, before Lady Patricia went down to dinner in the evenings, which, Chloe gathered from various things she had overheard, was the extent of the daily contact between mother and child since their removal to Applewood. If she could not help the mother, at least she could be of service to the child, Chloe resolved as she descended the stairs. Her companionship would go some way toward alleviating Emilie's loneliness—if the earl did not forbid their future association after today's incident. The thought that he must now consider her irresponsible hurt, and there was still Lady Montrose to face. Lady Patricia had not uttered words of censure to her, but one never knew how much of what went on around her the widow actually assimilated in her numbed state.

Chloe was about to take a chair in the saloon when Lady Mary said abruptly, "Your hair looks different, very attractive."

"Does it? I'm afraid I didn't really look at it closely. It's Tillie's doing. She kindly helped me to dry it."

"Were you caught in the rain, Chloe?" Lady Montrose asked in apparent concern.

She would never have a better opening to get her confession behind her, Chloe saw with a mixture of dismay and resolution. A surreptitious glance at the earl showed him staring at the cup in his hands. She steeled herself and said, "Yes, ma'am, and so was Emilie. We were down by the stream and I'm afraid I simply failed to note the warning thunder in time. I am sorry to have exposed Emilie to a wetting, but she seems to have taken no harm. I have just come from the nursery, and Lady Patricia has gone there to have her tea with Emilie. She asked me to carry her excuses to you for her absence."

The look of polite concern had vanished and a coldness had spread over Lady Montrose's classic features. "I cannot deny a certain measure of disappointment at the irresponsibility that could place Emilie's health at risk, but I shall say no more on that head. You have quite properly owned your fault, but you should have come to me rather than distressed my daughter with this tale."

Reduced to about an inch high by this dressing down, Chloe still felt obliged to lodge a mild protest. "I thought it my duty to inform Emilie's mother of the incident, ma'am," she said, meeting the countess's eyes bravely.

The earl spoke up then before his mother could. "I have come to believe that we are doing Tricia a disservice by shielding her from any worrying news, Mama. This retreat from living, though perfectly understandable in the beginning, cannot be permitted to continue to the point that it endangers her health or Emilie's well-being. Let us take heart from the fact that she has gone to see for herself that Emilie has taken no ill effect from her little adventure. I'd like to indulge the hope that this very proper action by Miss Norris today will mark the beginning of Tricia's return to assuming the primary responsibility for Emilie's welfare."

"Naturally I shall be overjoyed if this should prove to be the case," Lady Montrose said, but there was no increased warmth in the deep blue eyes when they passed over Chloe's person.

The subject was allowed to drop then, for which favor a subdued Chloe was most thankful. Once again she owed the lessening of tension to the thoughtful intercession of Lord Montrose. If not wholly exonerated in his eyes, which her carelessness did not deserve anyway, she was emboldened to think that her action in owning her mistake had gone some little way toward earning his better opinion of her as a responsible adult. In seeking crumbs of comfort she must also list the fellow feeling she was *almost* sure she had seen in Lady Mary's face after her mother's clear-cut denunciation. On the other hand, it was not pleasant to know that she had sunk in the countess's esteem. Truth to tell, although Lady Montrose had been unfailingly pleasant and gracious toward her, she had never been able to persuade herself that she was personally liked. The graciousness was too studied perhaps to come from the heart. She really wished not to have to believe this when she was trying so hard to like her hostess.

The rest of the day passed smoothly, on the surface at least. The entire family was present in the drawing room after dinner, an unusual occurrence at Applewood. Lady Montrose proposed a rubber of whist, inquiring whether Chloe played, and that unfashionable young woman had to confess to yet another social deficiency. She had never learned to play any card games at all.

"Are you and your father dissenters, then?" Mr. Keeson asked in a voice tinged with horror. "You aren't against dancing too, are you? I've been looking forward to dancing with you at Mary's party."

Chloe laughed. "No, not Methodists. It is simply that my parents never played cards, so who was there to teach me? I do play chess, however, and I love to dance."

"Well, if it's chess you like, then Ivor's your man, but if I may be permitted the license within the family, I'll alert you that I'm your best bet on the dance floor. Ivor has two left feet and has even been known to step on the same young lady's dress twice in the same evening. No word of a lie," he proclaimed, holding up his right hand. "All the girls develop the headache when they see my brother approaching. There's a general exodus for the ladies' retiring room."

Lady Montrose was laughing and shaking her head in protest. Lady Mary was smiling for once, and even Lady Patricia looked faintly amused.

"Is this really true?" Chloe asked the earl, whose face wore a look of rueful humor.

"Near enough," he admitted, "but if you can be persuaded to trust yourself to me after Ned's glowing testimonial, Miss Norris, I believe I can promise not to tear your skirt, in any event."

"Thank you, sir. In the interest of civility, and to prove my courage, I'll take the chance," she replied with equal solemnity.

"Meanwhile, since that pleasure is still in the future, perhaps you will give me a game of chess one evening soon?"

"I'd be glad of a chance to play," Chloe replied with the smile that, did she but know it, transformed her quiet good looks into something approaching real beauty.

"But not tonight," the countess said gaily. "If you would not object to being left on your own for a bit, my dear Chloe, I'd dearly like to take advantage of having everyone present to play a little whist."

"Of course, I should not mind, ma'am. I have my sewing with me, which I have been neglecting."

Lady Mary was pressed into service to make up the table very much against her inclination, if her sulky expression was a fair indicator of her mood. She had been in an uncertain humor since their walk into the village the previous day. Chloe's hopes that

that expedition might break the ice between them had suffered immediate eclipse after the chance meeting with the minister's daughter. Her best guess was that the news of Mr. Thomas Trainor's return to the neighborhood had strongly affected Lady Mary, though the reason for this had not yet become clear. The girl had never been forthcoming, but she had warmed up slightly on their stroll into the village. All that had changed with Miss Vessey's announcement, and Lady Mary had been acting strangely ever since. What Chloe had come to think of as her customary apathy mixed with sullen resentment of her mother's demands had been replaced by a manner more consistent with an irritation of the nerves. She was preoccupied and jittery by turns, tensing up at every sound outside the room she happened to be occupying at the moment while remaining unaware of half of what transpired in the company of which she was physically a member. Her performance at the card table was consistent with this new behavior and caused her younger brother, who had the misfortune to draw her for his partner, to bemoan his fate on more than one occasion over the next hour as her inattention caused the score to mount up against them. Her responses varied from a muttered apology to a snapped retort that earned her a reproof from her parent.

Chloe and Lady Patricia sat together in silence for the most part, but by the time the refreshment tray arrived, Chloe could congratulate herself on having drawn three little stories about her daughter out of the widow by her artless references to Emilie's many charming qualities. It had taken patience and perseverance to elicit anything resembling sustained conversation from Lady Patricia, but Rome wasn't built overnight. She dared not pride herself that this might be the true beginning of the widow's recovery from her prolonged affliction, but any small step in that direction must be hailed as hopeful.

Chloe was more than ready to seek her bed when the time came to retire. It had been a seesaw kind of day and had taken its toll on her customary equanimity. Before lunchtime she had been rather in the boughs with the prospect of making a real friend at Applewood. That euphoric state had given way to an equally irrational despondency after the misadventure she had

shared with young Emilie during the storm and its consequent
censure, first from the earl and later from his mother. The
surface equilibrium had been restored for the moment, but as
she climbed between the smooth sheets of the large bed in her
pleasant bedchamber she was assailed by a premonition of a
major upheaval to come, though she would have to confess
herself at a stand if asked to articulate the nature of the upheaval.

Chapter Eight

THE WEATHER had improved dramatically by the next morning, but the early part of the day was less than dramatic for Chloe, who spent two hours after her solitary breakfast creating new flower arrangements after she had checked on Emilie and found the little girl in bouncing health and about to continue her campaign to win Tigre's affections. Working with flowers was a soothing and satisfying occupation and Chloe was humming softly to herself when Lady Mary wandered into the small room near the garden entrance that Mrs. Meggs set aside to this purpose.

"So here you are," said the girl with an indifferent glance about the room crammed with flowers in a multitude of containers.

"Were you looking for me?" Chloe looked up, a stalk of delphinium poised above an alabaster vase.

"Yes . . . no . . . not exactly."

Not knowing what reply to make to this muddled offering, Chloe resumed her task, but her eyes followed Lady Mary's movements as she slowly approached the large deal table that took up most of the space in the center of the room. A half-dozen completed arrangements were crowded together at one end of the table, their outer flowers nearly intermingling in the necessity to conserve as much working space as possible. Discarded cutting baskets lay about on the brick floor, and pails full of water in which the remaining cut flowers awaited their ultimate disposition stood on either side of Chloe's feet. On the table a pile of leaf-and-stalk cuttings at her right elbow grew denser with every snip of the shears. These snips were the only sounds in the room for a long moment. Chloe had ceased her humming at Lady Mary's entrance and the girl seemed in no hurry to explain her appearance as she looked over the finished arrangements, idly fingering a flower here and there.

"Take care, there is a large urn on the floor behind you," Chloe warned suddenly as the other girl circled the end of the table, her eyes—but not her mind, Chloe guessed—fixed on the assorted vases on the table.

"Oh." Lady Mary pulled in her skirts and turned to examine the waist-high arrangement. "It's very pretty. You've used only white, blue, and yellow flowers." She squatted down to get a look at the huge blue and white Chinese urn. "Is this for the hall table outside the drawing room?"

"Yes. I thought it would complement the blue and white Chinese rug in the hall."

"You are very clever at this, aren't you?" Lady Mary commented. "The most I can do is grab a handful of flowers and stick them in a vase."

Chloe chuckled. "Often that's all that is required. Flowers are so intrinsically beautiful they generally arrange themselves in a pleasing fashion. Have you never helped your mother with the arrangements?"

Lady Mary looked at the worker in momentary amusement. "Mama? Mama scratch her beautiful hands slaving over flower arrangements? I wish I may see it."

"One can wear gloves," Chloe said, and added matter-of-factly, "Your mother does have lovely hands. As long as she employs Mrs. Meggs, who is so very capable, she might as well preserve them for the drawing room."

"Why are you doing this?" Lady Mary asked bluntly, spreading her hand in a gesture that embraced everything on the work table.

"Because it affords me a great deal of pleasure, for one reason. Just smell those heavenly roses. Also, I am used to having my days fully occupied. I cannot seem to accustom myself to doing nothing all day long."

Lady Mary had dropped her eyes after meeting Chloe's for a moment, and she pulled in the corner of her mouth. Chloe, fearing her tone had not been as neutral as she had tried to make it, hesitated, but an apology for seeming to criticize the life-style of Applewood's inhabitants would only make matters worse. She bent over the pail at her right foot, selecting several stalks of delphinium, and continued her labors in a silence that lasted until Lady Mary picked up a half-opened white rose and tucked it into a slender cobalt-blue vase holding a few choice white blossoms.

"That looks perfect," Chloe said approvingly.

"Where is this little vase going? It looks so insignificant among all these large arrangements."

"It's for his lordship's desk," Chloe said after an infinitesimal pause. "He might not care to spare the space for a larger vase."

"Oh, Ivor is like my father. The gardens are his first love. You should approve of Ivor at least. He is the only one of us who doesn't sit around idle from morning till night."

"Lady Mary, I never meant to crit—"

"I'm sorry, Miss Norris—Chloe—that was a horrid thing to say. I don't know what is the matter with me lately. Please forgive me."

She would have gone out of the room then, but Chloe said, "Lady Mary, wait!"

The girl looked back, her face young and unhappy.

"Did you want me for something? Why did you come in here just now?" Chloe added gently when Lady Mary continued to stare at her in an uncomprehending fashion.

"I . . . I heard you humming. I was trying to avoid Mama, who wishes to discuss more new bride clothes."

"Would you like to go for a walk, perhaps?"

"But aren't you busy here?" Lady Mary indicated the messy scene with a wave of her hand.

"This is the last arrangement for today. The only condition under which Mrs. Meggs could be persuaded to transfer the flower arranging to me was that I should leave the chore of cleaning up to the maids. The footman places the arrangements where they belong. I don't think I could even lift that Chinese urn when there is water in it. I'd love to get outside in the sunshine for a while . . . ." She let her voice trail off.

"Yes, sunshine," Lady Mary exclaimed eagerly. "I'd love to escape from this house for a bit. I'll take you to a place where you can see the ocean, shall I? Unless you have already walked in that direction before?"

Chloe assured the girl there was nothing she'd like better than a glimpse of the sea, and they set off a few minutes later.

Their way took them through the orchard on a gradually rising course. Because she didn't feel as if she were climbing a hill Chloe was surprised when she glanced back over her shoulder some twenty minutes later to see that Applewood was considerably below their present elevation. Looking forward again, she could tell now by the shrinking of the rather featureless sweep of ground that had stayed before them that they were about to attain the broad, rounded top of a gentle hill.

"The ground drops more steeply on the other side," Lady Mary said, breaking the silence that had reigned between them for much of the way. For the most part the too-pale, too-slender girl had mechanically put one foot in front of the other, her eyes on the ground and her thoughts obviously divorced from her physical movements.

Chloe had made no attempt to initiate a conversation, sensing that her companion's troubles were beyond taking relief from momentary distraction. She did not reply now until they had reached the middle of the grassy area at the summit. Having pivoted slowly around to appreciate the complete view, she expelled a breath of admiration and said, facing toward the gray-green ocean in the distance, "Oh, it is a splendid sight. If I lived here I'd want my house built on this spot."

"Not enough accessible water, I understand," Lady Mary reported.

"Whose house is that?" Chloe pointed to a structure that could be seen with difficulty through an extensive grove of trees that began on the far side of the hill on which they stood.

"That is the manor. All the land between the hill and the sea belongs to the Trainors."

"So that is where we shall be going tomorrow evening?"

"Yes, but it is much longer by road. There aren't many roads in this part of the country."

"Mr. Keeson said you and he grew up with the Trainors."

"Yes, and the Vesseys. Ellen has an older brother who is at Cambridge now. Not Ivor or Tricia because they were too much older to pay us much heed. We all used to meet here for games sometimes, and there is a special place where you can sit and watch the sea. It's on Trainor land actually. We go into the grove over there."

Chloe followed willingly after her guide into the trees. She was struck by the quietness and peace in the grove of tall pines after the breezy hilltop.

"Yes," Lady Mary replied when Chloe mentioned this in a hushed voice, "there is generally a lot of wind on the hilltop, which is very exposed. The place we are going is more sheltered and the grownups never found us there, which we considered a decided advantage when we were dodging governesses and tutors. It isn't much farther, just around this hump. We go underneath that uprooted tree. Watch your head."

Their feet made no noise in the carpet of pine needles as they angled to their left and suddenly found themselves facing the sea again from a spot somewhat below the grassy hilltop. Chloe, entranced by the view through the treetops, was slow to perceive that they were not alone in the sheltered area that was like a bite taken out of the hill by a prehistoric giant. When her first soft exclamation of pleasure drew no response from her companion she turned her head and saw Lady Mary standing perfectly still staring at a man who had apparently just risen from the ground where he'd been sitting with his back against the hillside. The man, who was staring back in equal fascination, spoke first in a pleasant soft voice.

"For a moment I thought I was dreaming, Mary. You are even wearing the same dress you wore when we said good-bye. It's wonderful to see you."

"Tom!"

For a long second the harsh whisper was the only sound the fair girl uttered, and Chloe tensed her muscles to leap to her aid; she was so colorless as to suggest an imminent swoon. The man, whom her intuition had identified immediately as the squire's son, must have shared her apprehension, because he took a step forward, his eyes never leaving his old friend's face.

This seemed to steady Lady Mary, for she forced a smile to ashen lips and said, her voice now under control, "I am sorry to seem so stupid, but I was told you were not expected home until today."

"Yes, that is what I told the family so my mother and sisters would not get in a stew if I could not make it earlier, but I arrived yesterday evening as I had always intended. I apologize for

. . . for startling you." For the first time the young man glanced at Chloe, who felt self-consciously *de trop,* but there was literally no avenue of escape from this little aerie.

Following his glance, Lady Mary's eyes lighted on her companion and she blinked in surprise, evidently having forgotten her existence in the shock of coming face-to-face with this friend of her childhood. Summoning her mother's training to her aid, she said, "Chloe, may I present an old friend, Mr. Thomas Trainor? Miss Norris is staying with us at Applewood for a few weeks, Tom."

The two strangers took each other's measure while murmuring appropriately. Chloe had no trouble deciding that she liked what she saw. Mr. Trainor was a man of about her own age, tall and lithe with a look of whipcord strength despite a deceptive leanness. The marks of an extended stay in a more tropical climate were visible in his healthy suntanned skin and the numerous streaks of gold that highlighted his light brown hair. When he smiled, his teeth seemed extraordinarily white in contrast, and his eyes were a deeper blue than Lady Mary's. Despite his civil assurance of his great pleasure at meeting her, Chloe suspected he wished her, if not at the ends of the earth, at least elsewhere.

"You and Lady Mary must have much news to exchange, Mr. Trainor. If you will excuse me, I shall start walking back to Applewood," she said pleasantly. As she stepped forward to pass Lady Mary, however, the younger girl took her arm in a tight grip.

"No, don't go, Chloe; that is, we must both be going or we shall be dreadfully late for lunch." Lady Mary's tones had taken on confidence as she spoke. "I am very glad to see you safely returned, Tom."

"You will be at this dinner my mother is giving tomorrow?" he asked quickly as she would have turned away.

"Yes . . . yes. We'll see you then. Good-bye, Tom."

No words were exchanged between the girls as they retraced their path through the pine grove and up the hill; indeed, Lady Mary set such a grueling pace, her hand still gripping Chloe's arm as if she were a prisoner contemplating escape, that it is doubtful whether they could have mustered the breath to converse had they desired to do so. Chloe's thinking apparatus was functioning at full capacity even in the face of this handicap. She felt the mystery of Lady Mary's unsocial behavior was now abundantly explained. She studied the girl at her side in silent sympathy without any fear of being considered rude. Lady Mary was lost in a bleak private world and unaware of another presence. Her delicate profile looked pathetically vulnerable as she kept her gaze on the ground beneath her feet.

When they had crested the grassy hilltop and could see the Applewood orchard in the distance, Chloe pulled to a halt, disengaging her arm from Lady Mary's slackened grip. "So sorry," she said mendaciously. "I have a stitch in my side."

The pale girl in the gray dress her mother hated halted perforce and looked around her like a sleepwalker awakened suddenly. When her eyes met Chloe's, soft with sympathy, Lady Mary's rigid control gave way entirely. Her eyes brimmed over with tears and her face crumpled. "What have I done? What am I going to do?" she moaned.

"You love Mr. Trainor?"

"Yes. I always have, but I told myself it was just a childish attachment that would not hold up under such a long separation. I *prayed* that what I had felt would be gone when I saw him again." Lady Mary put her hands over her face and began to weep in earnest.

Chloe looked around in dismay. They were still a good quarter of a mile from the orchard, but anyone in that vicinity might wonder what was transpiring and come nearer to see if any help was required. The only possible concealment this empty landscape offered was a solitary tree off to the right of the path. It was a large spreading chestnut. Whether it was large enough to shelter them from curious eyes was a moot point, but they did not have the luxury of choice. Chloe put her arm around the girl's waist and led her unresisting over to the tree, keeping on the far side of it as she gently pushed Lady Mary down to the ground and sat beside her.

Chloe made no attempt to talk to the sobbing girl while the storm raged. She was ready with her handkerchief when Lady Mary raised her head presently. Her eyes were red and swollen and her mouth still trembled, but the torrent of tears had dried to a trickle as she accepted the white linen square and blew her nose and mopped at her face. "Th . . . thank you. You are very good. I . . . I beg your pardon."

"No need. You were entitled to a good bawl. It clears the air if nothing else." Chloe's lips curved slightly but her eyes were somber.

"It's all so hopeless!"

"Nothing is ever quite hopeless while there is breath in one's body, but it is certainly an . . . awkward situation."

The inadequacy of this choice of description seemed to grate on Lady Mary's nerves. "*Awkward!* Impossible would be closer to the truth," she said bitterly.

"How did it come about, if you do not mind my asking? I do not wish to pry into what doesn't concern me."

Lady Mary dismissed Chloe's scruples with a wave of the hand clutching a soaked handkerchief. "It's all right. Actually it is almost a relief to have another human being to talk to."

"No one in your family is aware of . . . this unfortunate situation?" Chloe said awkwardly.

"No. I might have confided in Tricia, but she is—well, you've seen how she is."

"Yes," Chloe agreed, noting but not commenting on the lack of reference to the girl's mother. "Did you have an understanding with Mr. Trainor before he left for Bermuda?"

"Yes . . . no—that is, Tom asked me to wait for him, but it was said almost in a joking way," she added with painful honesty.

"Joking?"

"He warned me not to go and get married behind his back, and he . . . kissed me good-bye. I was barely seventeen when he left and he was only supposed to be gone for a year."

"Did you consider yourself pledged to Mr. Trainor in your own mind?"

"Yes." There was a long silence while Lady Mary stared at her thoughts and Chloe exercised quiet patience. The younger girl looked up at last, her eyes tormented. "It was not so bad at first, though I missed Tom abominably. My father died that winter, so my come-out was postponed. Then I learned that Tom would not be returning at the end of the year, and no one could say how much longer he would have to stay away."

"Did you never hear from Mr. Trainor directly?"

"No, how could I? An unmarried girl cannot receive letters from men who are not related to her. Occasionally one of his sisters would pass along his compliments to me when she had received a letter."

"And this spring you made your come-out," Chloe prompted when Lady Mary had again fallen silent.

"Yes, and I might even have enjoyed it—all the parties and the theater and pretty clothes—if Mama had not made it so clear that she expected me to form an eligible connection while I was in town."

"Would she not consider Mr. Trainor eligible?"

"A mere esquire? Not Mama. You have heard the slighting way she speaks of Mrs. Trainor. Mama's family is one of the oldest in the country, though hers is a cadet branch and untitled. She is a fearful snob and expects all of us to make a social alliance rather than a marriage."

"Oh, dear. And Lord Thrale, what is he like? Do you like him?"

"A nonentity. There is nothing to like or dislike about him."

"Does he lo . . . care for you?"

"No. How could he? I tried to appear as much a nonentity as he all season long after I realized how determined Mama was to marry me off to the most eligible suitor she could snare. I was as missish and insipid as I knew how."

"And still Lord Thrale proposed?" Chloe permitted herself a small smile.

"Yes, which just goes to show you how little feeling entered into his decision to offer for me. I am persuaded he liked Mama better. At least she was charming to him and flattered him, and she is still very beautiful."

Chloe was silent, unable to think of any words of comfort that would be acceptable to the unhappy girl.

They sat under the tree for another minute or two, then Lady Mary got to her feet, followed by Chloe. As they brushed dirt and grass from their skirts, Lady Mary looked at her confidante with an anxious air. "You will say nothing of this to my mother, will you, Chloe?"

"Of course not, my dear. I just wish there were some way I could help you."

"You may believe me when I say it has helped just to be able to talk with someone. I have felt so solitary for so long, and I've been utterly miserable since I allowed Mama to persuade me to this wretched betrothal." Lady Mary pressed her lips together against further speech and set off toward home with Chloe trailing along a half-step behind.

The final segment of their walk, though taken at a more reasonable pace, was accomplished in a silence only slightly less total than on the previous leg. Chloe's mind was awhirl, going back over all that Lady Mary had just disclosed. She was not as shocked as she might have been. Observation had already convinced her that the young girl was not happy in her betrothal, and she had been alerted to expect some significance beyond that of an ordinary neighbor in Mr. Thomas Trainor. Unfortunately, preparedness did not lessen dismay at the enormity of the impending disaster. Lady Mary was desperately unhappy; the unknown Lord Thrale, unless he were of a singularly phlegmatic nature, was not going to find his marriage a source of much domestic satisfaction; and if Mr. Trainor was in love with his old playmate, the upcoming wedding would raise the total of miserable creatures to three. If, on the other hand, Lady Mary should decide to cry off from her engagement, there was the matter of some fourscore invitations to a pre-wedding ball that had been mailed last week.

The two young women were back in the orchard before Chloe finally accepted that Lady Mary was not going to breach this latest silence. She increased her pace to catch up, putting out a hand to detain her companion. "Pray forgive the impertinence, Lady Mary, but what are you going to do?"

"Do?" The girl blinked reddened eyelids, seeming at a loss.

"About your betrothal, of course."

"I don't know." Lady Mary shook off the hand and continued walking. "I must discover Tom's sentiments toward me."

Passing over for the moment the delicacy of obtaining this

kind of information, Chloe persisted. "What will you do if Mr. Trainor says he loves you?"

"I'll marry him, of course."

"And if he does not return your feelings?"

This time the reply was longer in coming, but after a moment Lady Mary said, "In that case, I shall have no choice but to marry Lord Thrale."

"I beg your pardon, Lady Mary, but there is one other choice you have overlooked. You can elect to remain unmarried until you meet someone for whom you can hope to cherish those warm feelings that promise felicity in marriage."

"If you think that, you don't know my mother. She would simply wait until the scandal over my broken engagement had died down. Then she'd set about making the most advantageous match still possible under the circumstances. Heaven knows what the next candidate would be like, and I'd have to endure the condescension of all the more popular girls again. Life with Lord Thrale would be preferable to that."

Chloe could find nothing to say in the face of this coolly rational analysis of the situation.

They were almost at the house before Lady Mary spoke again, and then it was only to inform her companion that she would not be going down to lunch. "I always look a perfect wreck when I cry, and I could not face Mama's questions today. You may tell her I have the headache," she said, parting from Chloe on the words.

Left standing alone in the shrubbery, Chloe sought the sanctuary of the white garden in the short time remaining before the luncheon bell would sound. Today, however, the lovely setting failed to exercise its customary tranquilizing effect on her spirit. As she stared at the creamy roses, her mind was preoccupied with a picture of Lady Mary huddled at the foot of the chestnut tree, giving way before a storm of emotion that had no doubt been brewing since Miss Vessey's announcement of Mr. Trainor's expected return to the area. Unnerving though she had found the experience from the point of not being able to translate deep pity into any practical succor for the poor girl, Chloe could still be thankful the breakdown had happened today.

Had Lady Mary not come upon Mr. Trainor unexpectedly this morning, what must her reaction have been on meeting him for the first time tomorrow evening amongst a horde of neighbors? She generally maintained a level of control over her emotions, as witnessed by the fact of having kept her unhappy sentiments about her betrothal to herself these past months, but the added weight of seeing the man she loved after an absence of two years had tipped the scale and shattered the fragile defenses she had erected to mask her unhappiness.

Chloe shivered involuntarily as she recalled her presentiment of impending trouble at Applewood. It had come true with a terrible swiftness that left her reeling. At the moment she was the only person who was aware of the potential for catastrophe that existed in the unresolved boy-and-girl attachment between Lady Mary and Mr. Trainor. Lady Mary had flatly stated her intention of marrying Mr. Trainor if he should ask her. Never having met him before today, Chloe could not hazard an opinion on his feelings with any confidence in the acuity of her judgment. She closed her eyes and summoned up an image of a very attractive man, startled but definitely affected by the sudden appearance of his old friend. He had said he thought he was dreaming at first. He had recognized the gray dress—now the girl's mysterious attachment to it was explained—as the one she had worn when they had said good-bye two years before. Surely that was significant, when one considered that most men had little appreciation for the details of women's fashions. Could she take that as evidence that he did indeed love Lady Mary? And if he did, would he speak of it in view of the fact that she was to be married shortly? Would honor hold him back?

When the bell sounded for lunch a few moments later, Chloe found herself with no trustworthy answers to any of the vital questions that would have to be resolved in the immediate future. Even more worrisome than this, however, was the knowledge that the time for resolving the issues was frighteningly short. The invitations to Lady Mary's ball had been sent out all over the country.

Chapter Nine

LUNCHEON PASSED MORE SMOOTHLY than Chloe had dared to hope. Always uncomfortable when deviating from the truth, she had dreaded being questioned by the countess about her daughter's reported indisposition, but Lady Montrose had accepted without comment the excuse of a headache.

As she had come to expect, the earl's presence guaranteed that the conversation would rise above the level of insipid commonplaces that prevailed when Lady Montrose was in sole command. Chloe had forgotten her initial wariness when her host turned to her with a smile and said, "I understand I have you to thank for the charming floral arrangement that now graces my desk, Miss Norris?"

"Why . . . yes, sir, and also Lady Mary, who helped me," she replied in some confusion, hoping the slight warmth in her cheeks was not visible to all eyes.

"I've never known Mary to turn her hand to flower arranging before," Lady Montrose said with a gracious smile. "It must be your beneficial influence, Chloe."

"I'll wager you had to hit her over the head and drag her into the flower room to get her to dirty her hands," Mr. Keeson suggested with a grin.

"Nothing of the sort," Chloe retorted with an answering twinkle. "Your sister volunteered to help me finish the arrangements so we could go for a walk together. It was a gorgeous morning to be outdoors."

Lady Montrose frowned. "And yet Mary has finished with a sick headache? She must have overexerted herself."

"I . . . I believe she'd hoped a brisk walk would be just the thing to clear her head, but, alas, it did not answer," Chloe offered feebly, conscious of being dragged deeper into a quagmire of deception.

"Where did you walk?" The casual question from his lordship

helped stiffen her resolve to appear as natural as possible.

"Lady Mary took me to the hilltop from where you can see the ocean."

"Did she point out the manor to you?"

"Yes, indeed." Chloe's assumption of nonchalance was a triumph of acting, considering the queasiness that overcame her at the mere thought of the upcoming dinner party on this estate. Once more she had reason to be grateful for the earl's skill at steering away from shoals as he monopolized the conversation with a description of the terrain between Applewood and the sea for her benefit.

Lady Mary finally put in an appearance at tea. To her mother's queries regarding the headache that had prostrated her earlier, she assured her that it had gone. When Lady Montrose pronounced it ill-advised to walk so far when she was feeling unwell, she shot a frightened look at Chloe, who said in a calm tone that it was too bad the crisp breeze on the hilltop had not entirely banished the headache as they had hoped.

"It did help, though, Mama, and the headache had quite vanished when I woke up from my nap," the girl said eagerly.

She took such pains to present a picture of bouncing health and spirits from that moment that Chloe felt compelled to take her aside on the way into dinner to caution her against over-playing her role.

"Your mother is watching you closely, and the earl has bent several thoughtful looks on you also."

"I scarcely know what I am doing or saying," Lady Mary admitted. "I cannot keep my mind fixed on what is going on around me, I am so anxious about what will happen tomorrow night."

"Why not offer to play the pianoforte after dinner? That should remove you from close scrutiny and save you from having to participate in the conversation."

Lady Mary seized on the suggestion with gratitude and managed to extend her offer to play for the company in an unexceptional manner that drew no unwelcome attention to her.

Lord Montrose preempted any proposal to play cards from the countess with the announcement that he intended to challenge Miss Norris to a game of chess if she were disposed to oblige.

"I thought it might be amusing to give Chloe her first lesson at whist tonight, Ivor," his mother countered swiftly. "With all of us to help her, I am persuaded she will master the basic principles in no time at all. It is a social skill that you will be glad to possess in your future life, my child," she added, turning to her guest with a brilliant smile.

"If you say so, ma'am," Chloe replied, trying to conceal her instinctive reluctance for the proposed tuition. No doubt Lady Montrose's intentions were of the kindest in taking pity on her own deplorable social liabilities, but the thought of having her initial bungling subjected to the scrutiny, even the kind scrutiny, of three such expert cardplayers was surprisingly distasteful. She had not realized until this moment that she was so proud as to be ridiculously sensitive to implied criticism on her lack of social accomplishments.

While Chloe was attempting to convince herself of the salutary effect upon her moral fiber of such a humbling of her pride, Lord Montrose rendered the exercise superfluous. "In less than a fortnight the house will be full to bursting with whist players and I shall not be free to indulge in chess games. Besides, with so many tutors, Miss Norris will be overwhelmed with no doubt conflicting advice. If you do not wish to give her a disgust of the game at the outset, Mama, it will be far better for you to lay out the cards some afternoon and give her the benefit of your undivided attention. If you really wish to play cards tonight I am persuaded Ned will give you a game of piquet, won't you, Ned?"

The countess's younger son assenting good-naturedly in this suggestion, Lady Montrose was forced to concede herself out-maneuvered for the present. "If you find yourself hopelessly overmatched after a few moments, Chloe," she said gaily as the earl went off to fetch a chessboard from the library, "you may call out for rescue and we can still have our whist lesson."

"Thank you, ma'am; I'll remember that." Chloe's tone matched that of her hostess in gaiety.

Fortunately for her pride and self-esteem, if not for her moral fiber, the chess match with Lord Montrose was a contest in the real sense of the word. Playing white, she made the conventional opening move of the queen's pawn and settled down to the game with a fierce concentration that must have appeared rather forbidding. After several minutes of playing in total silence, Lord Montrose said mildly, "May I inquire if your competitiveness is of such a high order as to preclude the exchange of all conversation between opponents, Miss Norris?"

He watched with masculine appreciation as thick dark lashes swept upwards and fluttered once while soft lips bunched together on a surprised and nearly soundless exclamation.

"Of course not, sir! I was paying strict attention so that I did not find myself ignominiously defeated in the first ten minutes of play."

"There is scant likelihood of that. You have not given me the slightest opening to press an attack," he said, moving his knight to threaten her queen.

"Now that sounds remarkably like a man trying to lull his opponent into a false sense of security so she will drop her guard and make a careless move," Chloe declared with a provocative flick of her lashes before bringing up reinforcements.

The earl smiled but returned no answer as he considered his next move. Scraps of conversation drifted over from the game table where the countess and her younger son were engaged in a lively game of piquet. Lady Patricia had excused herself directly after dinner and the only other sounds in the drawing room were the notes of a Beethoven sonata being played by Lady Mary.

"I assume it was your father who taught you to play chess?" the earl mused some ten minutes later after taking longer than usual to decide on his move.

"Then you assume incorrectly; it was my mother." Chloe's intent gaze never left the board as her hand hovered over her endangered knight before settling on a pawn.

The heavy gold setting of the jade betrothal ring she wore gleamed in the candlelight each time she moved her hand. That ring was beginning to annoy him. It was too large and awkward for such a slender hand. "I can see that your mother was someone quite out of the ordinary," he said, determined to have more of her than her chess-playing skills.

That brought her eyes up to his. "Well, I think she was in some ways, though she led a most ordinary life. Her intellect was superior and her mind well informed throughout her life, but she did not attempt to produce any literary or intellectual writings. After her marriage she devoted most of her energy and talents to the practicalities of the life she had chosen by marrying a physician. She was a great help to my father in his work and she taught me more than any governess could have.''

"Except for minor drawing-room accomplishments?" he suggested slyly.

Chloe's radiant smile began in her large brown eyes at the shared humor in the situation and ended with a little gurgle of laughter. "Please, I beg of you, do not lay my sins of omission in this area at my mother's door. Mother had a lovely singing voice and she played the piano beautifully. At least I thought her playing superb, but she assured me it was only because I have such a poor ear that I did not detect the deficiencies in her performance. Be that as it may, I was most unwilling to apply myself and devote wasted hours to practicing when it was painfully obvious that I had no gift for making music. Poor Mother was eventually forced to admit that her chick was not going to turn into a swan.''

He smiled and quirked an eyebrow. "Are you much like your mother, apart from this tragic musical impairment, I mean?''

Her eyes gleamed in amusement, and he watched the pupils dilate, absorbing the lighter brown of the iris into the dense black before she blinked. "In appearance I am like neither of my parents, though I am said to have my father's eyes. My mother was quite beautiful, you see.'' She paused, a considering look in her eyes. "Did you mean am I like Mother in temperament and character?''

He did not reply in words but continued to smile in an encouraging manner as her face took on a look of bafflement. "Do you know, it is the oddest thing, but it is no easy task to describe oneself. I would say our minds were rather similar, but I am innately of a more practical disposition than Mother, who had to teach herself how to go along in a very different mode of life than that in which she was reared. A crucial difference between us is that my mother never ceased to expect that people would live up to the finest qualities of mankind. Therefore, she was often disappointed and distressed to find their behavior quite otherwise. I do not possess her lofty opinion of the basic goodness of humanity. I am more conscious of its many failings, I fear.''

"You have written off the human race, Miss Norris?''

"Oh, no, nothing so final as that, but I don't expect unselfishness and nobility of spirit from poor souls whose lives have been a struggle to survive, nor indeed from those persons who have been raised to believe that all the good things of life are owing to them by virtue of their exalted birth or great wealth. In my view humans are faulty, frail creatures and one must accept them as such without allowing it to overset one's spirits.''

"You do not believe mankind capable of redemption, then?''

She looked faintly shocked at this bald interpretation. "Yes, of course I do, but perhaps not all persons in all degrees. As for writing them off, well, one must just deal with them as they are and not always be expecting miracles of reform.'' Her gaze dropped to the chessboard again. "Goodness, we have wandered far from the game. I believe it is your move, sir.''

He thought she was a trifle discomposed at having been betrayed into talking about herself even to such a slight degree and judged he would get no more out of her that evening. "I believe you are correct, it is my move,'' he said with a smile, considering his options. A second later he said, "Check, Miss Norris.''

Unfortunately, his judgment was abundantly confirmed. She hastily moved her king out of check, and for the hour remaining in the match before he was able to defeat her, Miss Norris kept her attention focused on the game, refusing to be lured into any personal confidences. She was not shy, her manners were universally pleasing, and she comported herself with unself-conscious assurance at Applewood, which though not overly formal—he not having any taste for pomp and ceremony—must be more complex than a doctor's modest establishment. He did not think she disliked him or held him in awe, but hold him at arm's length, he was beginning to realize, she most certainly did. Her pleasant manner and genuine desire to be helpful and fit in with all her host family's activities was well designed to disguise the fact that she kept her inner self inviolate from them all. This was easily enough accomplished at Applewood; the girls were so self-absorbed these days they barely noticed her presence, and Ned's brand of charm, turned on all females without discrimination, was scarcely calculated to overrun Miss Norris's defenses. As far as his mother was concerned, he could only hope her young guest had no inkling of the real feelings beneath the surface cordiality she displayed toward her sister's goddaughter.

The earl saw no reason to repine, however. He felt he had made some small progress in becoming better acquainted with the unusual and intriguing young woman temporarily residing in his home as well as discovering a chess player worthy of his mettle. It did not occur to him to question his marked interest in a female who was not only beneath his social notice but betrothed to another man to boot.

On the day of the Trainor dinner party the Applewood post included a letter addressed to Miss Norris in her godmother's hand, written from Lavering Manor. Lady Dalrymple reported that Millicent had been successfully delivered of a seven-and-one-half-pound son. When Chloe announced the glad tidings at lunch, Lady Montrose confirmed that she had been in receipt of a similar communication. Oddly, the countess seemed to find personal vindication in the fact of the baby's late arrival. Chloe also reported that Millicent had done her the honor of inviting her to be a godmother, and she sought her hostess's advice on a gift suitable to the occasion. They discussed the virtues of a silver porringer versus a set of silver-backed brushes with engraved initials, and Lady Montrose assured her guest that there was a jewelry store in Woodbridge where such items could be purchased. Since Lady Mary still required several additions to her bride clothes, it seemed desirable to plan a shopping trip for the following week.

The threatening skies emptied into showers during lunch, spoiling outdoor activities. After reading to Emilie for an hour, Chloe retired to her apartment to pen a congratulatory letter to Millicent. Her quill fairly danced across the page as she gave expression to her participation in her friend's joy at the long-awaited event. Millicent had been married for more than four years, and Chloe was well aware that she had harbored a growing fear that she might be unable to conceive a child.

It was more difficult to compose a letter to her godmother, whose happiness at the safe arrival of her grandson had not been so all-consuming as to preclude a lively interest in the goings-on at Applewood. She had asked some penetrating questions about Chloe's reactions to the various personalities in residence, questions that demonstrated her awareness of possible cracks behind the smooth facade of the family's life.

As Chloe directed a vacant stare at the blank half-sheet below her first joyous effusions about the baby's safe arrival she was reflecting wryly that yesterday she could have denied any factual knowledge of trouble at Applewood without fear of perjuring her soul. It was otherwise today. She brushed the feather end of the pen back and forth across her lips, wondering what if anything of the pending situation involving Lady Mary she should divulge to her godmother. She had no intention of mentioning the girl's confession of love for Mr. Thomas Trainor. At this point it was impossible to predict whether this complication would result in any change of plans for the upcoming wedding. If Lady Mary's stated intentions could be believed, the failure of Mr. Trainor to return her feelings would mean she would go ahead with her scheduled marriage, even though she did not welcome it. She might in time grow to love Lord Thrale, but whether or not this desirable state was ever achieved, she would certainly not like her present lack of affection for her intended husband to become common knowledge. Every instinct of delicacy and propriety must be offended, not to mention concern for poor Lord Thrale's unenviable position. If Mr. Trainor subsequently advanced a claim for Lady Mary's hand that caused the present engagement to be broken, there was going to be considerable talk and unpleasant conjecture no matter how tactfully any such announcement might be handled. Meanwhile, nothing would be gained by giving those at Lavering Manor any hints of a possible scandal.

In the end, Chloe elected to gloss over the situation. She told her godmother that she had been made warmly welcome by the countess and was being treated like the most pampered guest. She did not feel she was being disloyal in writing that Lady

Patricia appeared still too prostrated by grief to take a normal part in family affairs. After a brief struggle with her conscience she stated it as her opinion that Lady Mary was not so happy as one would wish to see a girl who was about to be married, but that they had not reached that degree of intimacy that would encourage the exchange of personal confidences. Yesterday that would have been true. Today she felt like a monster of deceit as her fingers formed the words. It was an effort to force her hand to end this lying epistle with assurances of her affection and esteem. She could tell herself that there was no point in needlessly worrying Lady Dalrymple when that lady was powerless to change anything that might happen here. Chloe could protest to her conscience that it would have been a worse crime to betray Lady Mary's confidence. What she could not do was absolve herself of complicity in what might well become a tragedy.

Any mildly pleasurable anticipation Chloe had entertained at widening her acquaintance in Suffolk with the Trainor dinner party had vanished when she learned of the former understanding between Lady Mary and Mr. Thomas Trainor. Her reluctance to participate in an evening that might very well set disruptive forces in motion was increased later as she put the finishing touches to her toilette by the unpalatable knowledge that her appearance did her no credit. She reminded herself that personal vanity was to be deplored, that a striving to be always in the vanguard of fashion could be translated into an unadmirable desire to take the shine out of other females, but these high-minded pronouncements did not alter the dissatisfaction with which she regarded her image in the glass as she fastened her mother's pearls about her throat. Though the pearls were valuable and her black silk gown well made, in her own eyes she looked like the proverbial poor relation in comparison with the Keesons' splendor.

This was brought home to her a moment later when a soft tap at the bedroom door preceded the entrance of Lady Mary. The girl looked really lovely. She was wearing a tasteful and fashionable gown of aquamarine sarcenet over a white slip. An aquamarine ribbon was threaded through her golden-brown curls, which had been brushed and pomaded until they shone. A shimmering excitement deepened the color of her eyes and cheeks, giving the oval face a glow of vitality it usually lacked.

"Don't you look pretty in that lovely gown. The color is perfect for you," Chloe said admiringly, turning from the mirror as the girl advanced into the room.

"Thank you, Chloe. This is my favorite of the gowns we had made in London during the Season."

Another knock at the door heralded the arrival of the maid, Tillie, who stopped short when she spotted Lady Mary. "Oh, I beg your pardon, Lady Mary, I . . . I just thought I'd pop in to see if Miss Norris might need a little help with her hair."

Lady Mary had been inspecting her friend's appearance while Chloe's attention was distracted, and now she spoke up before the other could reply. "Yes, Tillie. Can you arrange Miss Norris's hair the way you did the day she was caught in the rain?"

"But there is not time enough, Lady Mary. We shall be late," Chloe protested.

"It won't take long," that young lady replied, "and if we are a few moments late, I'll tell Mama I was the one who was slow. Be quick about it, Tillie. I am going to fetch something from my apartment, but I'll be back directly."

Chloe was staring at the closing door in consternation when the smiling maid pushed her gently onto the dressing-table bench and began pulling pins out of her hair.

When Lady Mary reentered the room a few minutes later, Tillie was twisting the heavy red tresses into a coil once more after loosening some of the front hair and allowing it to wave back from Chloe's forehead. The girl laid a length of tissue paper on the bed and came over to the dressing table. "Do you have a pair of scissors?" she asked Chloe, after scrutinizing the maid's handiwork.

"Scissors?" echoed Chloe, looking decidedly uneasy. "Why should you want scissors?"

"Because it is a crime to confine the glory of that hair of yours. Trust me. I'll not do anything radical." When Chloe had divulged the location of her sewing scissors with discernible reluctance, Lady Mary said soothingly, "I am just going to snip a few tendrils over the ears. They will curl enticingly and soften the effect so that no one will mistake you for a governess in that black gown. There, isn't that better, Tillie?"

"Yes, my lady. Someday I'd like to really dress Miss Norris's hair, mayhap in curls like yours."

"Nonsense, Tillie, I am too old to wear curls."

Chloe's automatic denial was lost in Lady Mary's enthusiastic endorsement of this proposal. "Excellent, Tillie. You shall do that for my dance." A stricken look came over her features, and she turned away abruptly, heading for the bed. Her voice was husky when next she spoke. "I have brought you something to brighten up that gown, Chloe."

In the mirror Chloe watched Lady Mary unwrap the tissue parcel. When Tillie had set the last pin Chloe thanked her and rose to face the other girl. "Oh, that is lovely," she said, eyeing the long length of wide black ribbon embroidered heavily in gold thread.

"I bought it on impulse when it took my eye in a shop in London, but I have never found the occasion to wear it. If we tie it around the waist of your gown the ends will flutter when you move." She was encircling Chloe's slim waist as she spoke, her fingers rapidly tying a sizable bow in the center. *"Voilà!* Look in the mirror. The plain black gown can now be described as simple but elegant. I wish it did not have those long sleeves, though," she added, scowling at these appendages.

"Never mind. I feel quite like a peacock already," Chloe said on a laugh before Lady Mary could again demand the scissors. "Thank you very much, Lady Mary, and now we had best be going downstairs before your mother's patience is exhausted." She caught up her cloak and a black-netted reticule and headed for the door after thanking Tillie once more for her assistance.

They were halfway to the main staircase when Lady Mary seized her friend's arm and halted their progress to say urgently, "Chloe, I must have some private conversation with Tom tonight. My entire dependence is upon you."

"On me?" Chloe's eyes rounded. "What possible use can I be to you in this endeavor?"

"You can keep Mama away from us; make sure she does not become suspicious."

"Well, I shall try, of course, but I cannot guarantee that anything I might think of would divert your mother's attention. We must hope she becomes involved in conversation with other guests."

"I am counting on you," Lady Mary repeated as they reached the staircase.

The countess and her sons were already assembled when the young ladies entered the small saloon. Lady Patricia, not feeling up to going out into company, had requested a tray in her suite.

"Here you are at last, girls," Lady Montrose said. "You are late, but it was worth the wait. You are in very good looks tonight, Mary, and you look charming too, Chloe. That sash gives your gown a touch of distinction."

"Thank you, ma'am. It was Lady Mary's idea. She lent it to me," Chloe said with a smile.

The earl interrupted the fashion parade with a smiling bow. "As Mama has already said, you both justify the extra time, but now we had best be leaving before the horses take cold standing around. Fortunately the rain has stopped. You have your wraps?"

The girls indicated the cloaks over their arms and accepted the gentlemen's assistance in donning them as the party walked to the entrance hall.

It was still light enough when they arrived at their destination to see that the manor was much older than Applewood, the central section evidently Tudor in origin. They pulled up under a portico and stepped into the brightly lighted vestibule where they were aided in removing their wraps by the porter and a footman. The route they took to the reception rooms led up and down stairs and through numerous passageways and corridors before finally bringing them into a newer wing where they were ushered into a large, high-ceilinged room already full of people. Chloe noted that the announcement of the Applewood group brought almost every head around. A tall, powerfully built man with iron-gray hair and a ruddy complexion detached himself from a group near the fireplace and came toward them with hand outstretched, a broad smile on his face.

"Good evening, Montrose. Lady Montrose, it is a pleasure to welcome you on such a happy occasion. Good to see you, Ned, my boy," he boomed, laying a heavy hand on Mr. Keeson's shoulder. "Lady Mary, we do not see enough of you at the manor these days. Maybe now that Tom is home, eh?"

Chloe kept her eyes away from the girl but felt her stiffen at her side.

"Mr. Trainor, may I present my guest, Miss Norris," the countess said in her well-modulated voice.

By the time Chloe had been bidden a kindly welcome by the jovial squire, their hostess and her son had arrived at the periphery of the group and greetings were being exchanged.

When her turn came to greet the returned son of the manor, Lady Mary held out her hand with a smile. "It's wonderful to see you, Tom. It has been a very long time."

Mr. Trainor's eyes flickered once, but he picked up his cue smoothly. "Much too long, Mary. May an old friend be permitted the license to tell you you are looking very lovely tonight? Like my sisters, you have grown up when my back was turned. I understand that I am to wish you happy?"

"I . . . I . . . yes, thank you." Lady Mary's jaw sagged and she replied in a stiffled voice.

Chloe stepped in quickly, offering her hand to Mr. Trainor before Lady Montrose could perform the introduction. "How do you do, Mr. Trainor. I am Chloe Norris, a sort of family connection staying at Applewood."

Mr. Trainor responded gallantly, and the awkward moment passed as other guests came up to speak to the Applewood party. In the flurry of introductions that followed, Chloe pasted a smile on her lips and made the mimimal response to each, trying to fade into the background. She had sensed the countess's surprise and disapproval at what must have struck her as unladylike forwardness in speaking to Mr. Trainor before being officially presented, and she could only hope to mitigate this impression by maintaining a retiring posture for the rest of the evening. At least she had succeeded in distracting attention from Lady Mary, whose composure had been in danger of crumbling.

It would have been a most enjoyable evening had Chloe been ignorant of Lady Mary's inner turmoil. She met a number of

perfectly pleasant persons, including Miss Vessey's delightful
parents, and partook of a splendid dinner. At table she was well
entertained by her dinner partners, Mr. Vessey and the son of
a neighboring baronet recently down from Cambridge and
hoping for a political career. Unfortunately, once the ladies left
the dining room, Chloe's latent concern for her young friend
prevented her from entering wholeheartedly into any conversation. She was conscious of the increase in tension in the girl
as the gentlemen rejoined the ladies and there was a general
shifting around in the large room. Lady Mary's eyes had fixed
themselves on Mr. Thomas Trainor, willing him to come to her,
but after sending a casual glance around the room, he joined
a group which included Mrs. and Miss Vessey, the budding
politician, and one of his sisters.

Trapped between two garrulous matrons, Chloe leaned
forward and said meaningfully, "I believe Mrs. Accrington has
inquired as to the date of your wedding, Lady Mary."

Under Chloe's steady regard the girl, who had made a movement to rise from her chair, sank back and turned to respond
to the speaker. To her credit, she summoned up a smile and
answered readily after begging the lady's pardon for her
momentary inattention. She was careful to avoid her mother's
eye.

From her position Chloe gradually became aware that Mr.
Thomas Trainor's eyes frequently strayed to Lady Mary in the
next half hour, though he remained attached to groups on the
other side of the room. The girl had been steered in among the
dowagers by her parent. Chloe had stayed close to lend
assistance if needed. Her neighbors' loquacity allowed her some
freedom to monitor the shifting patterns among the assembled
guests. It was her impression that Mr. Keeson flirted elegantly
with each of the young ladies in turn, while the earl conversed
almost entirely with the other gentlemen. Lady Mary's contribu-
tions became fewer until the refreshment cart was wheeled into
the room. Chloe feared that it was taking all the girl's resolution
simply to conceal her agitation. She had come for one purpose,
the achievement of which was being denied her. It must be
considered a form of slow torture to have to sit politely among

the dowagers, pretending interest in their gossip while every nerve screamed out for release.

There was the one hope remaining that Mr. Trainor would seek out his old friend while coffee was being served and people were repositioning themselves for the final scene before the evening ended. He did indeed glance toward Lady Mary when he came forward to take his cup, but his eyes slid away again instantly on encountering her regard. At that moment Ned put a hand on his shoulder and led him away for a chat.

For Lady Mary the evening ended on this note of bitter frustration. For Chloe there was still the ride home where she attempted to take up the slack caused by the girl's silence by drawing the countess out about the various people she had met that evening, a not entirely felicitous subject as it turned out, for Lady Montrose evidently preferred to hold herself aloof from all of the surrounding gentry. It had crossed Chloe's mind on a couple of occasions to wonder why no one had called at Applewood in the fortnight she had been there. The countess's blunt dismissal of her neighbors as a parcel of country dowds cleared up that little mystery, though it left Chloe feeling decidedly uncomfortable. She was beginning to wish she had never come to Applewood.

Chapter Ten

CHLOE WAS NOT entirely surprised to hear a soft knock on her door a few moments after she had retired. She cast off the covers, slid out of the bed, and hurried over to the door, pulling it wide to admit Lady Mary, who was clutching a candle and shivering in a flimsy silk wrapper.

"I . . . I'm sorry to disturb you at this hour, Chloe, but I couldn't sleep. I just had to know what you made of Tom's behavior tonight." Recent tears had left wet tracks on her pale cheeks.

"You are not disturbing me," Chloe said, taking the candle from the girl's shaking hand and guiding her over to the bed. "You are cold, Lady Mary. Get right into the bed beneath the covers."

The younger girl reacted instinctively to the authority of her friend's tone, meekly climbing into the bed. Her eyes followed Chloe's movements as she deposited the candlestick on the bedside table and went over to the armoire, where she pulled out a velvet dressing gown, which she proceeded to wrap about her person, tying the belt tightly. She then dragged the dressing table bench over to the bed and perched on it.

"The evening was a disappointment for you," she said softly.

"Worse than that, Chloe," the girl on the bed exclaimed, clutching the edges of the sheet close about her shoulders as she sat forward in her agitation. "I knew I would have to dodge Mama's eagle eye in order to talk to Tom, but . . . but after our first greeting he never even tried to speak to me. In fact, I believe he actually avoided me!"

If Lady Mary hoped her friend might tell her she was imagining things or taking too gloomy a view of the situation, she was not left long with these hopes. "I think you are correct in that belief," Chloe replied calmly, "but I would advise you not to despair. Only consider the difficulties of trying to conduct a delicate discussion under the circumstances prevailing at the manor tonight.'' The other girl's eyes were locked on hers in painful anxiety as she continued in a soothing voice. "Naturally, everyone present desired to have a word with Mr. Thomas Trainor to express their pleasure and happiness in his safe return. That alone would have made it difficult to snatch more than a few seconds of his uncontested attention, but you put up another obstacle right at the beginning when you denied by implication yesterday's prior meeting. What was he to think except that, since you preferred not to acknowledge the meeting, it was more than likely you also preferred to ignore the attachment that had existed between you before his departure. In retrospect your obvious perturbation at that meeting would be seen by him as evidence that you did not wish to be reminded of this. Being a gentleman, what could he do but accede to your wishes?''

"But I had to do that, don't you see, Chloe? If Mama found out about that accidental meeting she would be bound to wonder why I had not mentioned it, and her suspicions would have been instantly aroused.''

"I see, of course, but how could Mr. Trainor? For anything he knows to the contrary, you might be completely happy in your betrothal and merely desirous of sparing him and yourself the embarrassment attendant on any mention of your previous attachment. As a gentleman he cannot choose but to remain silent.''

"But I *must* talk to him. I cannot rest—time is getting so short—'' Lady Mary was plucking at the sheets in her agitation, and Chloe leaned forward and placed a hand over the writhing fingers.

"I understand. I fear *you* will have to make the opportunity in the light of what has passed this evening. You cannot expect that he will approach you.''

Lady Mary waved aside this consideration. "That does not signify. I must find out if he still cares for me, but how? I cannot write to him, but perhaps I might bribe my maid to carry a note to the manor. I am persuaded she would not tell Mama.''

"I shouldn't think that shift would be necessary. Tonight Mr. Trainor's sisters were both kind enough to say they would be pleased to receive me at the manor. Could we not call there some morning? Mr. Trainor might be home at the time. A meeting might come about very naturally.''

"Oh, Chloe, thank you. Of course, that is what we shall do. We'll call tomorrow.''

The lines of strain faded from the girl's face as she swung her legs over the side of the bed and reached for the candle. She apologized again for disturbing her friend's rest and left the room on a whispered good night.

The next morning the skies, which had cleared briefly, clouded over again and proceeded to produce a steady rainfall that lasted for the better part of Saturday, canceling out any chance of walking over to the manor that day to call on the Misses Trainor. Though both families attended divine service on Sunday, the countess went directly to the Applewood carriage upon leaving the church. The young people had time for no more than a quick smile and bow in passing. This was perhaps a blessing in disguise, for the banns proclaiming the upcoming marriage had been read for the first time during the service. In her preoccupation with fixing a meeting with Mr. Thomas Trainor, Lady Mary had actually lost sight of the imminency of this traditional public announcement. Mr. Vessey's sonorous reading of her name from the pulpit had come as a complete shock. She had started violently, and only Chloe's steely grip on her arm had kept her upright in the rush of dizziness that had come over her for a few seconds.

By the time breakfast was over on Monday morning, Lady Mary's composure resembled a thin sheet of glass ready to shatter at the first sharp impact. Patience is a virtue not unduly esteemed by the young even in the abstract, and has little to recommend it in situations where the element of time is perceived to be crucial. It would scarcely be exaggeration to compare the reading of the banns in church to the ringing of a death knell in the unhappy girl's mind. The need to discover whether Tom's feelings for her had survived their two-year separation was a clamoring, all-consuming urgency by now.

The two young women were preparing to leave the breakfast parlor when Lady Montrose appeared in the doorway. This was a rare enough occurrence to provoke comment from any member of her family, but Lady Mary would have continued on her way out of the room after a surprised greeting had not her mother stayed her progress.

"Wait, Mary, come back and have another cup of coffee while I eat. You too, Chloe."

Chloe shook her head warningly behind the countess's back as her daughter opened her lips to protest, and Lady Mary reluctantly retraced her steps, seating herself at the table with an air of tethered impatience.

"Let me lift that heavy coffeepot for you, ma'am. I do not believe I have ever seen you in the breakfast room before," Chloe said chattily to distract Lady Montrose's attention from her restless daughter.

"I thought I had better have something more substantial than bread and butter if we are to drive into Woodbridge today to shop," the countess said, helping herself to a slice of ham.

"Woodbridge! Oh, not today, Mama!" cried Lady Mary.

Lady Montrose lowered the fork she had raised to her mouth and cast a look of astonishment at her protesting daughter. "Pray why not today when we finally have a clear day so the walking will not be sloppy?"

"I . . . I have the headache this morning," Lady Mary said wildly. "You know I cannot bear to be shut up in a carriage when I have the headache. By the time we reached Woodbridge I would be too queasy to shop. Can we not go tomorrow instead?"

"I believe we can expect the dry weather to hold for another day or two now," Chloe said tranquilly when the countess hesitated, her eyes fixed on her daughter's tense countenance.

"Very well, girls, we'll put it off until tomorrow. Meanwhile, you had best lie down on your bed, Mary. Shall I have Mrs. Meggs prepare a tisane for you?"

"No, and I don't wish to lie down either. What I really need is to take a brisk walk in this fresh air. Will you come with me, Chloe?"

"If you like." Chloe continued to sip her coffee in an unconcerned manner.

"I don't like these frequent headaches of yours, Mary," said the countess, frowning at the girl poised on the edge of her chair. "Perhaps we should have the doctor check you over."

"This is only the second headache I've had, Mama. It will be gone by this afternoon. I don't need to see the doctor."

"Well, you are certainly not yourself lately, jumping at every little noise," replied her mother. "You are living on your nerves. Perhaps the doctor can prescribe something to restore a more even tenor to your spirits."

Seeing her young friend about to escalate her protest, Chloe stepped in again. "My father would tell you, ma'am, that a girl about to be married is subject to the oddest humors, one moment feverish with excitement, then sunk in a lethargy the next, and neither state seeming to bear any relation to the reality around her—at least in the view of other disinterested persons."

"You may have hit on something there, my dear Chloe," Lady Montrose said with an indulgent little laugh, "but if these headaches persist, we shall definitely consult the doctor. For the moment we shall plan to have our day in Woodbridge tomorrow."

Under Chloe's restraining eye, Lady Mary curbed her impatience to be gone and exerted herself to carry on a desultory conversation until her mother had finished her repast.

Fifteen minutes later, the two young women were walking purposefully through the orchard headed for the manor. There was very little conversation between them; each remained busy with her own thoughts. Chloe's, it was true, were largely concerned with her companion's predicament. It was impossible not to enter into her feelings. The thought of marrying one man when one loved another was insupportable, though Lady Mary's stated intention was to go through with the marriage if she found that Mr. Trainor's feelings for her had withered. For the sake of the three people concerned, the best solution would seem to be for the childhood friends to marry and release Lord Thrale from an entanglement that promised little happiness, but there was no denying that this course must give rise to the sort of notoriety no family would welcome. The next fortnight was going to be difficult no matter what decision was taken, but for Lady Mary, nothing could be worse than this torturous period of uncertainty. Hopefully, today's call at the manor would see an end to this stage at least.

An hour later the two girls trudged home again in a silence even more desperate than that in which they had approached the manor. The young ladies had been delighted to receive them, but they had not been able to produce their brother, who was out renewing his acquaintance in the vicinity. The bitter disappointment had been almost more than Lady Mary could face with decent composure; thus it had been left to Chloe to bear the lion's share of the conversation that must occur before they could politely take their leave. Unfortunately, the only topic that Miss Jane and Miss Caroline desired to pursue was the exciting one of their friend's upcoming wedding. Chloe was pushed to the limits of her ingenuity and inventiveness in keeping a conversation going under the circumstances, and it would be difficult to say whether she or Lady Mary was actually the more relieved when they had at last secured their release from the relentless tyranny of civilized behavior.

They were nearly through the orchard approaching the nearest wing of the house when Chloe ventured to ask her preoccupied companion what she planned to do next.

"I'll have to find some other way to contact Tom, of course," Lady Mary said, and Chloe was relieved to note that the girl was in full command of herself once more. Interpreting her searching look, the younger girl added with a faint smile, "I think perhaps it would be better . . . kinder . . . if I did not burden you with specific knowledge of my plans to accomplish this. I have already involved you more than can be quite comfortable for you as my mother's guest."

"But you will tell me if there is some way I can help you?" Though sincere in her desire to be of service to the unhappy girl, Chloe could not deny a cowardly sense of relief at Lady Mary's unexpected consideration for her anomalous position in the household.

"Yes. You have already done more for me in the short time you have been at Applewood than anyone ever has before, and I am truly grateful, Chloe. I would like it if you were to call me Mary. Will you?"

"Yes, of course," Chloe replied with her warm smile, "but I have done nothing to deserve such fervent thanks."

"You think not?" Lady Mary observed with a twisted smile.

"That shows that you have not been long at Applewood."

This cryptic comment brought them to the house, where they separated to tidy themselves for lunch.

The rest of the day was uneventful enough that Chloe's taut nerves relaxed somewhat. Lady Mary's demeanor, though subdued, was not such as would cause her mother concern. The hypothetical headache was not mentioned again and the girl willingly engaged herself at the card table after dinner. Chloe was thankful to be left in the undemanding presence of Lady Patricia, who had been persuaded by her mother to lend a hand in hemming some of her sister's bridal linen. Chloe joined her in this mindless task, content to sit sewing in silence while her thoughts roamed freely.

The shopping trip to Woodbridge the following day took place under different circumstances than originally planned. This time it was Lady Montrose who was the victim of a sick headache, presumably real in her case. She sent a message to that effect to the breakfast parlor, which sent Lady Mary posthaste up to her mother's apartment, with the result that the two girls set off in the carriage an hour later unencumbered by a chaperone.

"How did you ever persuade your mother to allow you to jaunt off without her?" Chloe asked in real curiosity. "I would have expected Lady Montrose to be quite strict in her notions of propriety."

"In general she is quite Gothic in her notions of propriety, but I pointed out that Woodbridge was a far cry from London, its streets are perfectly safe, and we would have the protection of her coachman should anything untoward arise. And while she would never have permitted me to go alone, *your* sensible presence can be trusted to act as a brake upon any major extravagances I might be tempted to contract."

"Did she really say that?" Chloe did not quite trust the demure innocence in the light blue eyes of the girl sitting opposite her in the carriage.

"Actually it was I who put that comforting thought in her head," Lady Mary admitted, "but that was not the real clincher." She paused, gazing expectantly at Chloe, who obliged by asking, "What was the argument that tipped the scales, then?"

"Not an argument: *this!*"

With a flourish Lady Mary unfolded a long, narrow sheet of paper and held it out for the other's inspection.

After a puzzled interlude, Chloe burst out laughing. "Your shopping list? Good heavens, there must be dozens of items. We'll never accomplish all of that in one day."

"Most of it is a lot of nonsense I made up, counting on Mama's disinclination to read anything when her head ached. Just the sight of it changed her mind about the desirability of putting off the excursion until she could come with us."

"You do indeed have hidden depths, Mary," Chloe declared with assumed gravity.

The girl's responsive smile was brief. "A talent for deception, you mean. It comes of living under my mother's autocratic rule all my life."

Despite their warmer relationship of late, Chloe did not feel she should delve into this dark area, so she ignored the underlying bitterness in her friend's voice and made some comment on the passing scene. Lady Mary followed her lead, pointing out places of interest as they entered the town.

Armed with the formidable list, the young ladies scoured the shops of Woodbridge for kid gloves and sandals to complement several of the new gowns that had recently arrived from the London modiste who had been entrusted with the task of making most of Lady Mary's bride clothes. They bought ribbons and petticoats too, and stockings by the dozen pairs, at least Lady Mary did. Chloe had purchased only a single pair of silk stockings when Lady Mary, her basic needs disposed of, said at last, "What about you, Chloe? Would not this white, beaded reticule you admired be just the thing for my dance? What will you be wearing?"

Chloe blinked her long lashes in confusion. "Oh, I expect I shall be home in Cambridgeshire by that time, Mary. In any case, I could not attend so grand an affair. I have nothing suitable to wear."

"Then you must wear one of my London dresses. I was not so thin last spring, and we are nearly of a height. One of my ball gowns is sure to fit you. In fact, I know just the one to

set off that magnificent hair of yours. How fortunate that I
mentioned it today. There will be ample time to do any altering
necessary.''

Her determined friend refused to listen to any of Chloe's
protestations. She sent Chloe off to try to match Lady
Montrose's embroidery silk, which effectively cut short the
argument.

They still had not visited a jeweler to look for a christening
gift when Lady Mary declared herself famished and they
repaired to the Crown, where they had reserved a private dining
room on their arrival in Woodbridge, as per the countess's
orders. Glad to be free of the assorted packages they had
accumulated, Chloe did full justice to the quite satisfactory meal
the hotel keeper put before them. It wasn't until her first pangs
of hunger had been assuaged that she remarked that her friend
was merely picking at her food despite her earlier declaration.

"I seem to have acquired a fierce headache along the way,"
Lady Mary confessed. "If you do not mind going to the
jeweler's alone, Chloe, I think I shall stay here and rest until
it is time to send for the carriage."

She turned a deaf ear to all Chloe's arguments that she could
shop another time and they should send for the carriage
immediately. She would rather rest, she insisted, and give her
head a chance to improve before stepping foot in a carriage,
since riding with a headache always added nausea to her other
complaints.

The upshot of the discussion was that Chloe found herself
back on the streets of Woodbridge after lunch minus her
companion of the morning. The afternoon sun warmed her face
while a persistent little breeze kept her quite comfortable in her
old brown pelisse. She was conscious of a guilty little pleasure
in being entirely on her own in a clean, pleasant town, though
she would never have wished a headache on her friend in order
to achieve this enjoyable state.

Chloe sauntered along, aware of the bustle of vehicular and
pedestrian activity while she checked the shops for the jeweler
Lady Mary had directed her to. At that moment her eye was
drawn to a man some dozen paces ahead of her by virtue of

his unsteady gait. She was wondering if he were ill when he appeared to step on something that caused him to turn his ankle. His foot slipped off the flagway into the road just as an open carriage bowled around the corner ahead and came straight at the staggering man, who tried to jump back and ended by falling heavily on the cobblestones. By the time Chloe came abreast of the fallen man the tilbury had swerved around him and its driver was pulling his pair to a stop. She ignored all this, concentrating on the man who lay facedown in the street. He appeared to be stunned or even unconscious, and from the way he had fallen, Chloe suspected he might have broken his left arm. It seemed expedient to turn him over while he was still dazed and less able to feel the inevitable pain. She was attempting to put this plan into effect by herself, not having noticed anyone close enough to be of immediate assistance, when a voice behind her said, "Here, I'll do that, Miss Norris. Step back."

Paying no attention to Lord Montrose's order—for she had recognized his voice almost from the first syllables—Chloe supported the victim's left arm with one hand above and one below the elbow as the earl turned him over onto his back.

"You should not be here, Miss Norris. This man is inebriated. I'll take over. Wait for me on the flagway."

Chloe had not been unaware of the strong aroma of stale spirits that emanated from the man in the street and she said calmly, "He is also injured. I am almost certain his left arm is broken. Help me to take his coat off before he comes around. It will spare him some pain later. Quickly," she added, looking up when the earl did not obey her right away.

She met his fiery glance briefly, and when her fingers had unbuttoned the now-groaning man's coat, she found him ready to assist her as requested. She bent the injured arm at the elbow and gently laid it across the man's chest after running her fingers knowledgeably along the forearm. "Yes, the ulna is nearly through the skin here. I am going to align it as best I can without a splint. Would you give me the scarf around his neck and I'll fashion a sling to keep it as immobile as possible until he can be gotten to a doctor?"

By now the driver of the tilbury had come up, protesting that

the man had fallen into his path. "I didn't hit him," he insisted
to anyone who would listen.

"No, you were very quick in getting your horses safely out
of the way," Chloe said, sending the flustered young man a
warm look before returning to her knot tying. "There, that
should serve for a time. There is a lump coming up on his forehead, but the skin is merely scraped, thank goodness."

"Is there anything I can do, ma'am?" the driver asked, gazing
admiringly down into the soft brown eyes that swung toward
him.

"Do you think you could drive him to the nearest doctor?"
she asked diffidently, before turning back to assist Lord
Montrose in raising the still-dazed man to a sitting position.

"Happy to be of assistance, ma'am. By Jupiter, I've never
met a lady with such cool nerves before," he declared, sweeping
off his hat and holding out a hand to pull her to her feet.

Chloe smiled but was glad to make picking up the accident
victim's coat and hat an excuse for looking away. The incident
had drawn quite a crowd of onlookers by this time and she was
grateful when Lord Montrose said shortly that if the driver
would climb back into his vehicle, he'd contrive to get the
injured man into it also. He declined Chloe's offer of assistance
as between them the two men bundled the injured man to his
feet despite his groans. Now that he was fully conscious, his
foxed state rendered him far less pitiable and more repugnant
than an unfavorable nature had intended. Aware that there were
many who would deplore her recent actions as inappropriate
and unbecoming in a gently bred female, Chloe was now more
than willing to efface herself. To that end, she handed the man's
belongings to a loitering youth to bring to the carriage, and
stepped back onto the flagway.

She was brushing the last remnants of dirt from her skirt when
Lord Montrose joined her. As she glanced at him uncertainly
from beneath curling lashes, the stern lines smoothed out of his
face and he smiled into her wary eyes. "Naturally that affair
was not something one would ever wish to see a lady embroiled
in, but you being your father's daughter, one would expect
nothing less from you, Miss Norris. Accept my compliments
on a piece of work well done."

Chloe's radiant smile illuminated her face as she accepted his proffered arm. "Thank you for understanding that I could not walk past him, not when I had seen how he fell and guessed what had happened. It would have been infinitely worse if that broken bone had come through the skin from rough handling."

He patted her gloved hand on his arm. "What are you doing here anyway, all by yourself?"

"I came to town with Lady Mary, but she developed a headache and is resting in the hotel where we had lunch. I had one more errand at the jeweler's." She glanced around and pointed. "That is the store Mary told me about. If you have business in town, I am perfectly safe, sir, I assure you. The chance of two adventures in one afternoon is infinitesimal. You can leave me here with a quiet mind," she finished brightly.

In response he placed his other hand on the one on his arm and guided her toward the door to the shop. "But if I accompany you I'll have a contented mind, and that is more to be desired," he said blandly.

Bereft of words for the moment, Chloe entered the shop, conscious of the earl's presence in a way she had never been before. She gazed around the attractive displays, gradually focusing on her errand as a smiling clerk hurried forward to be of assistance.

Later, with handsome examples of silver porringers and brushes before her, she sought the earl's opinion on which to choose.

"I believe I should pick the brushes," he said. "It's true that your godson will not be able to use them for some little time, but when he does graduate to them, he will think of you. On the other hand, the porringer will be in use during the period when he won't care if his food is served from a coconut shell."

This original line of reasoning found favor with Miss Norris, who decided on the brushes. When they had agreed on the style of engraving for the initials, the earl proposed going somewhere for coffee.

"Oh, but your sister will be wishing to return to Applewood. She knows I had only the one errand and will worry if I am not back directly."

"It is much more likely that Mary has taken advantage of the respite to have a restorative nap. Far from worrying, she is more apt to be annoyed at having her nap cut short," he said persuasively, as he drew her into a coffeehouse.

Chloe could not mount a convincing opposition to his suggestion for the simple reason that she was enjoying herself hugely and was much disinclined to listen to the promptings of conscience. Her nose took over when they had seated themselves on opposite sides of a table placed between high-backed benches. The small room was very dark after the brightness of the street, but the scent of coffee brewing was suddenly ambrosial, and she breathed it in deeply.

"Have you ever been to one of these places?" he asked, noting her interested glance around the sparsely tenanted room where she appeared to be the sole female customer.

"Yes, in Cambridge once with my father and some of his friends."

"I can't think of another woman I would bring in here," he said with an odd little smile. "Mama would be scandalized."

"Oh, I don't think so," she replied, taking him seriously. "Though it would not do for a female to come in without a male escort, perhaps."

They spoke idly of her impressions of Woodbridge until their coffee was served. His eyes were trained on her as she stirred sugar into her cup before taking a sip and pronouncing it delicious.

"If forced to defend my action in bringing you to a public house of sorts I would point out that you were desperately in need of a restorative after your unnerving experience," he said lightly.

Chloe chuckled. "Then I wonder you did not administer said restorative *before* we went shopping, sir. That cock won't fight." She sent him a glance of pure mischief.

He refused the challenge, becoming serious again. "The driver of the tilbury was right; you handled that situation with the greatest skill and coolness. You are a most unusual female, Miss Norris."

She rejected this hypothesis categorically. "No, I am not. Only my upbringing was a trifle unusual compared with that of the females of your acquaintance. I do not believe women are inherently less capable than men of taking practical action when the situation demands it. It is simply that the training . . . the preparation for life, if you will, differs according to the society into which one is born. My complete lack of those feminine accomplishments which are valued in the society in which you move is a case in point.''

"That is patently absurd. You know full well you have no slightest difficulty in fitting into the society in which I move, to use your words.'' He was glowering at her, but Chloe refused to be cowed.

"The fact that I was taught the ordinary manners and deportment obtaining among the upper classes merely supports my position that all is a matter of training,'' she persisted.

"All, Miss Norris? Remember, he that diggeth a pit shall fall into it.''

She grinned at that but was not deterred. "Since you are partial to biblical quotations, what of this one? 'Train up a child in the way he should go, and when he is old he shall not depart from it.' Within the inescapable bounds imposed by the degree of inherent intelligence, I contend that any child trained from birth will fit easily into that class for which the training was intended, as long as he is living among that class.''

"Radical indeed. I had no idea I was harboring an anarchist in my home.''

"You aren't,'' she said coolly. "I am not an advocate of the forcible reduction of the upper classes to the state of the masses.''

"Should I take comfort in the fact that you are not prepared to lead an uprising at Applewood?''

"Well, I think you might,'' she replied tranquilly, while twin devils danced in her eyes. "And now, sir, much as I have enjoyed our jousting, I think it is time we got back to Mary before she alerts the constabulary to search for me.''

She put down her thick cup, indicating that the delightful interval was at an end, and he was constrained to accept her decision, which he did with a palpable reluctance that any young lady could be pardoned for assuming was a tribute to the pleasures of her company.

Chapter Eleven

IT WAS AS Lord Montrose and Miss Norris were approaching the room in the Crown where Lady Mary awaited her friend's return that the gentleman said softly, as if to himself, "The day has turned out rather well after all."

Chloe's hand stopped in mid-air before her knuckles could strike the door panel and she looked back over her shoulder. "Did the day begin badly for you, sir?"

"No, no, nothing of the sort." His mild annoyance was, she felt, directed against himself for raising an issue, but she persisted.

"You sounded as though you had expected it to turn out badly."

"No." As she waited expectantly, he gave a snort of defeated laughter and admitted, "It is just that today is my birthday."

"I see," she said, drawing out the last word as if it were a great discovery. "And, of course, you have now reached such an advanced age that there is nothing ahead of you but imminent decline and decrepitude. I do indeed feel for your plight, sir."

"Little wretch!" He chuckled. "Not that thirty isn't a milestone of a less than agreeable sort."

"Calling for a period of understandably depressed spirits, I agree"—she nodded wisely—"but I trust your family's good wishes have helped to assuage the pain. May I add my felicitations, sir?"

"You may be the first," he said dryly.

"The first? You mean no one has remembered your birthday? Oh, of course! Lady Montrose has been prostrated with the headache today and Mary and I have been gone since shortly after breakfast. I imagine there will be a festive dinner tonight."

"Do you? I shouldn't count on it." The same dry inflection brought a troubled look to Miss Norris's countenance and her lips parted, then firmed again. She had turned back toward the closed door when his quiet voice said, "Miss Norris?" This bringing no response except the raising of her bent hand toward the door again, the earl reached out and took her fingers in his. "Chloe?"

This time his voice compelled acknowledgment, and she turned to look at him with a shade of wariness. "Sir?"

"I forbid you to say one word about my birthday to anyone at Applewood. Is that clear?"

"How did you know . . . ?"

"Sometimes, my dear, you are perfectly transparent, especially when your compassion is aroused, but I am not an object for your compassion. Do I have your promise to obey me in this?"

A brief intense clash of wills occurred before the brown eyes looked away and she nodded, albeit with reluctance. He released her fingers and knocked on the door himself.

Alone in her bedchamber that night, Chloe finally admitted that she could not like Lady Montrose.

The ride home from Woodbridge had been enjoyable. Lady Mary had greeted her gaily, free of her headache after a short nap. She had been pleased to see her brother, who had ridden into town that morning on estate business and now proposed to accompany the carriage back to Applewood. They had arrived in time for a late tea presided over by the countess. She was looking a trifle pale but claimed the worst of her headache was over. She was interested to hear all about their purchases in town. On Lady Mary's advice, Chloe omitted any description of her visit to a coffeehouse. Her own reticence had already precluded any disclosure of her action with regard to the inebriated accident victim.

No mention had been made by anyone of Lord Montrose's birthday at tea, but Chloe had remained confident that there would be some family acknowledgment of the occasion at dinner. To her acute distress, however, nothing was said then or at any time during the rest of the evening. Chloe had sat among the Keesons in gathering indignation which she battled to conceal every time her eyes lighted on the earl's faintly smiling countenance. He had been at his urbane best, which

had had the odd effect of concentrating her rising hostility on
him, the victim of the oversight. He need not have been so
grievously neglected had he not put it beyond her power to drop
a hint in Lady Mary's ear on their way home from Woodbridge,
she decided with questionable logic as she pummeled her pillows
in an effort to compose herself for sleep. She was annoyed—
nay, furious—with him for acting like a small child cutting off
his nose to spite his face, but her severest censure was reserved
for Lady Montrose.

How could any mother worthy of the title forget the anniver-
sary of the birth of her first child? It was unnatural, that's what
it was!

As Chloe's heated reaction to the slight to Lord Montrose
cooled enough to permit rational analysis, she could see that
the incident had crystallized a number of half-formed and duti-
fully rejected impressions that had flitted in and out of her
consciousness during her stay at Applewood. After sober
reflection she was left with the immutable conclusion that Lady
Montrose was indeed an unfeeling parent; in fact, hers was a
cold, self-absorbed nature beneath the surface charm and
compelling physical appeal. Even the affection she sometimes
displayed for Ned could be explained by the fact that he flattered
her, and his male version of her own beauty pleased her
aesthetically. Patricia was beautiful too, but she was not a source
of possessive pride at present, thanks to her prolonged and
uncompromising grieving that disturbed the even tenor of her
mother's existence.

Chloe had come to Applewood predisposed in favor of the
sister of her dear godmother and had been guilt-ridden up to
now to realize that she could not wholeheartedly like the lovely-
looking woman, despite her caressing words and the seeming
consideration she displayed toward her guest. She had never
been able to subdue a niggling little suspicion that *au fond* Lady
Montrose looked on her, if not with disdain, then at best with
condescension. She had rebuked herself repeatedly for such
unkind thoughts, blaming an unbecoming pridefulness that was
too ready to see condescension where none was intended. As
she lay in her bed, her mind still too active for sleep, Chloe
made the reasoned decision that it was time to stop trying to

explain the countess's character and behavior in the light of her own wishful thinking. It was more than time to stop castigating herself for her own negative feelings and accept the situation as it was in reality. The countess's ubiquitous charm was a sham; in fact, her whole life seemed to be one of pretense, but it behooved Chloe as a guest to play the role assigned to her. In the short time remaining she could certainly do that without needless heart burning.

There was real relief in taking this sensible decision. Chloe turned over on her stomach and promptly went to sleep.

The resolution she had taken with regard to her hostess was effective in shielding her from the occasional verbal pinpricks she sustained over the next day or two. Ned's flirtatious attentions, performed, Chloe was convinced, in a spirit of pure devilry, were the cause of the countess's playfully expressed little cautions that a young lady who acquired a reputation for levity was courting social disaster. The undeserved admonitions, expressed generally rather than directed openly at Chloe, would have hurt her feelings and caused her to search her conscience the previous week, but now they had no power to lower her self-esteem, though she always sought to avoid those occasions she knew would arouse the countess's protective jealousy. She also took care to disguise her annoyance at Ned for the provocation, her instincts warning her that he would intensify his teasing if he succeeded in rattling her composure. Instead she parried his overtures with her blandest smiles and mildest comments.

What bothered Chloe more than Ned's and Lady Montrose's behavior was the retreat, if that was the apposite term, on Lady Mary's part from the tentative friendship that had been developing between the two girls. Though maintaining the air of friendliness that seemed sincere when they were in company together, Lady Mary was again proving elusive. Chloe had been slightly surprised to see the girl wander off on her own, sketchbook under her arm, on the days immediately following their trip to Woodbridge. No invitation to accompany her had been forthcoming, and Chloe had too much delicacy to propose herself as a companion under the circumstances. She admitted to a feeling of disappointment, for she was well aware of Mary's basic unhappiness and would have liked to befriend her.

Only with young Emilie did Chloe feel completely at ease during this period, for she remained quite illogically piqued at the earl and was aware that she was treating him with a touch of reserve that had not existed before. She was glad of the child's companionship and gladder still to see Emilie beginning to recover the eagerness for living that properly belongs to childhood.

Two days after the trip to Woodbridge, Chloe was strolling about the grounds in the early part of the afternoon. She headed in the general direction of the stables, knowing Emilie went there daily in search of Tigre. She was preoccupied with Lady Mary's unfortunate situation as she often was to a degree, but part of her mind was in the momentary expectation of being hailed in a childish treble, which was why she froze in horror for a second when a piercing scream tore the drowsy silence to shreds. It was a high-pitched, agonized shriek, and Chloe was in no doubt that it came from Emilie. She set off at a dead run, stumbling at first until she had succeeded in hiking her skirts up high enough not to impede her progress. Her heart was thudding, and the succeeding screams rang in her ears as she headed mindlessly toward the horrible sounds, closer now as she neared the kennels.

Chloe rounded the corner of the stables to see Emilie desperately trying to pull the padlock off the gate to the dog pens. She could distinguish words now—*"Stop! No!"*—and over and over again: *"Tigre!"* Her eyes sought explanation inside the dog pens.

What seemed to Chloe's frantic eyes to be dozens of yapping hounds were engaged in tearing something to pieces. Nausea rose in her throat and nearly gagged her as she comprehended that the object of their frenzied activity was Emilie's cat, or what was left of him.

It took almost all of Chloe's strength to pry Emilie's fingers from the padlock before she could pick up the wildly struggling child and carry her a few feet away, out of sight, if not sound, of that sickening scene of carnage. She sank onto the grass, cradling the screaming child in her lap, murmuring crooning sounds that were not words, for of what use were words to Emilie at this moment of black despair?

At first the little girl struggled frantically against the confining arms, heedless of the soothing voice, the chaotic words tumbling out of her indicating that she had not yet accepted the finality of the tragedy.

"It's no use, dearest, you cannot save Tigre. No one can save him." Chloe repeated the words several times before she could sense a lessening in the child's resistance.

"What has happened? I heard that ungodly screaming. Is Emilie hurt?" demanded Lord Montrose, striding up to the pair on the ground at that moment.

Shaking her head, Chloe was too intent on gaining Emilie's crucial acceptance to attend to the man for the moment. She repeated the words, "You cannot save Tigre, dearest. No one can."

The child's wild flailing about had stopped and she looked at Chloe as if seeing her for the first time. "They killed Tigre!" she wailed, and burst into a storm of weeping.

"What's going on? Is she hurt?"

Lord Montrose had hunkered down on his haunches. His eyes went from the hysterically sobbing child to the woman who gathered her closer and began a rocking motion.

"Not physically," Chloe replied. "The dogs just killed her her kitten in front of her eyes."

"*Good God!* How did it happen?"

"I don't know. The cat was inside the kennel enclosure. I heard Emilie scream and saw her trying to pull the padlock off the gate. Thank God it was locked."

The man and woman exchanged a look of mutual horror at the thought in both their minds. The earl got to his feet staring helplessly down at the pair on the ground, rocking to and fro the few degrees possible in the awkward position, while the woman continued to murmur soothingly and the child sobbed and gasped out disjointed protests.

"I am going to get to the bottom of this," he promised savagely, turning on his heel.

"No, not yet!" When the earl continued to walk away with rapid strides, Chloe raised her voice, "Ivor, please, wait!"

He stopped and turned slowly and their eyes met again in wordless communication.

"I . . . I don't think I can carry Emilie all the way up to the nursery," Chloe explained, "and she should really be put to bed. She has had a frightful shock and the wind is turning chilly."

"Of course. I'll take her."

This was easier said than done. At the first touch of his hands on her back Emilie went rigid and clung more tightly to Chloe, who said, "It is only Uncle Ivor, dearest. He is going to carry you to the nursery. I shall come too, of course, and help Addie put you to bed," she added, sensing that the issue hung in the balance for an instant.

"You won't leave me?" Emilie cried as she felt herself scooped up by her uncle's strong arms.

"Not until you are asleep," Chloe promised recklessly.

By this time she was half running in order to keep up with the earl's long step and rapid pace. She knew from the muscle that twitched in his cheek that he was imposing a check on his emotions for Emilie's sake and understood the male need to take strong action to relieve the feeling of helplessness one was left with in a situation of this sort. Emilie was quieter now, but her slight frame shook spasmodically with the heartbroken sobs she could not yet control.

"I . . . I loved Tigre," she said once on a hiccuping gasp.

"I know, my sweet. He was a lovely kitten."

"I'll get you another cat, sweetheart," said the earl. "Tomorrow."

"I don't want another cat—ever!" Emilie's tears burst out afresh. "Nobody can take Tigre's place."

Chloe shook her head when the earl would have argued, and he pressed his lips firmly together, maintaining a grim silence until they reached the nursery.

"If you will put her on the bed, sir," Chloe said, "Addie and I will take care of her now."

He did as requested, staring broodingly down at the tear-drowned child, who had reached immediately for Chloe while Addie came clucking in from the day nursery, full of questions and concern. This was obviously no place for a man, but he delayed his exit long enough to ask Chloe in an undertone to come to him in the library in a half hour.

"I will if Emilie is asleep," she replied.

"That is understood." He sent one last glance at the clinging child and walked out of the room.

It was closer to an hour than thirty minutes when Chloe knocked on the library door. As she approached the desk the earl's gaze appraised her somberly, taking in her shadowed eyes and drooping lips.

"Sit down," he said, coming out from behind the desk as she looked at him without speaking.

She sank limply onto the chair he indicated and watched with incurious eyes as he went over to a side table and poured something from a cut-glass decanter into a stemmed glass.

"Drink this," he said, pressing the glass into her unwilling hand. "It will put some life back into you."

She obeyed mechanically, pulling a face when the fiery liquid made its presence felt.

"It's only brandy. Drink it all," he ordered, standing over her until she had complied rather than argue. When she had finished, he took the glass from her fingers and placed it on the desk as he circled behind it to take his seat again. "I assume Emilie is asleep?" he asked with a lift of one black brow, and when she had nodded, posed another question. "Should we send for the doctor?"

She gave this her serious consideration before replying in the negative. "Sleep is the best medicine at the moment. Perhaps tomorrow if you or her mother feel uneasy you might wish to have your doctor see her." She raised her head and looked him in the eye. "I plan to spend the night in the nursery in case she wakes up."

He could tell she was prepared to defend her position, but his quick agreement with the wisdom of this course made that unnecessary.

"This is a damnable thing to have happen to that child," he burst out, not even bothering with a *pro forma* apology for the violence of his language. The gravity of her expression as her eyes met his steadily showed her essential agreement with his sentiments.

"I think," she began, groping her way, "that this wasn't just about the death of her pet, although that would have been sufficiently appalling to send any child into hysterics.''

"Her father?" he suggested, quick to take her meaning.

"I'm afraid so." She sighed, and tears filmed her eyes for a moment. "What makes it so particularly unfortunate is that Emilie was just beginning to brighten up. She was beginning to . . . to trust life again . . . to look forward to each new day as children are meant to do. That kitten was largely responsible for this."

"Then we'll get her another kitten, and this one will live in the nursery," he declared fiercely.

"In time, of course, but for the moment, I fear that Emilie is not going to allow herself to love another creature the way she loved Tigre. Love makes one very vulnerable. Though she doesn't comprehend this with her intellect yet, I fear she has learned a sad truth one could wish long delayed."

"It is understandable that she should be so shattered at present, but children bounce back quickly," he asserted, trying for her sake to put more confidence than he actually felt into the words as a picture of the sad little ghost that Emilie had been for the past months appeared behind his eyelids.

"I would be pleased to think this will be true in Emilie's case, but she has lost so much lately." Chloe fell silent, and after a moment she ventured hesitantly, "I do not wish to seem to criticize or to intrude into matters that are not my concern, sir, but I cannot help but feel that in a large measure Emilie has lost her mother as well as her father. Believe me, I pity Lady Patricia most sincerely," she added hastily, perhaps sensing some withdrawal in him, "but if she could only be brought to see how desperately Emilie needs her mother's loving concern and interest on a constant basis, I am persuaded she would rally to provide this. It is obvious that she loves her daughter dearly, but at present she cannot seem to rise above her own personal grief to help Emilie, and it is now that Emilie requires love and support." Her voice trailed off and she bit her lip. "I beg your pardon if I have offended you."

"Kindness could never offend me," he assured her, "and in the event you are still unaware of something I have known for ages, let me make it clear that between friends there are no artificial barriers to the truth. You may say anything to me."

"Th . . . thank you." Chloe looked away quickly, and he wondered if it was merely maidenly confusion that kept her from meeting his eyes, but while he was wondering she turned back and said with the composure that generally distinguished her demeanor, "I am emboldened to hope you will not think I have overstepped the bounds by promising Emilie we should bury Tigre in the white garden with full honors tomorrow."

"I doubt there is enough left of the cat to bury."

She blanched at this frankness and swallowed hard. "Perhaps," she suggested, after a pregnant pause, "if we were to enclose *something* in a canvas bag or a small box with the lid nailed down it would satisfy Emilie's desire to render her pet formal homage."

"I'll see to it," he promised.

She smiled her relief. "Thank you. It may sound excessively morbid, but I am persuaded this ceremony will help Emilie to accept the situation and put it behind her. Did you find out how the cat happened to be in the kennel enclosure?"

"Yes. It's not a pretty story," he warned. She said nothing, leaving it to him to decide whether or not to disclose the circumstances.

"We took on a new stable boy lately at the request of my land agent, who wished to help the boy's family, a feckless bunch. Quite apart from the fact that the other boys all despise him, my head groom warned me just yesterday that the new boy was showing too much interest in Emilie. He'd overheard him trying to lure her into the barn with some hoaxing tale of a new litter of kittens. I decided to put the fear of God into him this morning by warning him that the next time he so much as spoke to Emilie would be his last day at Applewood." He paused at her look of dawning horror before adding grimly, "With the direct result that he took the first opportunity to be revenged on me by throwing Emilie's beloved pet to the dogs when he spotted her on her way to the stables this afternoon. I must hold myself personally responsible for what happened today."

"Oh, no!" she protested strongly. "Anyone who could do such a thing is clearly not normal and very likely represented a real danger to Emilie. As terrible as this episode was, and

as much as Emilie is suffering at present, I have the strongest
conviction that your quick action may have averted a far greater
tragedy. My flesh is crawling at the thought,'' she said on a
shudder, rubbing her fingers up and down her lower forearm
above the wrist in an unconscious and telling gesture.

As he gazed into Chloe's troubled countenance, the trouble
put there by a concern for *his* family that ousted the
serenity that was a reflection of her own nature, Lord Montrose
was seized by a desire to take her in his arms and comfort her,
to kiss away the shadows in eyes of brown velvet and replace
the droop of that soft mouth with the curve of passion—

"Is something wrong, sir?"

Lord Montrose blinked and refocused. "Wrong?"

"Just now you looked as though you had sustained a shock
or suddenly remembered something of importance."

"It was more in the nature of a discovery than a recollection, but you are correct about the shock,'' he owned in a voice
whose timbre was uneven at present.

"Then I shall leave you to do what is necessary," she said,
rising from her chair. "And do not worry about Emilie tonight,
sir. It is to be expected that she will have a disturbed night,
but she seems to find my presence comforting, so I shall be
there if she wakes."

"Above rubies," he murmured.

"I beg your pardon?" She paused at the door and looked a
question at him.

He shook his head. "It doesn't signify," he lied gravely, and
watched her glide out of the room with neat grace and a friendly
smile.

At the moment it was beyond his powers to produce a similar
smile in response, though somewhere too near the surface for
comfort lurked derisive laughter clamoring for release. And he
had believed himself immune from those darts and pangs that
had plagued mankind down through the ages!

She had said he looked like a man who had sustained a shock,
so his expression must have accurately mirrored his reaction
to the discovery that his feelings for Chloe Norris were no longer
the pleasant pallid ones of friendship and shared interests. There
was nothing pallid about the sensations caused by the blood

pounding through his body at the mere idea of locking her into his embrace and kissing her until she responded with matching ardor.

He surged out of his chair and paced—or stalked—the length of the long room. This was utter madness! How else explain the suddenness of this full-blown desire to possess a woman who would never have attracted him in the past, not because she was unattractive but because there was about her no awareness of her attractions, nor, to his chagrin, any awareness of him as a potential lover. There was simply nothing seductive about Chloe Norris. Her nature seemed too matter-of-fact and practical to cherish romantic notions, her appearance was so unfashionable as to make her conspicuous in the circles in which he moved, and she did not possess the outstanding beauty that could negate the other objections.

Lord Montrose stood at the French doors looking out on the rose garden while he examined that statement and found it essentially correct but supremely irrelevant. If madness accounted for this blood singing in his veins, did he then wish to be cured of it?

The answer to this question was much longer in coming. If Chloe were to return to Cambridgeshire his life would soon return to the pleasant pattern her presence had interrupted. Though cherishing no illusions about the female sex, he had always accepted that it was his duty to marry eventually, and indeed he desired a son of his body to carry on the name. Females had been casting out lures to him—and his father's honors—for years, so it was no immodesty to say he could have his pick of this or any Season's most sought-after success. It was cold-blooded, but the fair lady of his choice would doubtless be operating on the same basic principle, so there would be no harm done.

Chloe had spoken more truly than she knew when she equated loving with vulnerability. He had been a lifelong witness to the power his mother had wielded so callously, by virtue of his father's helpless love for the beautiful, well-mannered, and heartless woman he had chosen for his wife. That was a trap Lord Montrose never intended to be caught in.

Unarguably rare, there *was* such a thing as mutual love,

though, unless all the poets had lied down through the ages. For instance, the man Chloe loved would possess a bit of heaven on earth. The warmth and generosity of her loving spirit shone out of those incredibly beautiful brown eyes.

The earl shook his head to clear it of a persistent picture of Chloe's lovely face. Good God, when had his earlier definition of his present condition as a case of simple masculine lust for a desirable female changed to one of undying love? He was going too fast down a road he had never wished to travel, caught up in a tidal wave of exhilaration he did not wish to acknowledge. And worst of all, he was doing this against all reason and sense. He was well aware that Chloe's present feeling for him was one of friendship uncomplicated by any nuances of romance, and what was potentially far worse, she was betrothed to another man.

It crossed the earl's mind to wonder why this last fact had so little power to cast him into the dumps. He knew Chloe was a person of shining integrity. He had been drawn to this quality in her from the beginning. Unlike many women he could name, it would never occur to her to break an engagement because of a better matrimonial proposition. On the other hand, that betrothal could not have reached the five-year mark if the parties to it were motivated by a strong romantic attachment, not unless extreme external circumstances beyond their control dictated the delay. He frowned blackly as a flaw in that theory presented itself. It was entirely possible that *one* lukewarm party to a betrothal could stall a marriage; this was certainly true if the tepid party was the man. He paused to consider Chloe as he had seen her in the admittedly short but concentrated span of their acquaintance. There was nothing about her to suggest the lovesick girl pining for her fiancé, but that was not in any case the figure a girl with any pride would desire to cut in public. His intelligence rejected the quick thought that Chloe's nature might be essentially passionless like his mother's. He had witnessed her warmth on too many occasions, even directed toward an unlovable drunkard, to doubt that hers was a loving heart.

The strength and nature of Chloe's attachment to this Captain Otley was something he would make it his business to discover in the immediate future. Her father would not be in Scotland much longer, and they could not reasonably hope to keep her at Applewood when Dr. Norris returned to Cambridgeshire. Considering the cool reception she had received from various members of his family, it would be wonderful if she had not already written to urge her parent's quicker return. She was, he suspected, not as blind to his mother's thinly veiled disdain as her good manners in not noticing would indicate. In a very few days this house would be packed with guests, most of them of his mother's choosing. It would scarcely be a propitious setting for the nominal host to conduct a difficult courtship.

His frown deepened into a scowl and the foolish euphoria of the last half hour evaporated as the myriad complexities made their presence felt, leaving him a prey to mixed feelings of hope and doubt. He stood irresolute in the middle of the room, then on an impulse headed to the mahogany stand where the large family Bible reposed. His fingers fumbled for the section he sought, then paused as he located the relevant passage in Proverbs:

Who can find a virtuous woman? for her price is far above rubies.

The words had sprung into his memory a few moments ago when Chloe had declared her intention of remaining in the nursery in case Emilie woke up in the middle of the night needing comfort. He read through the entire chapter; then his eyes returned to the verse over which they had lingered earlier. He read the words again. *The heart of her husband doth safely trust in her, so that he shall have no need of spoil.*

Chapter Twelve

EMILIE WOKE UP crying in the middle of the night, but Chloe had been prepared for this. She sent Addie down to the kitchen to fetch warm milk and bread and butter, for the child had slept through her dinner hour. She soothed and petted the little girl and washed her face and hands to make her more receptive to the food when it arrived. They discussed plans for Tigre's funeral in great detail until Emilie was ready to go back to sleep.

Chloe spent most of the following day with Emilie, taking her on a long, purposely tiring ramble about the estate and the village after the tearful obsequies for Tigre had been concluded, with Addie and Lord Montrose as the other mourners. The earl's presence was a welcome surprise. He had informed Chloe at lunch that he'd had a coffin made for the cat's remains and asked when the funeral was to take place, which had necessitated an explanation of the pet's demise to the rest of the family, with the exception of Lady Patricia who was not present. Mild exclamations of sympathy for Emilie's loss had been expressed by her aunt and uncle before they resumed their meal, while Lady Montrose had cited the present unhappy situation in proof of her belief in the folly of allowing children to become attached to domestic animals. She strongly deplored the holding of a funeral for a cat, claiming it was morbid and highly undesirable for a sensitive child like Emilie, who would be bound to dwell more on the death of the animal than would otherwise be the case. Sensing that the countess was working up to a refusal to allow the burial, Chloe sent an imploring look to the earl, who promptly took issue with his mother's point of view. His calm and determined championship of the event as an opportunity for the child to accept and express her natural grief carried the day over the countess's repeated objections. Though she herself had not said a word during the discussion, Chloe could not help but see from the unfriendly glances sent in her direction that Lady Montrose considered her responsible for the earl's present refusal to defer to his mother's opinion on something she considered a household matter. It could not be helped, however, and Chloe had gone past the point of caring for Lady Montrose's good opinion, except that it made life smoother at Applewood to be in agreement with her hostess. Fortunately it would not be much longer that she must endure being an unwanted guest, for by now she was convinced that the countess desired to see the last of her. She would be glad to leave, she told herself, for her own sake, though she would like to know Lady Mary and Emilie were in a way of being happier before she finally shook the dust of Applewood from her shoes.

When Lord Montrose requested a chess game that evening, Chloe begged to be excused. Since she had anticipated that he would at some time or other ask for a repeat of their very satisfying contest, she was prepared with a string of reasonable excuses that tripped easily off her tongue. He did not press her, accepting her refusal with his usual equanimity, but she was left with the feeling that her glibness had been to no avail and might on the contrary have convinced him that there was a personal reason for her refusal behind the socially acceptable ones she had cited. There wasn't, of course; it was merely that she preferred for everyone's sake not to incur the countess's displeasure, and any private intercourse between herself and either of her ladyship's sons was the quickest route to earning her displeasure. Chloe had her reward, if such it could be considered, in being left with her fancywork in the company of the inanimate Lady Patricia while the others played whist at Lady Montrose's instigation until it was time for final refreshments before retiring. The idea of private instruction in whist to correct one of the many gaps in Chloe's social education had not been pursued by the countess, to the great relief of the proposed beneficiary.

Chloe and Emilie were putting fresh flowers on Tigre's grave the next afternoon when Lord Montrose came into the white garden.

"Aha, just the ladies I was seeking," he said affably. "I have something to show you down at the stables, Emilie. You might

wish to come along too, Miss Norris,'' he added, shaking his
head slightly at her quick look of consternation. It seemed he
had guessed, in that disconcerting way he had of reading her
mind, that she was afraid he had gone ahead and procured
another kitten, and was reassuring her that was not the case.

She projected brisk enthusiasm for the sake of the hesitant
child. ''How exciting! Come along, Emilie. I wonder what the
surprise can be?''

Lord Montrose would give no hints, so they were indeed
surprised a few moments later to see a sturdy little pied pony
standing in the saddling yard.

''Ohhhhh!'' Emilie said on a long exhalation. Heartbroken
she might be, but she was not proof against the pony's soft
brown eyes turned inquiringly in her direction, and she needed
no urging from her uncle to reach out a hand to stroke the velvety
head. The pony promptly nuzzled its nose into the child's
shoulder, eliciting a little laugh from one who had not smiled
in days. ''Oh, you are so beautiful,'' crooned Emilie. ''What
is his name, Uncle Ivor?''

''*Her* name is Star because of the white mark on her
forehead.''

''*Étoile*! Is she for me, Uncle Ivor?'' Eagerness rang in
Emilie's voice.

''She is indeed for you, sweetheart.''

''Oh, thank you, Uncle!'' Emilie turned back to the pony,
who seemed to be attending, and switched to French. ''*Entends-
tu, Étoile? Tu seras mon poney.*''

The pony whickered softly and nodded its head, for all the
world as though giving its approval of the arrangement.

''How do you feel about a French-speaking horse, Miss
Norris?'' the earl asked in an amused undervoice.

''I think it is wonderful, sir,'' she replied, smiling in him
with shining eyes. ''Just the thing to cure her melancholy.''

''And ponies have the double advantage of longevity and
reasonable freedom from accidents,'' he added whimsically,
before addressing his enraptured niece again. ''There is only
one thing about owning a pony, Emilie. ''Étoile will need to
be exercised regularly. Otherwise, she will eat her head off and

get fat and lazy, which is bad for her health. She needs to be ridden nearly every day.''

"But I don't know how to ride." Anxiety crept into her eyes, and Emilie moved closer to her new pet as if afraid Étoile would be snatched away again.

"Then learning to ride will be the first order of business. Sawyer, my head groom, will teach you. He sat me on my first pony, and your mother, as well as your aunt and uncle in due course. And now it is your turn. Do you like the idea?''

"Oh, yes, Uncle Ivor. I'm not afraid of falling off or anything—at least, not much afraid.''

"Everyone takes a toss now and then, it does no harm," her uncle assured her. "Étoile is used to carrying children. She is a well-mannered animal.''

Evidently the idea of a horse with nice manners struck Emilie as amusing, for she giggled, looking all at once the picture of carefree childhood, her enchanting little face alight. Over her head the man and woman exchanged a look of deep satisfaction before the earl said, "Run into the tack room and check with Sawyer about when it will be convenient to schedule your lessons, Emilie. He will also tell you what to wear.''

"Yes, Uncle Ivor. Then I must run to tell *Maman* about Étoile.'' The little girl disappeared into the stable after a last pat for the patient pony.

"Yes . . . *Maman*," the earl said thoughtfully.

"You don't think Lady Patricia will forbid the riding lessons, do you, sir?''

"She won't forbid them," he replied firmly to dispel the little cloud of worry that had appeared in Chloe's eyes. "Emilie needs something constructive in her life at this time, some activity that will demand concentration and application. It is more than time that Tricia started putting her child's welfare before other considerations.''

But that was precisely what she was doing in withholding permission for her daughter to have riding lessons, a tearful and plaintive Lady Patricia explained to her stern-eyed brother an hour later when he had come to her suite in response to an urgent summons carried by one of the footmen over half the

estate before he had finally tracked his lordship down outside
one of the cottages, discussing roof repairs with his tenant.

"Riding is too dangerous. She could be badly hurt if she were
thrown."

"Tricia, this is not a huge, half-wild race horse; it's a small,
shaggy, *slow* pony whose last owner outgrew her at the age of
seven. Emilie is nine years old. How old were you when you
sat your first pony—not a day over six, I'll go bail."

"It was different then. Father was there to supervise our
riding."

"And I am here to supervise Emilie's. Do you think I'd let
Emilie be hurt? Or old Sawyer, for that matter? You know he
is completely reliable."

"Terrible things happen sometimes, no matter how careful
people are. Emilie is all I have left, Ivor. I cannot lose her!"

"You are already losing her in a fundamental sense, Tricia."

The earl felt himself lower than a worm when he saw the effect
his deliberate words had on the person who had been closest
to him during the happy years of his childhood. Already wraith-
thin and corpse-pale, his once-beautiful sister looked fragile
enough to be broken by harsh words, but a glance around the
dim, choking atmosphere of her self-imposed prison steeled him
to perform the task he had set himself.

"Ivor?" She was staring up at him pleadingly from the chaise,
her hands clutching each other before her breast, her eyes
agonized. He moved his legs aside a few inches and sat down
beside her, taking cold skeletal fingers in his warm grasp.

"Death is not the only way we lose those we love, Tricia.
Emilie too has suffered this last year. She adored her father and
he was taken away from her. She has needed her mother and
her mother has not answered that need."

"But I brought her home! Her whole family is here, Ivor,
even if I have been worse than useless."

He was shaking his head during this attempt at self-justifica-
tion. "That might have worked with another kind of family for
a while, Tricia, but this isn't a family in the sense that matters.
You know what Mama is. Do you honestly believe she has been
cuddling Emilie in a grandmotherly lap these last months while
you have immured yourself in this room? Emilie has been more

or less abandoned to the care of servants, and that is no less true since Mama and Mary returned from London. When Chloe Norris arrived here three weeks ago the child was a pathetic, lonely little ghost drifting about the estate. Luckily for Emilie, Miss Norris is possessed of a warm heart, and her heart went out to the child. If you haven't noticed the improvement in your daughter's spirits lately, then you should have. She has blossomed like a flower in the sunshine under the influence of Miss Norris's warmth and interest.''

''I have noticed that Emilie seems brighter these days, Ivor, and I—''

''But two days ago something terrible happened,'' he said, ruthlessly interrupting her. ''Emilie's pet kitten was torn to pieces by the dogs in front of her eyes.'' Ignoring her gasp of horror, the earl went on to tell her the whole story and its aftermath, sparing her no unhappy detail including Emilie's disturbed night, the presence of Miss Norris in the nursery, and the cat's funeral.

''Why was I not told about of this, Ivor? I am Emilie's mother, and it is my right to be informed of everything that concerns her!''

''Would you have slept in the nursery that night and helped plan a funeral for a stable cat had you been told of the incident?'' he demanded, compelling her gaze. ''Emilie needed comfort and help *then*, and she needs it now. Her problems and unhappiness cannot be postponed until her mother feels able to resume her rightful role in her life. That is why these riding lessons are so important at this time,'' he added, gentling his voice as the tears welled up in his sister's eyes and spilled down over her cheeks unchecked. ''I want your approval to go ahead with the lessons.''

''Yes, of course.'' She turned her head away as he got up from the chaise.

''And I'd like you to do something for me, Tricia.''

''What is it?''

''Think back over our childhood and try to work out just why it is that none of us feels toward Mama today the way I believe you would like Emilie to feel toward you when she is grown up. Will you promise to do that for me?''

There was a significant pause then while Lady Patricia seemed to shrink into herself. Ivor remained standing by the chaise, and at last she turned her head and met his eyes. "Yes, I will," she said.

Chloe knew, but only indirectly, that the earl must have needed to convince his sister of the benefits of riding lessons for Emilie. The child had sought her out twice during the afternoon. On the first instance, finding Chloe reading in the white garden, she had made a tearful report of her mother's refusal to grant permission for the lessons. The little girl had been listless and resigned as she parroted Lady Patricia's fears of accidental injury. Chloe, fearful of taking liberties, had dared to do no more than counsel patience and lay stress on the pleasure of visiting and getting to know Étoile even if she could not ride her.

An hour later Emilie had come skipping into the garden, her face transformed with pleasurable anticipation. Awaiting the child's arrival from the wrought-iron settee, Chloe had lowered the book of poetry which had been competing for her attention with her own disturbed ruminations for the past hour.

"Let me guess," she began, smiling at the little girl. "Your mother has reconsidered her objections to riding lessons for you?"

"Yes, isn't it wonderful? Uncle Ivor reminded her that she was only six years old when she learned to ride. And guess what, Miss Norris? *Maman* has promised that she will come down to meet Étoile and watch my first lesson tomorrow morning. Will you come too?"

"I'll tell you what, Emilie. How would it be if I came to watch the *second* lesson? Then you will be able to show me what you have already learned?"

Emilie saw the virtue in this arrangement and went off happily to the nursery to regale Addie with the latest developments.

Chloe sat on for a few moments longer, a little smile on her lips and her book forgotten in her lap. A cautionary instinct warned her it would not do to depend too much on this *volte-face* on the part of Lady Patricia. In the recent past a brief show of maternal interest on the widow's part had invariably been followed by a retreat to her cocoon of solitary brooding. If she allowed herself to entertain a tentative little hope that this action might signal the beginning of a resumption of Lady Patricia's maternal role in Emilie's life it was because this time Lord Montrose had intervened directly on his niece's behalf. Perhaps during his talk with his sister he had done more than remind her that she had begun riding at an earlier age than her daughter's. It had been presumptuous beyond belief on her own part to call the unsatisfactory situation between Emilie and her mother to his notice, but it was a breach of etiquette she would not regret if some lasting good resulted.

It was when Chloe was returning to her room to change for dinner that evening that she heard piano music coming through the closed door to the unused music room that contained, in addition to a black lacquered pianoforte, a harp, several music stands, and two cases that might contain violins. Mrs. Meggs had shown her this room on her early tour of Applewood. She paused outside the door for a moment listening in surprised appreciation to a Mozart composition being played with an artistry that proved that Lady Mary could not be the performer. Of course, for all she really knew of the musical accomplishments of the Keesons, the musician might be someone other than Lady Patricia, but Chloe went on upstairs much cheered by the hopeful thoughts going around in her head.

She was humming as she entered her own room, but the humming and the cheerful thoughts both ceased abruptly at sight of the figure slumped in the wing chair.

"What has happened, Mary?" she asked, hurrying over to the dull-eyed girl facing her, though whether Lady Mary really saw her or not was something on which Chloe would not have cared to lay a wager.

"I have seen Tom."

The irrelevant thought that here was an explanation for Mary's sudden interest in sketching popped into Chloe's mind and was instantly banished. She waited in sympathy and uncertainty, for her friend's demeanor was a far cry from what one would expect of a girl happily reunited with her lover.

"Actually I have seen him twice since the day we spent in Woodbridge," Lady Mary said, glancing fleetingly at Chloe before turning to stare into the fireplace. "I did not have a headache at lunch. I just said that to get rid of you so I could write to Tom to arrange a meeting."

He doesn't love her, Chloe thought with a sinking sensation in her stomach. What could she possibly offer in the way of comfort in the face of such unhappiness?

She had not been granted any inspiration when Lady Mary turned toward her again, her words tumbling over each other. "It's not going to work; he doesn't understand. I don't know what else I can say to convince him . . ."

Thoroughly confused by this spate of words whose meaning eluded her, Chloe blurted, "Convince who . . . whom . . . of what?"

"Convince Tom that our only course is to elope. He won't listen to me."

Chloe's jaw dropped and she swallowed, regrouping her scattered faculties. "Are you saying that Tom—Mr. Trainor—still loves you? You looked so miserable when I came in that I thought . . . I feared he no longer cared."

Lady Mary's expression lightened and she said softly, "He told me he has been miserably unhappy ever since his mother wrote to him of my betrothal. He began trying to make arrangements to return to England right away, not knowing if he would be in time."

As the younger girl's face took on a dreamy aspect, Chloe, having assimilated the pertinent facts, returned to her questioning. "Then why were you looking so despondent when I came in, and what is all this about eloping?"

The dreaminess vanished and Lady Mary said urgently, "Believe me, Chloe, it is the only way Tom and I will be able to marry, but he won't listen to me. He wants to come here and confront Mama and tell her we wish to be married."

"But surely that is what a man of honor would do in his position, Mary. Naturally, your mother is not going to be pleased to have you break your engagement at this late date. There will be a deal of talk, I imagine, but an elopement would give rise to real scandal. You cannot have thought what that would mean for you both and for your families. You would not wish to subject them to such an experience."

Lady Mary was shaking her head slowly from side to side. "It is you who do not understand, Chloe. I know an elopement will cause a terrible scandal, but I know also that it is the only way Tom and I can ever be married."

Chloe was impressed against her will by the absolute conviction in her friend's face, despite her faulty reasoning, for of course it must be faulty. She had been standing in front of Lady Mary, but now she walked over to the dressing table and brought the bench back to the area in front of the empty fireplace. There was no sound in the room at the moment as the younger girl waited with set features for whatever argument Chloe might advance when she had settled herself on the bench.

"Let us approach this problem from another angle. For the moment, forget about marrying Tom. Take it one step at a time. The first thing that must be done is to bring your betrothal to Lord Thrale to an end. It will not be a pleasant experience, I warrant, but there is no escaping the necessity. After a decent interval, when the talk has died down, you and Tom may tell your families that you wish to marry."

Lady Mary was shaking her head again, calm certainty in her face. "That is not what would happen, Chloe. In the first place, my mother will not permit me to break my engagement to Lord Thrale."

"Nonsense, Mary. No one can compel you to marry, not your mother, not anyone."

"You do not know the strength of my mother's will or the way she has bent me to her will all my life. Do you think I wished to become betrothed to Thrale in the first place?"

"Then go to your brother. Tell him the truth about your feelings. You must know he will see to it that you are not dragged to the altar against your will."

"I thought of that, Chloe, and perhaps Ivor could prevent Mama from making me marry Lord Thrale, but it is Mama who will be my guardian for the next two years, not Ivor. She will see to it that Tom and I are separated. She will whisk me off somewhere immediately, and then next Season I will be paraded on the Marriage Mart once more and it will all begin again. I will have to listen to all those well-connected people commiserating with her because I do not possess her beauty or

Patricia's. I used to shrivel up inside when I overheard them this spring. I don't think I can bear any more of that. I would rather marry Lord Thrale. At least that way I would get away from her!''

"You are overwrought, Mary. Think of what you are saying. Marriage is for the rest of your life. Can you seriously contemplate wedding Lord Thrale when you and Mr. Trainor love each other?''

As Chloe sought to hold her friend's wavering glance, the clock on the mantel chimed the half hour. Lady Mary leaped out of her chair. "I must go, or we shall be late for dinner and there will be all sorts of questions from Mama.''

"Mary," Chloe said imperatively as the girl hastened over to the door, "you must talk to your mother—"

"I must find some way to convince Tom that an elopement is our only chance at happiness," Lady Mary replied, her hand on the door handle.

"If you feel you cannot face your mother, then go to Ivor," Chloe persisted, but the closing of the door shut off her words, and she was persuaded her young friend had long since shut her ears to her voice.

Chloe dressed that evening in a perfectly distracted state. How was it all going to end? Mary seemed to be marching straight into a tragedy that to an outsider's eyes appeared entirely preventable. The exaggerated dread she had of confronting and opposing her mother was clouding her judgment so that she could see no way out of her dilemma except flight, in this case an elopement that would plunge three families into quite unnecessary scandal.

After reviewing their unavailing conversation in her mind, Chloe could not delude herself into hoping her arguments had had the least weight with the girl. There was a little pleat between her eyebrows as she clasped her mother's pearls about her throat without even the fleetest glance in the mirror. Mary was afraid to make her desires known to her mother or even her brother, and she would not listen to her friend. That left her would-be husband, Mr. Thomas Trainor, as the sole influence for reasoned action. The fact that he opposed an elopement showed him to be an honorable and sensible man.

For the sake of all concerned, Chloe could only pray that he would be able to bring his befuddled beloved around to a saner way of thinking in the very near future.

The next afternoon brought this forlorn hope crashing down about her ears. Chloe was wandering about in the orchard, her mind occupied with her friend's predicament, when she nearly stumbled over the girl literally. Lady Mary was the picture of despair, huddled at the base of an apple tree with her legs crossed at the ankles, her bent knees enclosed by her elbows, and her face in her hands. She was sobbing with the abandon of a heart-broken child.

"Mary!"

The girl was too wrapped up in her own pain even to be surprised at discovery. "I have had the most dreadful quarrel with Tom and it is all over, Chloe."

"Over?" Chloe had been fishing her handkerchief out of her pocket. She stood another second staring into drenched blue eyes and a pale set face that struck her oddly as containing nearly as much anger as despair. She sank down to the ground, sitting tailor fashion, and proferred the handkerchief.

"Over and done with." Lady Mary accepted the handkerchief and mopped up her face. "Obviously Tom does not love me enough to make a push to secure my hand—"

"You mean elope?" interjected Chloe, straining to follow.

Mary nodded and said bitterly, "He just kept endlessly repeating that he would go to my mother and Ivor and every-thing would be fine eventually, even if he had to wait for a while to become engaged. He wouldn't believe me when I told him how impossible that was, so at last I said if he really loved me he would be willing to elope, and . . . and then *he* said if *I* really loved *him* I would not ask him to do anything dishonorable, and . . ."

"And the quarrel escalated from there." Chloe nodded, needing no further enlightenment. "What will you do now?"

"I shall marry Lord Thrale," the other girl replied through clenched teeth.

"Did you say this to Mr. Trainor?"

"Yes." The monosyllable came out with an edge of defiance.

"What did he reply?"

''For a long time I didn't think he was going to say anything at all; then he bowed very formally and said that if I should have a change of heart I had only to send him a message to that effect and he would instantly present himself to my mother with a formal application for my hand. Then he walked away without once looking back.''

Chapter Thirteen

GUESTS BEGAN ARRIVING at Applewood the following day for the pheasant shooting and wedding festivities. The domestic machinery of the household had been humming along with increased concentration for days, gearing itself for the influx of visitors above and below stairs, for the number of servants to be accommodated would actually be greater than the number of guests, what with personal servants and grooms and coachmen who must be fed and housed for the duration, not to mention the horses.

Chloe had no dealings with the kitchen staff, but she found unobtrusive ways in which to lend the hardworking Mrs. Meggs a hand about the house. She had helped her supervise the maids in readying the guest rooms, and now on the morning of the expected first arrivals she was doing a final check to make sure there were fresh flowers in the rooms these guests would occupy.

Her arms were full of towels as she exited from one of the guest chambers in the main wing. Intent on balancing her burden while closing the door with one hand, she did not really register the sound of another door closing farther along the corridor and was therefore unprepared to see Lord Montrose coming toward her. There was a slight frown on his generally unrevealing countenance, and Chloe stiffened, watching his approach with a touch of wariness. Underneath his usual suavity he had been annoyed with her last night, a new experience for her and one she did not care to repeat.

It had begun innocently enough at dinner when Lady Montrose and she had been comparing notes on the status of the guest rooms. At tea Chloe had given her the final list of rooms allotted by Mrs. Meggs, based on the housekeeper's earlier conferences with her mistress. The countess had apparently found it satisfactory except in one particular.

"I see that Lady Miranda Smythe has been put in the same corridor with Miss Ellicott and Martha Claven, who are to be Mary's bride maids."

"Yes, ma'am. Mrs. Meggs thought you'd like to keep the younger ladies together for ease of visiting back and forth."

"Hmmmm. I am having second thoughts about that after all. Lady Miranda is only slightly acquainted with the other two girls, who are bosom friends. It might be more tactful to place her nearer her mother. Let me see." The countess took a list of room assignments from her reticule and perused it swiftly. "No, that won't do," she said with a sigh. "We have put Lady Mallory in the orchard wing, and there are no empty rooms there."

Chloe had been thinking ahead while Lady Montrose studied the list. She recalled that Lady Mallory had been given the room next to her own and was in no doubt that Lady Montrose, having had the list in her possession since tea, would already have made herself familiar with the room assignments. Her own duty was clear. She summoned up a cheerful smile and said in the tones of one who has just glimpsed a solution to a problem, "Then nothing could be simpler, ma'am. I believe Lady Mallory is to have the room next to mine, so I shall move to another room for the few days remaining of my stay and Lady Miranda can go into my room. They are not due to arrive until the day after tomorrow, so there is ample time to make the switch."

"It is very sweet of you to offer, my dear Chloe, but I could not ask you to give up your apartment," Lady Montrose said dulcetly.

Knowing that her insistence would eventually be allowed to overcome her hostess's resistance, Chloe had just taken a fortifying breath to play out the rest of the scene when Lord Montrose's voice came clearly from the other end of the table. "Of course not, Mama, nor could I permit Chloe to sacrifice her comfort. We'll have Mrs. Meggs change another guest out of the orchard wing to make room for Lady Mallory's daughter."

"It is certainly not the least sacrifice on my part, sir," Chloe had said on a gay laugh. "My visit is nearly at an end, you

know. I shall be hearing any day now from my father that he
is on his way home."

"I am persuaded Dr. Norris would not dream of dragging
you away from us before the dance you have been at pains to
arrange," the earl had replied with a cool smile.

"But I never had any intention of attending the dance, sir,"
she had protested. "I brought nothing suitable with me to
wear."

"But, Chloe, I thought we agreed that you should wear one
of my ball gowns," Lady Mary had chimed in. "You cannot
leave us so soon."

"Indeed you cannot," Ned said in a determined voice, "when
I have promised myself the pleasure of dancing with you."

Even Lady Patricia had expressed the hope that Chloe would
delay her departure until after her sister's dance.

"That makes it unanimous," the earl had declared, seemingly
unaware that his mother's voice had not swelled the chorus.
"We are all quite decided that you shall not be allowed to run
off so soon. If your father desires your presence before then,
we shall be very happy to welcome him at Applewood. There
is more than enough room."

Defeated by *force majeure,* Chloe had weakly thanked him,
but despite his smile, she had been aware of a dangerous glitter
in eyes that seemed suddenly to have darkened to the color of
steel. Then, after riding roughshod over her arguments, he had
retired from the conversation; in fact, he'd had nothing to say
to her for the rest of the evening.

Now Chloe hesitated, undecided whether to call out a brisk
good morning and hare off or stand her ground as he bore down
on her.

"What are you doing with those towels?" he demanded in
lieu of a greeting.

She looked at him in surprise. "These? I was just checking
to see that the guest rooms are well supplied."

"Why should you be doing anything of the sort? Where is
Mrs. Meggs? This is not the province of a guest, and so I shall
tell her."

"Don't you *dare* say one cross word to Mrs. Meggs!" Chloe

flashed back. "The idea! You'd have thought I was cleaning out the grates or scrubbing down the walls!"

Those straight black eyebrows shot up at this impertinence. "So you do have a temper after all," he drawled. "I can see I do not know you quite as well as I flattered myself I did."

"I . . . I beg your pardon, sir, for the intemperance of my speech," Chloe said, eyeing him askance. "I should rather have said that if you value your well-run house, you will take care what you say to Mrs. Meggs, who is a veritable treasure, and to be treated accordingly."

"You need not humble yourself because I spoke a bit abruptly, Miss Norris, and I would have you know that there is an excellent understanding between Mrs. Meggs and myself."

"I am not in the least humble," she retorted, "but I think you, sir, are in a teasing humor for some reason."

"You know, I believe you are right. It must be that I see so little of you that two minutes of privacy have gone to my head." He smiled at her with a warm light in smoky eyes that held her mesmerized as he took a step closer. "Why wouldn't you play chess with me, Chloe?"

Chloe could feel herself getting hot all over as those magnetic eyes continued to hold her rooted to the spot.

"Oh, there you are, Miss Norris. Thank you so much for bringing the towels I forgot earlier."

The voice of the housemaid who stuck her head out of the next door along the hall released Chloe from the spell Lord Montrose had cast over her. She tore her eyes from his and made some reply to the maid as she hurried forward, pleasantly surprised that voice and legs still functioned normally. She was aware that the earl had turned and walked off in the opposite direction.

Though Chloe did her best to appear her usual cheerful self that day and succeeded quite well, a percipient eye might have detected a hint of effort behind her smiles and a suspicion of strain in the depths of her eyes. She couldn't pin a name to this unease of the spirit that had been creeping up on her. There had been Emilie's loss and Mary's unhappy situation, of course, but honesty compelled her to admit that this present vague malaise was on her own account.

She really should leave Applewood. She was becoming infected by the aura of personal disenchantment radiating from its inhabitants that chipped away insidiously at her previous contentment with her lot in life. Best to go before her long-anticipated future as the wife of a sea captain lost all its remaining patina of promise. A month ago she would have thought herself the last person in the world to get ideas above her station and she was appalled to find that she was not above air dreaming. And all this because the Earl of Montrose had amused himself with a little—a very little—harmless flirtation this morning. Heavens, Ned had availed himself of every tiniest opportunity to flirt outrageously with her since the first hour of their acquaintance, and she had not allowed that to cast her into confusion. Where had her vaunted good sense gone? The fact that until today the earl had never shown any inclination toward idle dalliance should not be permitted any weight. It merely proved that no man was immune from the temptation, given the right circumstances. He had discovered her in an upstairs corridor with her arms full of towels like a chambermaid and had treated her as chambermaids had been treated from time immemorial.

The blatant injustice of this callous description of the earl's conduct did not seem to occur to one who always prided herself on her impartial judgment. Having explained away the earl's behavior and censured her own, she redoubled her efforts to play the part assigned to her in the social charade that was life at Applewood.

This was becoming increasingly tricky as far as her relationship with Lady Montrose was concerned. The countess had been of two minds about Chloe from the start of their acquaintance, welcoming her assistance while considering her beneath her notice socially. She had been able to conceal her condescension behind a gracious manner until an element of personal dislike crept into her feelings. At first Chloe's unfashionable attire and her lack of accomplishments, together with her engaged status, had protected her, but as time passed and the countess recognized that her guest's deferential manner and willingness to be useful did not extend to unilateral agreement with all her hostess's opinions or prevent her from

airing her own, her attitude had hardened against the young
woman her sister had foisted on her. She chose to conceal her
feelings for the sake of expediency and because a singular dislike
of an inoffensive nonentity did not correspond with the picture
of benevolence she wished to present to the world. Chloe had
been intuitively conscious of this dichotomy and had gradually
come to a sounder intellectual grasp as her understanding of
the complex character of her hostess evolved. When Lady
Montrose first began to dislike her Chloe could not say with
certainty, but there had been a touch of resentment over
Chloe's interest in Emilie that deepened as her involvement with
the child did. Add to this the accumulation of slights Ned had
inflicted on his mother by his teasing attentions to Chloe and
what appeared on the surface to be an unreasonable dislike
became more comprehensible.

Pursuing this line of reasoning, Chloe saw as if in a flash
of light that Ivor's insistence on holding the cat's funeral and
his refusal last night to allow Chloe's room to be changed would
be seen by his mother as the crowning indignities. Her interest
had been set aside in favor of those of an encroaching nobody
with no claim upon his loyalty. The countess was finding it
nearly impossible to maintain her facade of cordiality toward
Chloe. Conversation with Lady Montrose today had all the
appeal for Chloe of picking her way through a patch of thorns.
She persevered doggedly, but she could not help looking forward
to her deliverance in the form of the expected influx of people
who would divert her hostess's attention.

By teatime the company had been swelled by the arrival of
Mr. and Mrs. Rudolph Claven and their pretty blond daughter
Martha, who greeted Lady Mary with squeals of delight, Sir
Digby Ellicott, a fashionable young buck of Ned's age, with
his sister Susannah, another squealer; and Sir Watson Oglivy,
a distinguished-looking gray-haired man who greeted his hostess
in a courtly fashion. With the addition of two lively young
females the afternoon ritual took on the air of a party.

The young ladies eyed Lord Montrose with respect tinged
with shyness, but it was evident that their real interest was in
Mr. Edmund Keeson, who smilingly obliged with flattering
attentions to both. Lady Mary, who had avoided Chloe since

her last unhappy meeting with Thomas Trainor, had been roused to give a passable performance as a carefree young woman on the eve of her marriage. Chloe was wearing the white lace collar she had bought in the village in an attempt to soften the severity of her old brown dress, but she could see that the young ladies had dismissed her as negligible after one assessing glance. There had been a time, not so very long ago, when, secure in the esteem of those persons she valued, she would have been completely unmoved by the casual judgments of those persons whose opinions she had no cause to admire or respect. It slayed her to admit this was no longer the case, that such a short exposure to those who inhabited the world of fashion should have so corrupted her scale of values.

Chloe spent the period between tea and dinner in taking herself firmly in hand. These people with whom she was mingling at present were not of her world and this experience was an aberration in her life. She did not find them particularly admirable; on the other hand, they were unlikely to be more prone to moral laxity than some individuals one came up against in the country. Human nature did not vary greatly between town and country settings. The really painful discovery was a heretofore unsuspected streak of vanity in herself that bitterly resented being found sartorially deficient by these same people. This was a thoroughly contemptible quality which she should be ashamed to own up to—and she was! Unfortunately, the admission did not also mean the remission of the vice, and she put the last pins in her hair with a jabbing motion that reflected her general dissatisfaction with everything about herself today. She snatched up a clean handkerchief and hurried out of the room to get away from her thoughts and her dull image in the mirror.

On crossing the threshold into the main drawing room, Chloe found the place still untenanted. A quick glance at the French mantel clock revealed that she was more than ten minutes early in her desire to escape from her own company. There were some periodicals on a side table against the wall to the left of the door and she drifted over to look through them. She rejected the fashion journals with a pettish push of her fingers and was about to take a copy of the *Edinburgh Review* when a step at the door

announced the end of her solitude. She fastened a polite smile
to her lips as she turned to meet the interested gaze of a total
stranger. There were two male guests expected, Mr. Bartholomew Ransom and Lord Landers, in addition to Lord Thrale,
who was not due to arrive until the next day.

As the man came toward her, Chloe knew instantly that it
could never be Lord Thrale, because not even a girl already
in love with someone else could describe this man as a nonentity.
He looked to be about thirty years of age and was tall and straight
with an understated neatness about his appearance that suggested
that he might have been in the military. His raven-dark hair
was worn a bit shorter than the current fashion and kept firmly
under control, as opposed to the windswept effect sought by
men with pretensions to *à-la-modeté*. His eyes were as dark
as his hair, and his skin was more deeply tanned than Mr.
Thomas Trainor's, giving him an almost piratical air.

"Good evening," the stranger said in an attractive low-pitched
voice, while intelligent eyes swept over Chloe's long-sleeved
black gown. "Do I have the honor of addressing Lady Patricia
Roberts?"

Chloe shook her head, ruefully accepting that her sober attire
had put him in mind of mourning. "No, sir, I am Chloe Norris,
a family connection of the Keesons, a rather remote connection,
actually."

"How do you do, Miss Norris? I am Bartholomew Ransom,
an old school friend of Ivor's, and I am strongly in favor of
remote family connections."

Mr. Ransom's attractive smile drew a spontaneous gurgle of
laughter from Chloe, who liked the twinkle in his eyes that
proclaimed that he did not expect her to take his nonsense
seriously. She proceeded to inquire about his journey to Suffolk
and discovered that he came from Devon and had met none of
his friend's family save his brother. They were getting along
famously when the earl appeared in the drawing room in advance
of his guests. His generally unreadable face was transformed
by a rare full-blown smile on seeing the room's occupants.

Circumstances might have kept them from frequent intercourse in the years since the end of their school association,
but it was apparent to Chloe as the two men greeted each other

that theirs was a genuine friendship of the comfortable sort that could be resumed instantly after long separations. She would have slipped away to allow them their first reunion in privacy, but the earl caught her hand, arresting her progress. He avoided her surprised eyes, saying easily to his friend as he drew her to his side, "I see you have already met our visiting good angel, Bart."

"There seems to be a discrepancy here, Ivor," Mr. Ransom replied with a straight face. "Miss Norris introduced herself as a remote connection, not a heavenly one."

"Modesty is not the least of Chloe's virtues, but the simple truth is that the Keesons have been blessed to enjoy her delightful presence and harmonious spirit these past few weeks since she came to help my mother prepare for the current festivities."

Chloe stood stiff and silent with her eyes averted and her senses alerted and registering conflicting messages. She could feel the heightened interest in Mr. Ransom's gaze, and why not, when the earl, under the guise of general praise, seemed to be binding her to himself with a handclasp that was sending unnerving tingles up her arm. A nearly submerged sense of identity, or decency, demanded that she announce herself to be an engaged woman, but could anything be more crude or gauche than a pronouncement of this nature? She was filled with impotent irritation at the untenable position the earl had placed her in when he broke off his remarks to say, "Ah, here you are, Mama. I was just telling my old friend Bartholomew Ransom how indebted we all are to Chloe for her invaluable assistance."

With her back to the doorway, Chloe had tugged hard to free her hand at his first words to his parent, but an involuntary glance at that cold perfect face told her the countess had not missed the gesture. It required all her pride and resolution to keep her from betraying her inner perturbation during the next few minutes until several other persons entered the room simultaneously and rescued her from a situation fraught with awkwardness.

There was one additional guest at dinner, Lord Landers, a supercilious-looking individual somewhere between thirty and forty years of age who was too impressed with his own

consequence to bother being pleasant to others. The party was
not complete until the next day, however, when Lady Mallory,
a bosom bow of the countess, arrived with her daughter; and
the bridegroom, Lord Thrale, made his long-awaited entrance
trailing in his formidable mother's wake.

Lady Mallory, though not gifted by nature with Lady
Montrose's exceptional beauty, had through the expert use of
art and cosmetics succeeded in preserving her considerable good
looks well into middle age. From the top of her sleek dark head,
free of any strands of gray, to the tips of her fingers no detail
of grooming or fashion had been neglected in the determined
pursuit of eternal youth. Her slender and elegantly attired
daughter might have been termed beautiful except that her
heavily lashed light brown eyes were set a bit too close together
and her aristocratic nose and chin were a smidgeon longer than
strict beauty allowed. Even these minor defects might have been
obliterated had Lady Miranda's well-bred smile engaged a few
more facial muscles so as to lend animation to her fine features.
Such did not seem to be the case, though, so despite shining
dark ringlets, pretty teeth, and a graceful form, she remained
in Chloe's opinion an attractive rather than lovely girl.

At least the Mallory ladies exerted themselves to play the role
of guests willing to be pleased by the entertainment and exertions
put forth for their benefit by their hosts. The same could not
be said of Lady Thrale, whose aloof manner proclaimed her
as high in the instep as Lord Landers. Her restless gaze
appraised the rooms and furnishings constantly, and Chloe
received the decided impression that she would have been
pleased to find them lacking in some respect. She made a point
of stressing her delicate digestion before each repast, and her
sour expression indicated a congenital difficulty in figuratively
digesting social amenities also. Chloe could not help wondering
if it was this quality in his mother of being impossible to please
that was responsible for Lord Thrale's seeming eagerness to
please (or appease) the company in general. She found him much
as Mary had described, so ineffectual as to possess neither
positive virtues nor vices, both of which demanded more passion
than one could credit him with, at least on slight acquaintance.
His physical appearance did nothing to mitigate this impression.

His average height, narrow-shouldered frame, poor posture, and spindle shanks must have challenged his tailor's ingenuity. The not-entirely-successful solution was coats of extravagant cut and thickly padded shoulders, an aggressive choice of colors, and extra-wide cravats to disguise a scrawny neck. His countenance was not ill-favored, his skin was pale and blemish-free, his features were undistinguished, and his thinning brown locks were carefully arranged in the windswept fashion. He wore an air of always desiring to please despite little expectation of accomplishing this objective—perfectly understandable when one considered that he resided with his maternal parent. Chloe pitied him from the bottom of her heart.

The earl, who was meeting his sister's affianced husband and his mother for the first time, welcomed them with his usual courtesy, but Chloe, who knew each slight change of expression by now, unrevealing of emotion though they generally appeared, thought she detected dismay. Over the next few days he seemed to be studying his prospective brother-in-law but, as far as she knew, he kept his own counsel as to his conclusions.

Meanwhile the men went off pheasant shooting each day, leaving the females to their own devices until late afternoon. The feminine contingent tended to split along generational lines with Lady Montrose assuming charge of the elder ladies while Lady Mary, aided by Chloe, took the younger set in tow. They took advantage of the pleasant weather to stroll about the grounds and into the village. Having learned how close Applewood was to the coast, the young ladies clamored to see the sea. Chloe could sense her friend's reluctance to walk in the direction of the manor, but it was actually less trouble for Lady Mary to accommodate the wishes of her guests than to explain away her disinclination for the activity. In any event, they met no one along the way to the grassy hilltop where the young ladies could indulge their fancy to gaze at the sea to their heart's content, or, on this particular day, until the chill wind off the water drove them back to the house.

Lady Patricia did not join in any of these group activities. Sometimes she appeared at the lunch table, but she had taken to having afternoon tea in the nursery with Emilie. She did grace the drawing room with her presence in the evenings. Though she still dressed in unrelieved mourning, she had begun to take more pains with her hair, and Chloe could see that she made a heroic effort not to cast a damper on the congenial atmosphere of the company. She avoided the younger females and the men, gravitating instead toward Mrs. Claven, a matronly woman with kind eyes and a gentle manner. After a couple of days it became clear to Chloe that Lady Montrose had had her elder daughter's future in mind when she had included Lord Landers in the party. Though too much the mistress of the social scene to allow her maneuvering to become obvious to the casual eye, the countess saw to it that that well-connected gentleman was placed in close proximity to Lady Patricia at dinner or whenever there was a change of activity that produced a shuffling of the company. Equally clear to Chloe was Lady Patricia's discomfiture at this jockeying on the part of her mother. The young widow still shrank instinctively from any but the most impersonal contact with others. It was still an effort for her to focus her attention outside of herself long enough to assume full part in a real conversation with anyone, but apart from this general problem, Chloe suspected Lady Patricia had taken the proud and predatory Lord Landers in actual aversion. When she found the young widow's eyes seeking hers in a beseeching manner, she could not ignore the plea for help. As unobtrusively as possible in those first few evenings she managed to break up several tête-à-têtes he had forced upon Patricia, even knowing she was chalking up another mark against herself with the countess in so doing. Her reward was the widow's fervent though unspoken gratitude conveyed by her eloquent sapphire eyes. Chloe did not trouble herself in the least over Lord Lander's ill-concealed dislike of her disruptive activities. On the second occasion in as many days when she had insinuated herself into a private conversation, or monologue rather, that Lord Landers had forced upon Lady Patricia, Chloe received a discreet wink from the earl as he watched the disgruntled baron go off in a huff to a more receptive audience of younger ladies. The warm glow that spread through her at this sign of approval chilled quickly, though, when she inadvertently encountered the countess's watchful eyes and read the naked enmity there before her ladyship turned away abruptly.

With such a large party assembled there was a wide choice of evening activities. Cards, whist in particular, always drew a few addicts even when the company in general had chosen to have a musical evening. Sir Watson Ogilvy and Lady Thrale led the card contingent, the rest of the table being made up by those hardy souls who decided the pleasure of a well-fought contest outweighed the drawback of close exposure to Lady Thrale's acid tongue.

Lady Montrose was an experienced hostess who provided opportunities for various forms of entertainment and allowed her guests to choose whether they desired to participate. One evening there was a boisterous game of speculation going on that involved most of the younger set, while two tables of serious whist players contested in near silence in the small reception room next door for nearly three hours.

It was a musically accomplished company on the whole, and music making was often the preferred entertainment of an evening. Miss Claven played the harp. Lady Miranda possessed a better-than-average soprano voice and accompanied herself at the piano. Several of the men enjoyed singing catches and glees, even Lord Thrale joining in with a reedy tenor at his mother's urging. The most accomplished musician in Chloe's opinion was, surprisingly, the earl's old friend, Mr. Ransom, who could produce breathtakingly beautiful sounds from the violin. She listened raptly to the soaring melodies he coaxed out of the instrument and experienced a minor melancholy each time he set it down.

It was only during the musical evenings that she could relax completely and forget for a time the undercurrents beneath the prevailing surface amiability. Only during the musical interludes was her mind entirely free of the day's impressions, impressions of Lady Mary, whose forced gaiety became less convincing each day and more thickly overlaid with desperation; of Lady Montrose tirelessly maneuvering Lord Landers into Patricia's path and Lady Miranda into Ned's; of those beautiful deep blue eyes of the countess following her own movements at the periphery of the party with an inimical expression she no longer bothered to disguise.

Meanwhile Chloe battled against surrendering to the sense

of creeping disaster that invaded her thoughts whenever she was not actively engaged. Half the time she found herself longing to be home with her father, safely away from the impending crisis, and the rest of the time she sought vainly for some way to avert the tragedy she saw in the making. Though Mary demanded her presence whenever she was with the three youngest ladies and accepted Chloe's help in keeping them contentedly occupied, she took care to give her worried friend no opportunity for private conversation in which to resurrect the subject of her coming marriage.

The one hopeful note at present was provided by Lady Patricia, who was looking less pale and strained as the days went by. She had taken over the supervision of Emilie's riding lessons and she was gradually increasing her personal interaction with her mother's guests. Chloe noted that after a few days she no longer required assistance in dealing with the unwanted attentions of Lord Landers. Chloe could not know to what degree Lady Montrose was committed to her matrimonial plans for her widowed daughter and younger son, but the plan had misfired in Patricia's case. Though Chloe took no interest in Ned's future, there was no doubt in her mind about his ability to emerge untethered from any matrimonial maneuvering on his behalf.

She was totally unprepared, however, for the rather crude method he chose to employ in bringing his mother's machinations to a crashing halt.

Chapter Fourteen

CHLOE TOOK HER TIME in checking the various drawers and cabinets in the small reception room. She had volunteered to locate an old set of spillikins for the challenge thrown down by Sir Digby Ellicott to all comers at tea, but she was in no hurry to return to the drawing room. Ned was in one of those teasing humors when he flirted blatantly with her under his mother's fulminating eye. The longer she stayed away the more likely it was that his grasshopper mind would flit to some other interest. After she unearthed the box of spillikins at the back of an ebony cabinet, she lingered a few moments longer. Too long as it turned out.

She was getting to her feet from her knees, box in hand, when she became aware that she was no longer alone in the room. "There you are, my pretty one," said an ardent and carrying voice.

Chloe looked up, scowling impatiently at the blond Apollo hurrying toward her. She opened her lips to give him a piece of her mind, but before she could utter one of the scathing comments clamoring for release, she was seized and silenced by virtue of a rough kiss being pressed on her unwilling mouth. Hampered by the box, she was holding in both hands, it took several seconds of twisting and turning to wrench her mouth free of this assault. She was gathering breath for her attack on his insufferable complacence when her eyes were drawn by movement beyond his shoulder. She found herself staring into the shocked face of Lady Miranda Smythe and the furious one of Lady Montrose, both of whom were standing frozen in the doorway.

Anger, defeat, and humiliation were the most prominent of the emotions that washed over Chloe as she comprehended in a flash what this scene must have looked like from where the women stood. Her unwillingness to participate would have been screened by Ned's back. For another second that seemed an eternity everyone remained fixed in place, Chloe with her eyes closed in an agony of humiliation. When she opened them the doorway was empty.

Her gaze returned to the handsome half-triumphant face above hers. "You can let me go now," she said with discernible bitterness. "Your audience has left."

He released her shoulders immediately and had the grace to look ashamed. "I am really sorry for involving you, Chloe, but Mama has been pitching that girl at my head since she got here. The situation called for desperate measures. I overheard Mama telling the chit she wanted to show her that miniature of me when I was a child that she keeps in this room. When I remembered that you had come in here to get something, I was struck by a brilliant notion of how to get her off my neck and I sprinted in here before they left the room."

"Congratulations. Your measures were crude but efficacious. I doubt Lady Miranda will be a willing party to any further machinations along that line. You don't care whom you sacrifice in pursuit of your comfort, do you, Ned? Your mother already disliked me heartily before this little episode."

He looked increasingly uncomfortable, which was some small satisfaction. "Oh, I say now, that is pitching it rather too strong, Chloe. Of course Mama don't dislike you. It is just that she is bound and determined to see all of us make good matches, you know, in a worldly sense, which I am prepared to do in my own good time. And I won't choose a milk-and-water pattern card of propriety like Miranda Smythe when I do decide to tie the knot either."

Chloe stared at him, her anger falling away. What was the use? His congenial insensibility was better protection than a suit of armor against her puny efforts. "Will you do me one small favor at least?" she asked wearily. "Will you allow me to go back in there alone?"

"Yes, yes, anything, Chloe," he assented, eager to make amends. "I'll take myself off. And I really do apologize for making things a trifle awkward for you with Mama." He bestowed on her the brilliant smile that had laid countless female hearts at his feet and went off whistling, his conscience repaired.

Chloe moistened dry lips, straightened her spine another degree or two, and assumed a mask of unconcern as her reluctant steps took her back to all those alien people in the drawing room.

A number of mental reminders of her innocence plus exhortations to hold her head high were insufficient to alleviate the distress Chloe endured for the remainder of the day. Only a grim determination not to cave in enabled her to participate minimally in the evening's socializing. Lady Montrose had looked through rather than at her when she reentered the drawing room with the box of spillikins. Pure pride had kept her own eyes steady under the insult, and she had not permitted herself to evade the avid curiosity in Lady Miranda's face, which she met with a stony mask of calm applied over clenched teeth. Any attempt at explanation would be worse than useless. It was definitely a case of the least said the soonest mended, though she had little expectation that the titillating morsel of gossip would go no further. After dinner, when Miss Ellicott casually asked if her unusual ring was a betrothal ring, she knew Lady Miranda had been unable to resist the temptation to whisper the story into at least one ear. She recalled having told Lady Miranda of her engagement in response to a direct question. The return of the gentlemen saved her from undergoing an interrogation artlessly initiated by Miss Ellicott in pursuit of further scandalous revelations. She sat in a corner of the settee in a frozen state of humiliation during the musical program that followed, very little of which pierced her misery except for Mr. Ransom's poignant violin playing that nearly succeeded in oversetting her precarious control.

Things never look quite so black after a night's sleep, even a disturbed night's sleep, and Chloe woke to a day of clear blue sky and sunshine, determined to put the unfortunate incident behind her. Today promised to be of more than customary interest, for the men had agreed to forgo their shooting in order to accompany the younger ladies on an excursion to Framlingham Castle with its great curtain wall and thirteen towers. It would be wonderful just to get away from Applewood for a few hours, but the ruined castle itself was reputed to be one of the most impressive military buildings in England and certainly worth a visit while she was in East Anglia.

If Chloe did not exactly bound out of bed, at least she greeted
the day with a sense of anticipation she would not have believed
possible twelve hours before, which only went to prove that
no misfortune was as black as it might seem on first impact.
Today she could examine her stricken reaction to yesterday's
humiliation and wonder at her own excessive sensibility.

Chloe's newborn optimism was destined to be short-lived.
She was just leaving the breakfast table when Hawkins presented
Lady Montrose's compliments with a request that Miss Norris
oblige her with a brief visit to her apartment as soon as
convenient. Chloe's first thought, that the countess had decided
to send her home in disgrace after the incident she had witnessed,
drove the natural color from her cheeks, but she steadied her
trembling lips and thanked the butler quietly.

As she left the table and headed for the main staircase, rising
anger at the unfairness of the situation provided the stiffening
she needed to present a calm front to Lady Montrose when she
was ushered into her presence by an abigail.

Lady Montrose was seated at her dressing table having her
hair arranged when Chloe came slowly forward. She greeted
Chloe's mirror image as the abigail resumed her task. "I must
begin with an apology for the favor I am about to ask of you,"
she began in a purring voice, pausing expectantly.

"Yes, ma'am?" Chloe could read nothing in the beautiful
face of the woman looking at her in the mirror.

"Hawkins tells me that the flowers in the dining room and
main reception rooms are looking dreadfully wilted this
morning."

"The flowers, ma'am? But . . . but I made up those arrangements only yesterday," Chloe said, confused by this unexpected
turn of events.

"It is very strange, to be sure, but they must be refreshed
before the rooms are used today. I'd ask Mrs. Meggs to do it,
but she has so much extra work on her hands with all the guests
in residence." The countess paused again, and it dawned on
Chloe that she was neatly trapped. The tacit request, though
put in the form of a favor, was actually the countess's way of
punishing her for the kissing incident. A refusal to make this
sacrifice on the part of one who had been treated like a daughter

in the house was unthinkable, while acceptance of the chore could be taken by the countess as an admission of her guilt. One of the maids or Lady Montrose herself could have freshened the bouquets this once, but no such suggestion was possible from her.

"Yes, of course I shall be happy to restore the arrangements, ma'am," she said, conceding defeat.

"Thank you, Chloe. You are most accommodating. I hope you were not too eager to go to Framlingham today? The castle is little better than a ruin actually. You won't be missing much."

"It doesn't signify in the least, ma'am. I'll get started on the flowers right away," Chloe replied politely, denying her opponent the final satisfaction of visual proof of what the capitulation had cost.

Fury on an order of magnitude of which she had not known herself capable coursed through Chloe's veins as she made her way to the garden room, detouring only long enough to tell an uninterested Lady Mary that she would not be going on the outing to Framlingham. This latest sample of Lady Montrose's behavior when crossed did not spring from condescension or toploftiness or any other unbecoming trait shared by many members of the privileged class as a result of their upbringing. This was personal spite and nastiness of a sort one associated with the meanest characters in society. As fast as her anger had flared it abated, leaving her with an aching regret that she had not left Applewood last week when her father had written to say he was leaving Scotland. That way she would have been spared this painful knowledge, and some pleasant early memories of her stay here would have remained untarnished.

Chloe entered the garden room and let her eyes range over the dozen or so vases of badly wilted flowers standing about on the floor or placed on the huge table in the center of the room. Lady Montrose certainly had not been guilty of exaggeration. Not a single flower in a single arrangement could be revived. She would have to begin all over again. It was as if they had never been in water at all. For a second she wondered if she could have forgotten to put water in the containers, but such an oversight was impossible; the water went in first, at least most of it did. Some was added after the arrangements had been safely carried to their display locations. Even if the footmen whose duty it was to transport the vases had neglected to fill the containers, there should have been enough water already in them for a couple of days. Chloe shook her head in bafflement and proceeded to clear away all the dead vegetation. Fortunately the order for more flowers must have gone out to the gardeners early this morning, because there seemed to be sufficient stock in the pails to redo the arrangements, though they might not be as generous as she would like.

Chloe was placing the background greenery in the first vase when the door opened and the earl came in, stopping just over the threshold and sending a frowning glance around the room before resting it on the sober-faced girl behind the table. "Mary says you are not coming to Framlingham with us."

"No," Chloe replied, waving a comprehensive hand to indicate the empty containers. "All these arrangements need redoing." She continued with the placement of the leaves, keeping her eyes on her busy hands. Her first quick look had revealed that he was wearing gloves and a black beaver on his dark head, which meant the party must be getting ready to leave.

"Why should you be doing this?" he asked impatiently. "Let someone else take over for today. We'll wait while you get your wraps."

"I . . . I'm sorry, but I really cannot go. I promised your mother I would do the flowers this morning."

"What do you mean, you promised my mother? Why should she care who does the job?" Impatience still sat squarely on his countenance.

"Lady Montrose sent for me a little while ago and asked me to do this as a favor, and I promised that I would. It does not signify. I won't be missed in that large party, and Mrs. Claven is going along as chaperone." Chloe was concentrating so hard on keeping any trace of resentment out of her voice while keeping her eyes on her fingers that she was unprepared to find the earl beside her. She jumped nervously at the sound of his deep voice above her ear.

"I don't know what has happened and there is no time to find out now with everyone waiting for me." He took her by the shoulders and turned her gently to face him. "Look at me,

Chloe.'' When she refused to lift her eyes, he put one gloved hand under her chin and raised her face to stare down into over-bright eyes. "You are wrong about one thing, my dear. It does signify. It matters very much to me that you wished to go on this jaunt and cannot, but don't despair. I'll take you to Framlingham one day soon, I promise." He bent his head and kissed her quivering mouth gently but very thoroughly.

Chloe's eyelids had fluttered down and she was utterly still, not even breathing while his lips remained on hers, though aware of her heart beating frantically in her throat. Her heavy lashes had barely cleared her cheeks when the earl stepped back. By the time her eyes focused again, he was going out the door.

Had there been a chair in the workroom she'd have collapsed on it. As it was, she sagged limply against the table's edge for a few moments while she tasted the cup of despair.

This then was the explanation for her strange reluctance to leave Applewood even after the countess's dislike had become manifest. She had been insisting all along to that soft warning voice inside her head that her feelings for the earl were strictly those of friendship. Self-deception, yet another unsuspected weakness in her character, had succeeded in delaying the inevitable discovery that she was achingly in love with him. After weeks of denying that his physical presence had any effect on her, she had nearly succumbed to the first touch of his lips on hers. It had taken every grain of strength she possessed to remain passive when her senses were clamoring to return his kiss. Worst of all, this had happened even though she was fully aware that comfort, not passion, had been the motive behind his impulsive action. Her sufferings over a minor injustice and humiliation last night had been reduced to pinpricks compared with the misery she was experiencing at present. *Then* the knowledge of her innocence had insulated her innermost core; *now* the knowledge of her disloyalty to the man she had eagerly agreed to marry was a whip to lash her trembling spirits. She had no right to desire another man's love or take pleasure in his touch.

The sound of footsteps on the flagstone floor outside the garden room jerked Chloe upright with the stern power of propriety, and she reached blindly for a spray of leaves, which she proceeded to plunge anyhow into the vase in front of her. The interruption turned out to be one of the housemaids sent by Mrs. Meggs to assist her in her task. Chloe was grateful for the housekeeper's thoughtfulness and grateful as much for the cheerful company of her helper as for her actual assistance. Even lending half an ear to Alice's bubbling chatter meant she could not descend to wallowing in misery, not while there was work to be done, anyway.

The luncheon table was greatly depleted that day. Sir Watson, Lady Montrose's earnest cavalier, was the sole gentleman present, and only the dowagers and Lady Patricia among the women had remained at Applewood. The morning's greater disaster having driven yesterday's humiliation from her mind, it took Chloe most of the meal, for which she had no appetite, to realize that she was being treated with chilly reserve by Lady Thrale and Lady Mallory. Their disapproval had no power to disturb the calmness of despair that had descended upon her, but perhaps it was just as well that she could not know that her composure was taken as proof positive of her shamelessness and afforded the elder ladies increased scope for their gossip that afternoon. Lady Montrose played the charming hostess to perfection, affecting not to be aware of undercurrents, while Lady Patricia's usual self-absorption had given way to an aroused sympathy for the victim.

It seemed even Lady Patricia had heard the story of the stolen kiss in the small reception room. She took Chloe aside on their way out of the dining room to commiserate with her. "Ned's selfishness and irresponsibility are the outside of enough," she declared with unwonted spirit. "He considers it safe to flirt with you because you are betrothed, and he doesn't concern himself with what you are made to bear because of his lapses."

Chloe's smile was a trifle wan, but in truth she was a good deal touched by the young widow's championship. "You are very kind, but do not worry about me, Lady Patricia. It is not very pleasant to be treated like a pariah, but I shall be leaving Applewood soon and I promise you I shan't allow the present unpleasantness to overset me."

"It is you who are kind, Chloe, and I'd like to say I consider that you have been a friend to me by being one to Emilie. I

can see you are not very happy just now. I have no intention
of asking prying questions,'' she added, noting the other's
instinctive withdrawal, ''but if you ever wish to talk to someone,
please come to me.''

''Thank you,'' Chloe said simply.

She smilingly declined an invitation to sail leaf boats with
Emilie and her mother, citing some neglected correspondence
in excuse. It was true that she owed Lady Dalrymple a letter,
but it did not get written that afternoon. Chloe sought sanctuary
in her bedchamber, but even that was denied her at first. As
she entered the haven of her room, Tillie looked up from the
armoire where she was putting away some clothes that had been
freshly laundered.

''I was that surprised to hear from Alice that you was doing
the flowers together this morning, Miss Norris. I thought you
was going to Framlingham wi' the others.''

''I was, but a number of the flower arrangements had wilted
overnight and Lady Montrose asked if I would do them again.''
Chloe dropped into the wing chair with an unconscious sigh.
There was silence in the room for a moment and Chloe became
aware of the tiny sounds associated with putting things in the
armoire. She heard the doors click shut and turned her head
to say good-bye to Tillie, only to find the girl standing still,
indecision enveloping her person as she glanced at Chloe and
away again.

''Is something wrong, Tillie?''

''Well, I don't rightly know, Miss Norris, but I've been
wondering if I should tell you something queer that happened
last night.''

''Something that concerns me?''

''Well, at first I didn't think nothing of it, miss, but when
Alice told me what you and she had been at this morning, it
struck me as downright queer.''

Tillie took Chloe's mystified silence for encouragement and
hastened on, coming a bit closer as she spoke. ''You might not
know, miss, that Eldon the footman and I are promised. We're
going to get married in a year or two when we save up some
money.'' She accepted Chloe's felicitations with a dismissive
wave, saying, ''The point is, Eldon didn't get back to the

servants' hall last night before the housemaids were sent to bed.
This morning, when I asked him where he had been, he told
me that the mistress had come up to him before the tea tray
was brought in last night and told him he was to wait up till
everyone had gone upstairs. Then he was to take all the flower
vases out o' the main rooms and empty every bit o' water out
of 'em into the sink in the garden room wi'out disturbing the
flowers, and then put every single vase back where it belonged
before he went to bed." At this point Chloe emitted a little gasp,
but Tillie was not through with her tale. "That's not the end
of it, miss. The first thing this morning Eldon was to put some
water back in all the vases he had emptied it out of. That's what
he was doing when I found him, but the flowers was already
dead by then. I thought you ought to know, miss," she finished.

Chloe had to clear her throat before she could break the
expectant silence that followed Tillie's abrupt ending. "I . . .
I see. Thank you for telling me, Tillie. May I ask as a favor
that you and Eldon not mention this to anyone who doesn't
already know about it?"

"Yes, Miss Norris. I won't let him say a word to a soul,"
Tillie promised.

Chloe continued to stare blankly into the fireplace when the
maid had gone, reduced to numb misery again by this latest
revelation. She had known that spite lay behind Lady Montrose's
request to her this morning, but she had not allowed herself
to speculate on the reason for the complete collapse of so many
flower arrangements. She was appalled and chilled at the lengths
the woman would go to achieve her paltry revenge, but as she
turned the events over in her mind she decided it was more likely
that the countess had seen a chance to get the girl she detested
out of Applewood and had acted on it, assuming no one with
any self-respect would wish to stay around for more of the
treatment Chloe had received at lunch.

And she was absolutely correct in her assumption! Though
if things had been different, if she had been free to love Ivor
and he really wanted her, she would not have let Lady Montrose
drive her away so easily. As it was, she would seek out the
first opportunity to speak with the earl when the touring party
returned this afternoon and tell him she wished to leave Apple-

wood tomorrow. Mary's dance was the day after that, and she would like to be long gone before that event.

Alas for hastily conceived plans. Chloe found it impossible to have a private word with the earl that evening for a series of reasons, one of which, she strongly suspected, was his disinclination to grant her such an opportunity. The possibility that he was deliberately avoiding her rendered a mostly sleepless night hideous with additional humiliation. Did he fear she was planning to ask his intentions on the strength of one meaningless kiss? she demanded of the quiet bedchamber as she pounded her pillows into submission several hours after a dismal evening whose only saving grace was the quiet companionship of Lady Patricia while the rest of the company played round games or whist. Did he believe the great honor of joining the aristocracy would blind her to the principles she held dear and cause her to jilt her fiancé to leap at an offer of marriage from him? If Chloe did less than justice to the earl's principles and honor in her furious internal debates that night, it might be entered in her defense that she could not afford to credit Ivor with any virtue or attraction whilst engaged in whipping her own traitorous emotions into line with her principles. There would be oceans of time for memories and regrets when she was back in her father's home.

Chloe knocked on the door to the library after breakfast the next morning in her pursuit of a quick escape from Applewood. She almost withdrew when she saw that the earl was engaged with his bailiff, but Ivor put up a staying hand. "Don't go, Miss Norris. Halbertson and I will have finished our business in a minute or two."

Chloe felt the awkwardness of her position but could scarcely defy his command by leaving or enter into an argument when the earl had gone straight back to his conversation with his visitor. She wandered down the long room to give the men as much privacy as possible and stopped to study the portrait between the two windows on the end wall, which she had not noticed on her previous visits to this room.

That this was the second earl of Montrose was past doubting. The face that looked out of the canvas was so like Ivor's that her first thought had been that here was the present earl's portrait. Only on closer inspection did she discern that the man in the picture was probably some five or six years older than Ivor. The coloring was the same, as was the broad forehead and square jaw. The well-shaped nose, nicely carved mouth, and flat ears were admirable, but those straight thick eyebrows and the rocky chin added up to a strong rather than handsome visage, something equally true of the present owner of the face. The second earl's eyes were a darker gray than his son's and, despite the obvious strength of character, there was a hint of vulnerability about this painted face that Chloe had never spotted in the present-day version.

"In case you had wondered before, you can see that they didn't find me under a cabbage plant," said the earl, so close behind her that Chloe jumped.

"No, indeed," she agreed, mustering up a smile as she turned. "The resemblance is even greater than that between your mother and Lady Patricia."

"Yes, the family beauty bypassed me completely. Fortunately, the others all inherited my mother's looks."

"It didn't bypass you completely, you know," she said conversationally, indicating his hand, which had gone out to straighten the frame's alignment a hair. "You have your mother's hands."

He stared at his hands as though seeing them for the first time and rejected the comparison outright. "Nonsense, this is a farmer's hand like my father's."

Chloe laughed a little. "I beg to differ with you, sir. I noticed at our first meeting that your hands were like your mother's, narrow in width with long, slender fingers." She gestured at the painting. "Your father's hand is much broader than yours, and his fingers are not so long." She turned back from the portrait to find those pale eyes with the iris outlined in black fixed intently on her face, and an alarm tocsin sounded in her brain.

"Since you are so very noticing you cannot have failed to note that—"

"I promise you I did not interrupt your work to waste your time, sir," she said in a rather breathless voice she strove to make businesslike, "but to tell you that, if you do not object,

I should like to make arrangements to leave Applewood tomorrow, unless it is still possible to leave today?''

"*Leave!*" Those thick brows drew together. "Of course I object! Today is out of the question and tomorrow is the dance." As she opened her lips, he warned, "And I do not wish to hear again how you have nothing to wear. You and Mary are almost of a size. She will be happy to rig you out—"

A knock at the door silenced him for a second before he called permission to enter. They both watched Hawkins come in with his measured step, carrying a parcel about the size of a band-box. "This package was picked up at the receiving office this morning, my lord. It is for Miss Norris."

"For me?" Chloe made no move to claim her property, and the earl said with a touch of impatience, "Very well, Hawkins, leave it. You may go."

"Very good, sir." Hawkins retreated, dignity intact.

When the door had closed again, the earl said, "Go ahead, open it." He turned away.

"Later. Sir—" she began.

"Have you no normal feminine curiosity, Miss Norris?"

"Yes, I have. How did Hawkins know I was in here?"

Ivor gave a bark of laughter that set lights dancing in his eyes and took years from his age. "A good butler makes it his business to know where everyone is at all times. Why are you unwilling to open your parcel? Are you afraid it will prove to be some proscribed personal article from the absent Captain Otley?"

"Certainly not!" Chloe strongly resented his taunting words. She turned to the package, feeling she needed to reestablish the calm tone of the meeting. "It's from Lady Dalrymple," she said, examining the wrapping. He made no comment and she proceeded to tear away the wrappings, exposing a bandbox whose cover she removed with a growing sense of puzzlement. A second later she exclaimed, "Oh, how perfectly lovely!" and reached inside, eagerly now, to lift out a shimmering gown of white silk and gold lace.

"Well, this solves the apparel problem," Ivor said in a milder tone than he had previously employed.

"Sir, I really feel it is time I left Applewood," Chloe began earnestly, tearing her eyes away from the creation in her hands.

"I know it has been difficult for you here lately, Chloe; in fact, this entire visit had demanded more of you than any family has a right to expect even from a close family member. And then this damn house party! I am so tied by my position as host, but please bear with me a little longer. I need your sanity and tact to help us get through this mad press of social events."

"Your mother would really prefer that I left," she said softly, feeling mean, but determined to get it out in the open.

"My mother accepts that it is my wishes that must ultimately prevail at Applewood." He looked away from the understanding in her steady gaze, then turned back to say with a hint of uncertainty in his voice, "If you are . . . concerned that I might press unwanted attentions on you after yesterday, then let me assure you you have nothing to fear on that head."

"I . . . I don't fear it," she said, her head averted.

"Then . . . will you stay?"

There was a long pause during which Chloe bit her lip and looked everywhere but at the waiting earl. Finally she said, "Yes . . . for a little longer."

Chapter Fifteen

CHLOE REGRETTED her promise a half-dozen times before the first strains of music sounded at the long-awaited ball, the first time a scant minute after she made it. She had barely shut the library door behind her when she saw Lady Montrose in the hall. As the countess glanced from the bandbox in the girl's hands to the door from which she had emerged she raised one beautifully arched brow, her sole acknowledgment of Chloe's presence as she continued her passage down the hall. It was necessary for Chloe to remind herself that Lady Montrose's dislike was no longer her chief problem. Her main concern was to get through the next two days with her dignity and self-respect intact and without betraying her illicit feelings for her ladyship's elder son.

Even this unhappy truth could be ignored for the next half hour while she carried Lady Dalrymple's unexpected gift to her room for closer inspection. Chloe was not such an unnatural female that she was indifferent to the allure of the most beautiful gown she had ever clapped eyes on. It consisted of an opaque slip of white crape to be worn under a silk overdress of gossamer fineness trimmed with frothing gold lace at the hem. The dress was fastened down the front by clusters of pearls like rosettes, and its brief puffed sleeves were sewn all over with pearls. Chloe was holding the overdress up in front of her before the looking glass when a knock sounded on the door and Lady Mary came in at her bidding."

"My word, that's gorgeous! Where did you get it?"

"Lady Dalrymple sent it to me for your dance. Is something wrong?" Chloe asked, seeing the momentary animation produced by the sight of the gown fade from the girl's face at the mention of her dance.

Lady Mary gave a bitter laugh. "Only what has been wrong all along." She flung herself into the wing chair and looked at her friend with despairing eyes. "Chloe, what am I to do?"

Chloe did not respond immediately, taking her time in laying the gown out on her bed and smoothing out some of the travel wrinkles. Finally she turned to the pale girl staring beseechingly at her and said quietly, "My advice is what it has been all along—tell your mother or your brother how you feel."

"How can I with Thrale and his horrid mother here watching me like a hawk?"

"If you do not, you will soon find yourself living with Lord Thrale and his horrid mother," Chloe said hardily. Her conscience smote her as Mary shivered violently, looking quite sick, and she added on impulse, "Mary, would you like *me* to tell your brother? Or give him a hint at least that you are unhappy?"

The alarm that leapt into the girl's eyes was answer enough. Sighing, Chloe tried one more approach. "Have you heard from Tom in the past sennight?"

Lady Mary rose from her chair. "Not a word," she said, heading for the door, "which proves how correct I was when I said he didn't really love me."

"I would have said that a man who is prepared to confront the family of an engaged girl has rather demonstrated fair proof of his devotion." As the young girl still refused to look at her, Chloe said softly, "Your wedding is less than a sennight away, Mary, and I shall be gone from Applewood by then. There will be no one to talk to about the way you feel. Please go to Ivor. He will help you."

Lady Mary's shoulders seemed to sag, but she made no reply as she left the room.

Chloe would always recall the period before Mary's dance as one of uneasy waiting as if for an expected storm to strike. For herself it was a time of heightened perceptions, perhaps because she saw it as the lingering climax of an experience that had lasted too long. She helped Mrs. Meggs and the footmen to decorate the long drawing room, which was cleared of its furnishings for dancing. Two of the smaller reception rooms were to be used for cards and mingling by those who did not care to dance, and the dining room was to be the site of a buffet supper with the long table pushed to the wall and small tables set up about the large room for the convenience of the guests. Chloe kept her contacts with the resident guests to the minimum possible, gratefully accepting an invitation from Lady Patricia to take nursery tea with herself and Emilie. It was a pleasant, even mildly jolly occasion, with Emilie happily confiding that her mother was going to begin teaching her to play the pianoforte once the guests left after Aunt Mary's wedding.

When Lady Patricia regretted with a sigh that the age difference between herself and Mary, coupled with her own early marriage, had kept them from becoming close friends, Chloe took a calculated gamble and hinted delicately that she feared Mary did not quite fit the picture of a happy bride-to-be. It was all she felt she could do without betraying Mary's confidence, and little enough at that, taking into account Lady Patricia's habitual lack of involvement with her family, but time was fast running out and she was reduced to grasping at straws.

The night before the dance, for the first time since her husband's death, Lady Patricia had consented to play the pianoforte in company. Her masterly performance had been enthusiastically received, following which Mr. Bartholomew Ransom had beaten Lord Landers to a seat by Lady Patricia's side, a place he had not relinquished for the rest of the evening. It was the first time Chloe had witnessed sustained animation in the beautiful young widow's manner as she and her brother's friend discussed music for more than an hour. As she reviewed her time at Applewood, Chloe took comfort in the fact that she had seen an improvement in two lives, Lady Patricia's and her daughter's, during her visit, which went some way to counterbalance the enmity of the countess and the feeling of abject helplessness where Mary's future was concerned.

Everyone agreed that Applewood looked magnificent on the night of the dance in honor of the coming marriage of the younger daughter of the house. There was significantly less agreement on the appearance of the most humble of Applewood's guests that evening, the larger faction, predominantly masculine, holding on the evidence of its eyes that Miss Norris was second to none of the ladies attending in beauty and charm. A vocal minority, exclusively feminine, looked down its collective nose and agreed among itself that fine feathers did

not necessarily make fine birds. Chloe, who cared for no opinion
save one, though she had been greatly touched by Tillie's ecstatic
compliments when the little maid came to exercise her talent
for coiffeuring, remained curiously detached from the comments
and compliments her enhanced appearance evoked.

Lady Mary, looking lifeless in a pretty gown of deep pink
silk that should have lent her skin some healthy color, stopped
by Chloe's room before she went downstairs with a charming
gold lace fan she urged her to carry. Already wearing a pair
of her friend's dancing slippers, Chloe was warmed by the kind
thought, knowing as she did how much Lady Mary was dreading
this night. The girls descended together, a mistake that Chloe
recognized only belatedly when people began to rain
compliments on her. It was a natural enough reaction to the
contrast and surprise of her modish appearance, but the mother
of the guest of honor, her eyes glittering with suppressed rage,
could not be expected to enjoy seeing her daughter cast into
the shade on her special evening, particularly by someone that
same mother had come to detest. Chloe's gaze sought Ivor
against her sworn resolution to maintain a safe distance all
evening, and she had the tainted thrill of seeing his eyes aflame
with something deeper than mere admiration before she admitted
the danger and increased the distance between them.

There was no great difficulty in keeping herself out of the
earl's orbit once the party was swollen by the presence of dozens
of local families. Chloe met again all those who had been at
the manor to welcome Thomas Trainor and reconfirmed her
first impression that Applewood's immediate neighborhood was
populated by a pleasant set of people. Though she did not
recognize it as a conscious decision, she remained in the
company of various neighbors most of the evening, comforted
by their friendly acceptance of her.

Chloe did not lack for partners that evening; she had her pick
of the best dancers present and might have enjoyed herself
mightily under different circumstances. Mr. Thomas Trainor
solicited her hand for a waltz midway through the evening.
Chloe had made a covert study of this gentleman whenever he
had come into her line of vision and she had concluded that
behind his stiff exterior he was suffering as much as Mary. He

did not say anything for the first few minutes of their dance together, nor did Chloe attempt to initiate a conversation. Whether his jerky style was an indication of his tense mental state or the result of a lack of aptitude, she did not find him a very comfortable partner. Halfway through the dance he stepped on her foot and tendered a rapid apology.

"It is perfectly all right, Mr. Trainor," she said mildly. "It may be that your mind is not entirely on dancing tonight."

He flashed her a quick look and, finding nothing of a judgmental nature in her calm visage, said, "I'll try to do better."

His performance did improve for a few bars until he swung her into a glancing collision with another couple, who whirled off unscathed.

"Are you all right, Miss Norris? I am not generally so clumsy."

"Perfectly all right, sir. May I ask you something?"

"Of course," he replied automatically.

"Why did you come here tonight?"

He fixed her with a brilliant blue stare. "That is a curious question, Miss Norris. This is a celebration, is it not?"

"Purportedly." Chloe returned his stare and saw suspicion give way to comprehension.

"You know how it is with us, then?"

"Yes. Have you tried to speak with her tonight, to change her mind?"

"She is giving me a wide berth," he said bitterly. "I came here tonight because I could not believe she meant to go through with this mockery. Look at them together! It's as plain as a pikestaff that she can scarcely bear the fellow's company! I could shake her until her teeth rattle, but a pretty fool I'd make of myself going slap up to her mother and announcing it's me she loves when she threatened she'd deny it."

Hearing the helpless frustration behind the angry words, Chloe said, "Mary has an unreasoning fear of her mother's power to bend her to her will. I was hoping a week of close proximity to Lord Thrale and his dragon of a mother would be enough of a preview of the future to put heart into her, but it has not answered. She is looking almost ill tonight."

Chloe had not needed to direct her partner's attention to Lady Mary. His blue gaze, more furious than loverlike, was pursuing his childhood friend relentlessly as she silently danced nearby with her affianced husband. Mary was indeed looking unwell, and presently she left the floor after a whispered word to her fiancé.

"Have you considered approaching Lord Montrose instead of her mother?" Chloe asked hesitantly as her partner missed another step. "I really believe he would stand your friend."

"I might just do that tomorrow," he declared as the music ended.

Chloe joined her next partner feeling she had gone as far as she could without breaking her word to Mary.

His duties as host kept Lord Montrose busy until well into the evening. Chloe had been conscious that he monitored her progress around the rooms. After the one exchange that had seemed to banish the entire company, leaving them alone in wordless communion, she did not again allow herself the forbidden rapture of meeting his glance. Each stolen moment would have to be paid for with guilt and remorse when she returned to her real life.

If the best antidote for a brooding melancholy is to keep busy, then Chloe's ailment should have been cured that evening, for she kept constantly in circulation. When she was not dancing she was chatting with small groups of neighbors or procuring cups of punch for some of the more sedentary dowagers gathered in a corner of the ballroom.

It was fairly late in the evening when Lord Montrose came up to her while she was dancing with his brother. He told Ned his mother wished to speak with him and smoothly appropriated his partner, waltzing Chloe away before she could excuse herself.

"Is it my imagination or was Ned looking a bit disgruntled just now?" he asked prosaically enough.

"I believe your brother feels I do not fully appreciate the true artistry of his well-turned compliments," Chloe replied, aware of her thrumming pulses as she matched her steps to his.

"And is he correct in this belief?"

"I told him females preferred exclusivity to even the most

consummate artistry. He appeared to find that a perverse pecularity on the part of an otherwise charming species." Chloe knew she was chattering as a defense against meaningful communication, but her gay prolixity failed to divert him from a serious response.

"I prefer exclusivity also, and you may believe me when I say that to me you are the loveliest girl in the room. You would still be lovely wearing sackcloth, but in this white and gold creation, with your glorious hair dressed in that enchanting fashion, you take my breath away."

"Please, Ivor, don't," she whispered, wrenching her eyes from his in an attempt to evade the magnetizing force he exerted over her of late.

"Why not?"

"You know why." She glanced at him fleetingly to see a mulish set to his mouth and jaw.

"What I know is that there has always been complete honesty between us, and that must not change."

"But do you not see that it is dishonest of me to allow you to talk this way?" she cried, gazing up at him imploringly.

He emitted an inarticulate growl and pulled her close to avoid a collision as the music came to an end. Chloe could feel the wild beating of her heart—or was it his?—in the timeless moment that she was held clamped to his chest before the countess's decisive voice said, "The waiters are ready with the champagne, Ivor. It is time to make the toast to Mary and Thrale."

The earl released Chloe with a deliberation that did not go unnoticed by his mother as she waited for him to accompany her. She did not even glance at Chloe, but the flustered young woman could sense her disapproval. She evaded Ivor's hand as he tried to take her arm to bring her along with them and melted into the milling crowd of dancers who were accepting glasses of champagne from the waiters moving among them.

Chloe's personal despair gave way to renewed concern for Lady Mary as the moment she had dreaded arrived. This public toast to the affianced couple symbolically marked the end of the girl's hopes of happiness with Tom. The large room suddenly seemed stuffy as the heat given off by hundreds of candles and scores of dancers reached the point of discomfort.

Men's shirt points were beginning to wilt and ladies were plying their fans in an effort to cool flushed cheeks. Chloe slipped through the throng to a distant point where she had a long but relatively unobstructed view of the area in front of the musicians where Ivor had herded the couple to be honored. The young people were flanked by the dowagers—Lady Montrose beautiful and triumphant in celestial blue silk and diamonds, and Lady Thrale imposing and sour in purple velvet and towering plumes.

Chloe's attention shifted back to Mary and her heart skipped a beat. The girl really did look ill! She straightened her shoulders at a whispered word from her mother and in so doing, her downcast eyes gazed briefly out into the crowd. She swayed, and the countess put an arm around her waist. Chloe, noting Mr. Thomas Trainor's sun-streaked head in the first rank of spectators, had no doubts as to where Mary's eyes had lighted. Pity for the girl's plight flooded through her along with impatience at the spinelessness that had made this wretched mockery inevitable.

The earl raised a hand and a partial hush fell over the expectant guests. His voice was clear and audible, but Chloe heard none of his little speech. She was entirely given over to willing strength into his young sister, who, it must be obvious to all eyes, was being kept upright by her mother's arm. The countess's perfect features wore the control of a great lady who did not deign to recognize disaster approaching. A ripple passed through the room as glasses were raised in scores of hands at the earl's request. Chloe, her unwanted glass still held at waist level, was clenching her left fist so tightly that her nails were digging into her palms while she mentally exhorted her friend to hold on for another minute or two. The ordeal was nearly over.

Before the exhortation had finished framing itself, and before the majority of glasses had reached their owners' lips, Lady Mary broke away from her mother's grasp, crying, *"No, no, I cannot marry him!"* She took one step toward the astonished crowd of well-wishers and crumpled to the floor.

The earl thrust his glass into the limp fist of the bewildered bridegroom and leapt forward at the same time that Mr. Thomas Trainor sprang out of the crowd, but neither man was in time to catch Mary before she hit the floor. Like a flock of birds, wings beating in concert, gasps and murmurs rose into the overheated air of the ballroom following a tiny stunned silence. Some people surged forward and others fell back as dictated by their various natures, and the buzz of conversation increased in volume and intensity.

Chloe put her untouched glass on a passing waiter's tray and slipped out of the room at this juncture. Her presence could be of no benefit to Mary. Lady Montrose would see to it that her daughter was hustled out of the public eye while she set about trying to erase the impression the girl's hysterical outburst had made on the fascinated company. Chloe judged this goal to be beyond achievement, given the public nature of the incident. Applewood's reception rooms would continue to hum with surreptitious conjecture and speculation until the last local guest had departed, leaving the temporary residents to carry on in more comfort.

It was a thousand pities that Lady Mary had not been able to summon the courage to speak of her true feelings to her family before the house guests had arrived. There would have been some talk, of course, but nothing to compare with the full-blown scandal tonight's desperate declaration had already set in motion. Even the scheduled wedding could not entirely circumvent that now, and judging from Lady Thrale's furious face, which currently matched her gown in hue, she would oppose the marriage in the unlikely event the girl could be brought to recant. One did not need to be a prophet to see that there was going to be a great deal of unpleasantness over this fiasco.

Chloe trudged up the main staircase overwhelmed with tiredness all at once. The sands in the hourglass that marked her visit to Applewood were fast running out. Tomorrow, she promised herself, tomorrow she would leave, no matter what arguments Ivor put forth to keep her here. Even more overpowering than her fatigue was a longing to be in her father's calm, comforting presence again.

Chloe was seated at the dressing table the next morning listlessly brushing the tangles from her curly hair when a knock on her door proved to be one of the housemaids with a message.

Chloe's stomach muscles tightened as she read the curt request
that she present herself in her hostess's apartment *toute de suite*.
Her lips were tightened too when she resumed the task of
restoring her hair to its usual neat arrangement with fingers that
were unaccountably clumsy. It seemed she was not even to be
allowed her breakfast this time. Chloe could only marvel that
amidst the ruins of her grand plans for Mary's future, Lady
Montrose could still address herself to the supposed peccadilloes
of the despised upstart. As she knocked on the door to the
countess's suite about five minutes later she wondered idly if
the crime of *almost* kissing the elder son would be considered
greater or less than *actually* kissing the younger.

There was no abigail present this time, Chloe noted on
entering the beautifully appointed bedchamber and, conse-
quently, no need for any pretense of cordiality. The woman
staring coldly at her from a nest of lace-edged pillows possessed
the exquisite bone structure that guaranteed she would be
beautiful all her life, but without cosmetic aid she looked nearer
her age this morning as she set a delicate cup back on its saucer
with precision and watched her unwanted guest's quiet approach.

Refusing to be intimidated, Chloe came steadily forward and
stopped near one of the turned mahogany posts at the foot of
the bed. She stood there for a second with her hands loosely
linked below her waist, her gaze steady by dint of willpower.
"You wanted to see me, ma'am?" she prompted when the
countess did not immediately speak.

"I wish never to set eyes on you again," that lady replied
in icy clear tones. "I have never been so deceived in anyone
in all my life. A maid is packing your belongings at this moment
and I have sent to the stables for a carriage. You are to be out
of this house within the hour."

The natural color drained out of Chloe's face, the only visible
sign of damage from the blow she had just been dealt, but her
stomach churned and saliva flooded in under her tongue, while
a wave of dizziness threatened her balance. Accompanying these
unpleasant physical symptoms was a craven urge to remove
herself posthaste from the vicinity of such viciousness to a place
where she could lick her wounds and restore her *amour propre*.

She might have given in to blind instinct and fled had not

something in the malevolence of that blue gaze aroused a stubborn core of resistance against the injustice being done. She swallowed back the saliva, stiffened her knees, and tried to ignore the internal churning.

"I fail to see in what way I could be said to have deceived you, my lady," she said with commendable restraint, though her voice was not as steady as she would have liked.

"In every way! Coming here with that meek face and those drab clothes and that bundled-up hair of yours, pretending to be an engaged woman when—"

"*Pretending?*" Chloe's eyes rounded and her brows escalated. "I can assure you my engagement is no pretense." Unthinkingly she was twisting her jade ring, and the countess's eyes winged to the movement.

"You needn't bother to display that trumpery ring for my benefit. I am not so naive. If the so-called engagement was real, which I strongly doubt, it certainly did not keep you from setting out to entangle whichever of my sons might be more easily fooled by that pious pose. You cast out your lures for Ned first but—"

"These allegations are ludicrous—almost, I might say, the product of a disordered mind," Chloe snapped, stung into defending her actions. "It is scarcely my fault if Ned flirts with anything in skirts. My behavior has always been circumspect."

"Circumspect? Do you call that scene in the small reception room circumspect?"

"Ned staged that kiss because he resented having Lady Miranda thrust down his throat." Chloe softened her tone and went on more gently. "I know how it must have looked from the doorway, but he caught me by surprise as I was getting up with the spilliken box in my hands. I have never encouraged his attentions and I have nothing to reproach myself with on that head."

Lady Montrose's eyes were glittering with a feral light as she sat up straighter in her bed. "And have you nothing to reproach yourself with in Ivor's case? Can you deny you made a dead set at his rank and fortune when you realized that Ned's attentions were not serious?"

"I can and do deny it," Chloe answered evenly, aware of

heat in her cheeks but determined to keep a grip on her temper, though diplomacy had long since been cast to the winds in the face of continued insults. "Lord Montrose is fully cognizant of my engagement, and I have employed no deception of any sort while in residence at Applewood."

"You can say that when you have known all along of Mary's involvement with Tom Trainor and never breathed a word to me? Don't trouble to deny it; she has confessed everything."

This was a new charge and Chloe hesitated briefly, not wanting to say anything that would injure the girl. "Yes, I knew she loved Mr. Trainor, but I have urged her all along to confide in you. I could not persuade her to do so. As late as the day before the ball she told me she intended to go through with the marriage to Lord Thrale."

"You might have known the foolish girl would so something to ruin herself. You are no fool; you saw this scandal brewing and did not lift a finger to stop it. It was your duty to tell me what was in the wind and you deliberately kept silent. If that wasn't deception, I cannot find another term for it, unless it is betrayal."

Chloe was shaking by now and convinced at last that the countess's dislike of her was so great as to put her beyond the reach of reason. Nothing anyone could say or do would soften Lady Montrose on the subject, but she would not crawl away with any charges unanswered. That much she owed to herself. She lifted her chin and returned look for hostile look. "Mary is not a child and she had a right to expect that I would not betray her confidence. I am sorry that you see my silence as a betrayal of you, but I could not have done differently. I'll leave you now with my regrets that my visit was not a success."

As Chloe walked across the room Lady Montrose called indifferently, "Naturally, there will be money for your traveling expenses when the carriage arrives."

Her hand on the doorknob, Chloe whirled around. "I'd rather beg in the streets," she said through gritted teeth.

She was trembling visibly from reaction by the time she reached her room, but the presence of a maid methodically filling her valise deprived her of the luxury of giving way to her feelings. She forced a stiff smile to her lips and tried to give appropriate replies to the girl's several remarks while the part of her mind that was still functioning rapidly evaluated her financial situation. She had her return ticket on the stage, and Mr. Moore, the proprietor of the White Hart, would send her home in the inn's gig. The purchase of the christening gift had greatly depleted her purse, but she could just manage vails for the servants and tips for the coachman and guard if she limited herself to coffee when they changed horses. Her obstinate pride would not have to be further humbled.

In the next half hour Chloe prepared herself for departure and managed a quick farewell visit to the nursery. Emilie cried and clung to her but was eventually mollified by the promise of a faithful correspondence. Chloe kept to herself her reservations about the countess's swift countervention of any kind of continued contact with Applewood. Emilie would soon forget her in the improvement of her relationship with her mother and the excitement of her new activities.

After prolonged internal debate, Chloe knocked on the library door to bid the earl farewell, only to be told by Hawkins, who was passing in the hall, that Lord Montrose had gone off to the manor a half hour before.

There was no one save the footman Eldon to see her off the premises. Chloe entrusted him with a valedictory message and token for Tillie and accepted his help in climbing up into the carriage. She did not look back as the coachman gave his horses the signal to start.

The return journey from Applewood was not something Chloe ever desired to recall in detail. A miasma of dull, numb misery kept her insulated from the actual events of the long gray day. None of her traveling companions made the slightest impression on her consciousness, and she was mercifully unaware that the stage from Newmarket was rendered particularly uncomfortable for the passengers by a team of stumblers the coachman could not get to pull together. Only when she was being driven home by one of Mr. Moore's stableboys in the deepening twilight did the gnawing emptiness within her descend specifically to her stomach in a belated reminder that she had eaten nothing since a quick visit to the supper room during the dance the previous evening. The dull headache that had perched waiting behind her eyes all day had commenced pounding up through the top of her skull as the gig pulled up before her home. Stupid tears crowded behind her eyelids as she gazed at the shining brass knocker on the black door.

She had not mustered the strength to move when the door opened and her father's tall, lean and beloved figure came quickly down the steps. "Chloe, my dear child, why did you not advise me of your arrival?" he called out as he came up to the gig.

"Papa!" She held out her arms and was swung out of the vehicle and soundly embraced while the tears pushed harder behind her lids. She blinked one away as she smiled up into concerned dark eyes so like her own.

Dr. Norris set his daughter on her feet and turned her with an arm that encircled her shoulders. "My dear, look who has just arrived to surprise us."

Obediently Chloe glanced toward the open front door where a solid figure stood blocking the interior light, his face half-swallowed up by the evening shadows.

For the first time in her healthy existence, Chloe fainted.

Chapter Sixteen

CHLOE'S SWOON did not last more than a few seconds. Her father's arm was around her when her knees buckled and he simply held her tight against his long body, shoring her up until an intake of breath told him she was already recovering. The man in the doorway had hastened down to where they stood, and as Chloe's lashes lifted she found herself staring into the concerned face of her fiancé.

"Bertram," she said faintly.

"Are you all right, my dear?"

"Yes, thank you. So silly of me. I have been rocking in a stagecoach for hours and my legs were still a little shaky."

Dr. Norris's eyes had been making a thorough inspection of his daughter's pale face as she straightened upright once more. He kept his arm lightly around her while he said, "Hot food is what you need, my child."

"Oh yes," Chloe assented eagerly, "I have eaten nothing all day."

She could have bitten her tongue out for that hasty admission, for her father's gaze sharpened, but he only said mildly, "Bertram and I were about to go in to dinner when we heard the gig outside. Come along."

"That sounds wonderful," she said, hoping her voice did not sound as hollow as she felt. "If you will pay the boy, Papa, I'll join you both when I have taken off my pelisse and hat. I won't be five minutes."

Chloe avoided her father's eyes and gave Bertram an apologetic little smile as she slipped past him into the house. Her knees still felt decidedly shivery as she climbed the stairs rather more slowly than was her habit. Her brain was not in much better condition. It had seemed to shut down for a second on becoming aware of Bertram standing in the doorway and now it was awhirl with jumbled thoughts and impressions. For the last few miles, ever since the numbness that Lady Montrose's attack had cast her into had started to wear off, she had been consumed with impatience to reach her father and pour out the whole story of her disastrous sojourn among the aristocracy. The sight of her fiancé had been pure shock, and to her shame, she had proved to have no more self-control than Lady Mary. Even now her dazed brain was having trouble dealing with the evidence of her eyes.

Chloe entered her familiar bedroom, unfamiliar now with no welcoming fire or lamplight to greet her. There was just enough light to enable her to remove her outer clothing and ascertain that her hair should be brushed and repinned. She did not really need to see to perform these mechanical actions, and her sight turned inward again as she opened a drawer and took out an old hairbrush she had left behind.

What was Bertram doing here? She gave a shake of her head to clear it of extraneous material. The reason for his appearance after an absence of more than two years was not obscure. She was the woman he had asked to be his wife; naturally he would come to see her when he was in England. Her problem was that the events of her short stay at Applewood had banished Bertram to a dim shadowy past that she could recall only with the greatest difficulty. She had better apply herself to the task of recollection, however, because in a moment she must go downstairs and pretend not only that everything was normal but that she was thrilled and happy to see her betrothed after a long absence instead of shocked and guilt-ridden.

Mindful of her father's sapient eye, Chloe pinched her cheeks on the way down to stimulate some blood flow and entered the family parlor with a smile on her lips. "I hope I have not kept two hungry men waiting?"

"Not a bit, my dear," said Dr. Norris, holding up his glass. "We are enjoying another glass of Madeira and will enjoy our dinner all the more for your company."

Chloe smiled lovingly at her father, already experiencing a shrinking of the cold lump of misery deep in her being. She turned to the other man, her smile still intact. "Why did you not let me know you were coming home, Bertram? How long have you been here?"

"I arrived this afternoon, and your father has found my letter apprising you of my return. It came while you were both away. He did not send it on to the place you were visiting, he tells me, since he really expected you home before now."

"I was going to send Bertram off to Suffolk tomorrow to escort you home from Applewood," Dr. Norris interjected, "so it is fortunate you came when you did, my dear, or you might have passed each other en route."

Chloe barely repressed a shudder at the thought of Bertram arriving unheralded at Applewood in the middle of the present crisis there, perhaps to be told she had been sent away in disgrace. She murmured fervent agreement with her father's sentiments and was relieved that dinner was announced at that moment.

Chloe's relief was merely transient. The hour that followed was certainly one of the strangest and most unsettling of her life. There was about it the unreality of a dream where the essential self somehow stands apart from the person undergoing the dream experience, an observer as it were, though still a participant. Bertram, though essentially unchanged, his keen hazel eyes as alert and his weatherbeaten skin a trifle ruddier than she remembered, was yet unfamiliar to her tonight. Still quivering from the spiritual bruising that was the legacy of her stay at Applewood, she felt distant emotionally from this quiet dinner with the two most important persons in her life. She satisfied her hunger without tasting what she ate and participated minimally in a conversation that was primarily an exchange of recent experiences between Bertram and her father without assimilating what her ears took in. In response to polite queries she must have told them something about her time with the Keesons, but could never afterward recall the substance of her few remarks.

While the men talked easily, Chloe continued to watch Bertram. She remembered that habit he had of pulling in one corner of his mouth when he was considering a reply and the way his red-brown hair curled above his ears. Bertram was the same person he'd always been. Perhaps it was she who was the stranger.

The protective numbness in which she'd been enveloped

dissipated still further as she stared at the man she had happily promised to marry. In its place like choking smoke from a clogged chimney rose raw fear, instantly recognizable though she'd never experienced it before. She blinked rapidly and turned her panicky gaze on her father who came quickly to her rescue.

"I am going to suggest that you young people postpone your reunion until Chloe has had a night's rest after her difficult day," he said, smiling benevolently at them both. "We'll excuse you if you'd like to retire now, my child."

Chloe nearly jumped out of her chair, restraining her eagerness to escape with difficulty. "Yes, I find I am very tired tonight. Good night, Papa." She went to kiss her father good night, conscious that Bertram had risen also with the evident intention of opening the door for her. She forced herself to meet his gaze as she walked to the door, trying to stretch her stiff lips into the semblance of a smile. "Good night, Bertram."

As he opened the door he took her upper arm in his hand and bent to kiss her cheek. "Sleep well, Chloe."

Bertram's parting wish for her stood no chance of coming true. Chloe's mind and heart were much too troubled to permit the relaxation necessary to her tired body. Her bruised spirit had been granted no time to recover before she was confronted with the most important decision of her life.

Lacking evidence to the contrary, she must assume that Bertram was here to make plans for their marriage, and she did not know what to do for the best. If she listened only to her heart she would send him away. The one clear fact to emerge from the last hour was that her sentiments toward him had changed irrevocably. She was almost persuaded that she had stopped being in love with him before she met Ivor Keeson, but perhaps she would never have the comfort of knowing this was true.

It was insupportable to contemplate marrying one man while in love with another. Just a short time ago she had devoted much effort to convincing Lady Mary of this, being so convinced herself that the girl was wrong to marry Lord Thrale when she loved Tom Trainor. When faced with nearly the same situation herself she found it equally insupportable to break her pledged word. The vital difference in the two cases was that she had not been coerced into accepting Bertram's offer; she had done it willingly, even joyfully. It was bad enough that her love had not survived the test of time. Was she to discard honor too? Chloe tossed and turned for hours in a warring agony of self-disgust and yearning, falling at last into an exhausted sleep from which she arose less refreshed than ever in her life, her dilemma still unresolved.

Before leaving her room the next morning Chloe read Bertram's letter, which she found on her small writing desk. Apart from informing her of his expected arrival, it was just as impersonal in tone as his last few letters had been. It was a far cry from the outpouring one might expect from a literate man about to be reunited with the woman he loved. Chloe stared thoughtfully out the window, the letter in her hand, while she summoned up a picture of Bertram as he had appeared at dinner. He was as she remembered him, articulate, with the same quiet confidence that distinguished his bearing. She wished now she had not been too cowardly to meet his glance for more than an instant. In her guilty state she had not wanted to see the warm glow of love in his eyes, but would she have seen it? Bertram's manner were perfect, but how could this letter have been written by a man deeply in love with the recipient?

Chloe's heart was beating rapidly, but whether from trepidation or anticipation she'd have been loathe to decide. She tossed the letter into the desk and proceeded to wind her hair into its customary coil, confident suddenly that she would know what was the right thing to do once she and Bertram met face-to-face.

She was informed by the maid who waited on her at table that Dr. Norris had gone to see a patient after having breakfasted with his guest, and Captain Otley was taking a turn in the shrubbery. Chloe hurried through her breakfast and went out to join her betrothed.

He was leaning over the low wall that separated the kitchen garden from the shrubbery, staring into space, but he turned at her approach.

"Good morning, Bertram. I hope you slept well," she said with a smile.

"Yes, thank you, better than you, I should say." The keen

eyes searched her face, taking in the shadows under her eyes.

Chloe could feel the betraying color in her cheeks, but she met his look squarely, making her own survey. She saw no evasion in his eyes; neither did she see the warmth that had been there in the past.

"I am sorry it has been so long since our last meeting," he began.

A small smile curved Chloe's lips. "It did seem rather long."

His gaze became more intent, but she did not look away. "I could not refuse the chance to have my own ship. I hoped you'd understand."

"Of course not, and I did understand."

"Yes, well, I imagine you have guessed that I have come to make plans for our marriage . . . at last," he added with a whimsical smile.

Her steady gaze never wavered. "Is that what you wish to do, Bertram?"

His eyes flickered once; then he said, "Heavens, Chloe, we have been betrothed for five years. Do you not think it is about time we set a date?"

"That was not what I asked you."

"I shall be in England for a month this time. We can be married before I sail."

"You still haven't answered my question, Bertram. Is this what you wish to do?"

"I am perfectly willing to marry you tomorrow by special license if you prefer, so we might have more time together."

Chloe sighed. "I had not realized before quite what a disadvantage it is to be a gentleman in this kind of situation." Suddenly she flashed him a mischievous smile. "But rescue is at hand because I find I no longer wish to marry you either."

He took her shoulders in his hands and examined her upturned face. "Is that the truth, Chloe?"

"Yes. I am sorry that our feelings for each other didn't endure. They were real at one time, I think?" She searched his face in turn, her expression faintly sad.

He smiled. "Very real. I have never wanted to marry anyone else, Chloe, and that is the absolute truth, but the long separations make it difficult to sustain . . ." Words failed him here.

"Yes, it takes a greater love than we felt to survive the separations. I hope one day you will find such a love, Bertram."

"Chloe, I feel an utter cad to have wasted your youth like this," he groaned, looking so miserably guilty that she had to laugh.

"Not perhaps the most diplomatic of speeches," she teased.

He grinned at that. "When you smile like that you are so lovely it is a ridiculous speech also. Somehow I have no doubt that you, at least, will find a lasting love."

It was mid-afternoon when Dr. Norris returned to find his guest gone and his daughter sitting in the shrubbery staring into space. She started at his first words.

"Ah, here are you, my dear child."

"And where have you been all day?" she countered with up-raised brows.

"I thought you and Captain Otley needed privacy to settle your future," he replied, peering at her face, which was now carefully neutral. "Do I take it from his absence that the betrothal is at an end?"

"Yes, Papa. I hope you are not too upset?"

He gripped her shoulder briefly before seating himself beside her on the wooden bench. "My state of mind depends entirely on yours, Chloe. Are you unhappy over this breakup?"

"No, Papa, I promise you. It was entirely mutual."

Looking at his daughter's composed face, Dr. Norris read the truth in her eyes. He also glimpsed the deeper unhappiness in their depths. Her hands were clasping each other in her lap. He took them in his warm grip, noting their unusual coldness, and tugged gently until she was directly facing him.

"Now tell me what happened at Applewood that has made you so unhappy," he commanded.

As he rode back through the pine grove behind the manor, Lord Montrose was oppressed by an uncharacteristic lassitude, part physical, perhaps, but more likely the result of the

accumulated strains of the past few days. Even before last night's
debacle he had been concerned and uneasy about his sister's
imminent marriage after having observed the affianced couple
together since Thrale's arrival at Applewood. He was very
greatly at fault for not having invited Mary's confidence much
earlier. Had he not been so preoccupied with his own concerns
they could have avoided that calamitous scene at the party last
night. Always shy and quiet, Mary had been downpin ever since
coming home from London, and he should not have missed the
signs that she was unhappy. It was no justification for his
blindness that his mother had laid down a smoke screen to
conceal what she knew to be her daughter's dissatisfaction and
reluctance over her betrothal. Chloe had come among them as
a stranger and quickly discovered the truth. If only she had come
to him and hinted that Mary was not happy!

As his horse reached the grassy hilltop midway between the
two properties. Ivor pulled him to a stop and gazed unseeingly
out over the ever-moving sea, replaying in his mind the frenzied
hour that had followed Mary's desperate rebellion. His mother
had directed him to carry his sister into the library, which was
the closest room where they could escape from the hovering
guests. Mary was already reviving when he laid her on the
leather sofa, but he had resisted his parent's efforts to get him
to leave her daughter to her ministrations while he tried to scotch
the rumors spreading around the ballroom. Thank heavens that
he had been determined to learn the truth, or his mother might
possibly have been able to reassert the power she had wielded
over her cowed daughter for so long. Under his questioning
the whole story had come tumbling out of his hysterically
sobbing sister, though his mother had tried to stem the flow
by proposing to send the girl to her room and postpone until
the morning any discussion of the situation. His parent had not
conceded the ruin of her grandiose arrangements for her
daughter's future until Mary had confessed the attachment
between herself and Tom Trainor. The discovery that Chloe
had known about this affair had turned his mother rigid with
fury, which all Mary's prostestations of her friend's consistent
urging that she confide in her family had not served to mitigate.

The scowl that sat on the earl's face lifted somewhat as he

recalled how magnificently Patricia had risen to the occasion. She had come in while Mary was relating her tearful tale and had taken charge of her sister, whisking her away from her irate parent and conducting her to her room, where she put her to bed and stayed with her until she fell asleep. His mother had regained command of herself and had returned to the ballroom with him to face Lord Thrale and his enraged parent. He drew a veil across that vituperative scene in his memory, and the repetition of recriminations early this morning when he had helped Thrale tuck his hostile mother into their carriage as they left Applewood for good.

Ivor reluctantly turned his back on the sea and resumed his homeward trek. He had not met any member of his family this morning or Chloe. He had been so concerned with speeding the parting guests last night that he had brushed aside Tom Trainor's attempts to speak with him, promising to call at the manor first thing this morning. He had redeemed that promise as soon as the Thrales were off the premises. He had always liked the squire, and from everything he'd heard in the neighborhood his son was a promising young man. If Mary wanted him he had no objection, though he had warned Tom that there was to be no announcement of a betrothal until the spring at the earliest. The Trainors had been in complete agreement that the dust Mary had kicked up with her hysterics last night must be allowed to settle first.

As he approached the stables Ivor permitted himself the luxury of thinking about his own future. He was yearning for ten minutes of uninterrupted privacy with Chloe and determined that nothing and no one was going to prevent that from occurring this very day. Last night when he had looked for her after Mary's departure and the interview with the Thrales, Hawkins had informed him that Miss Norris had left the party and retired for the night. Their last few encounters had been productive of nothing save frustration. He had been ever mindful of his duties as host for what was supposed to be his sister's happy occasion, and Chloe had been obsessed (unhappily, he hoped) with her bethrothed status. It was imperative to clear the air between them before she left Applewood.

Five minutes later Ivor's inquiry to Hawkins as to Chloe's

present whereabouts produced the astounding intelligence that Miss Norris had departed an hour since.

Black brows snapped together. "Gone from Applewood?"

"The undercoachman took Miss Norris and her baggage away in the carriage, so I must assume that is the case, sir."

The cold mask slid down over the earl's countenance as his icy eyes examined the wooden-faced butler. "Who saw her off, Hawkins?" he asked in a dangerously soft voice.

"There was no one in the hall when Miss Norris left, sir."

"I see. Where is Lady Montrose?"

"Her ladyship has not yet come downstairs this morning, sir," replied Hawkins without expression.

Two minutes later Ivor was demanding entrance to his mother's apartment. He told the abigail who opened the door to go away until her mistress rang, and walked through the sitting room into his mother's beautiful bedchamber where she was seated in front of her mirrored dressing table. She glanced past him.

"Where is Marie?"

"I sent her away."

Ivor studied for a moment the still-lovely face of the woman who had borne him but could read nothing there. Her expression was one of polite inquiry. Her control was magnificent. He could only hope his own would be equal to this interview. Let this be the one thing in addition to the shape of his hands that he had inherited from her. "Why did you send Chloe away?" he began without preamble.

"I should think that must be obvious."

"I promise you it is not obvious to me. Enlighten me, please."

The countess resumed the careful application of rouge that her son's entrance had interrupted. "Would you have expected me to let her stay after Mary's disclosure last night? I keep no one under my roof who has betrayed my trust."

"Something Chloe did not do, but we'll let that pass for the moment while I remind you that this is no longer your house but mine."

There was the merest compression of her lips for a second before Lady Montrose said coolly, "Be that as it may, Miss

Norris was my guest and it was at my pleasure that she remained or left.''

"Do you really expect me to countenance cruelty to a guest in my house?''

"How dare you accuse me of cruelty!'' The countess put down the rouge pot and swept gracefully around on the bench to face him. "That girl came into this house for the sole purpose of assisting me, and instead she deliberately set about to undermine my authority, first with Emilie, then with Mary. She encouraged Ned to flirt with her and—''

"Everything you have just said,'' snapped the earl, interrupting his mother's catalog of Chloe's supposed crimes, "is a gross distortion of the truth, stemming from an irrational dislike of someone whose warm heart and generous spirit hold up a mirror to your cold unconcern for the true welfare of your children and grandchild.''

As the countess gasped out in shock at these unfilial accusations, Ivor clamped his teeth shut on any elaboration of his charges, saying in a milder tone, "I beg your pardon for voicing what it does not become me to say to my mother regardless of the essential truth. There is no point in continuing any discussion of Chloe Norris because we are unlikely to reconcile our conflicting views of her, but I had better warn you that I am going to make her my wife if she'll have me—''

"*Ivor, no!* That encroaching little nobody has bewitched you with her insinuating ways! You owe it to your father's name to select a wife from your own class, someone who—''

"Stop! You have said more than enough,'' Ivor declared, wearily running his fingers back through the hair at his temple. "I owe it to my father's memory not to repeat the mistake he made, and to my children's welfare to choose a mother who will love them. I will not ask you and Chloe to share a roof. You are welcome to the exclusive use of the London house. I will continue to pay the running expenses so your jointure can remain intact for your pleasures. I will be going to Cambridge-shire as soon as we get rid of this houseful of guests who came for a wedding that will not take place. Thrale and his mother left this morning,'' he added when her lips parted. He turned then and walked out of the room, giving her no opportunity to engage in argument or dissuasion.

It was three days before Lord Montrose could make good his pledge, and by that time he was surfeited with dispute and extraneous persons. His mother resumed her objections and arguments as soon as the last guest departed, and ended by resorting to tears and recriminations when she found all her children united against her in this instance.

When he had driven off this morning he had looked forward to a day of solitude in which to reflect and make plans. If only he could have been more assured of Chloe's favorable answer he would have thoroughly enjoyed the experience and the passing scene on a beautiful crisp autumn day. It was not that he doubted her feelings for him; her circumspect behavior not-withstanding, those beautiful eyes betrayed her in unguarded moments. What kept his nerves taut was the niggling fear that she would be guided solely by a sense of duty to the man to whom she had pledged her word so long ago. He did not even dare to contemplate how long it might take to establish contact with the peripatetic Captain Otley and secure her release once he had persuaded her to this course.

All things considered, the Earl of Montrose was not so sanguine about the outcome as a man hopes to be when approaching the lady he desires to make his wife. The servant who opened the door to him with the information that the doctor was visiting a patient smilingly ushered him into a small but lovely garden where Chloe was seated with her back to him. He dismissed the maid, saying he'd announce himself, and slowly walked toward the girl he loved, noting as he did so that she was setting an occasional stitch into some white material in her lap. As he feasted his eyes on a curling length of dark lash and an exquisite line of creamy cheek, his steps quickened and he kicked a piece of gravel in the path.

Chloe turned her head and stared. "*Ivor!*" One hand went to her throat and she jumped up from the bench with no thought to her sewing, which followed the law of gravity and slid to her feet.

As Ivor bent to pick it up his eyes lighted on the ringless fingers on her left hand and he tossed the fabric aside and seized her hand. Raising it to his lips, he kissed the ring finger deliberately, holding her gaze as he did so. "You have broken your engagement?"

"Yes," Chloe whispered. "Bertram was here when I arrived home. It was a mutual decision," she started to explain, but Ivor had heard all he needed to hear. The control he had expected to have to exercise was not required and he acted on simple desire, wrapping his arms tightly around her. He kissed her with relief and yearning, joyously aware of instant and total response from his beloved.

"My lovely girl," he breathed when that first kiss ended. "Will you marry me?"

He felt her stiffen and sudden dread made him lightheaded. He tightened his arms around her convulsively. "Chloe?" To his alarm he saw the great brown eyes film with tears. "What it is, my darling? Tell me!"

"Oh, Ivor, it's just that your mother dislikes me so much that I am afraid it might be a mistake to—"

"*Never!*" He silenced her with another kiss that drove all thought from her mind and melted her bones. Ivor chuckled gently as she sagged against him, relishing the heightened color in her cheeks and the confused mixture of pleasure and alarm in her eyes. He guided her down onto the bench and joined her, keeping her securely within one arm for a better arguing posture.

"We both know what my mother is, but I promise you she has no power to drive a wedge between us. She has lived her life the way she chose and must now allow her children the same free choice. The girls and Ned have made me the bearer of many loving messages for you, not to mention young Emilie, who is ecstatic at the idea of having you in the family permanently. My mother will make her home in London, which is the life she infinitely prefers. You may be sure she will present a contented face to the world about our marriage and Mary and Tom's. I believe you will find that you can rub along together well enough on the surface for those brief times when it will be necessary, and I know I can count on your good will."

"Yes, you can," she promised simply. Chloe had been studying his face during this earnest speech. She was immensely gratified that Ivor had known her well enough to be confident

that she would be able to release her grievance and do her part
in getting along with his difficult parent. She smiled at him
lovingly.

"I hope you don't want a long engagement," he began, and
then laughed outright at the horrified expression that crossed
her face. "That was a rather infelicitous choice of words, to
be sure," he agreed, hugging her to him exuberantly. "When
will you marry me?"

"Well, I do need some clothes if I am not to disgrace you
in the eyes of your family and friends."

"Anything but brown," he put in, eyeing her old dress with
disfavor, and was promptly pinched by his blushing fiancée.
"Though I fell in love with you in that dress," he offered in
an attempt at self-exculpation that she quite properly ignored.

"And I must find and train a housekeeper for my father—"

"If I am to have a housekeeper foisted on to me, then this
must be Lord Montrose," said an amused voice behind them.

The engrossed couple on the bench started, then rose to meet
Dr. Norris, who had nearly come up to them unnoticed.

"How do you do, sir?" said the earl with a rueful smile. "I'm
afraid it is not the most propitious beginning to our acquaintance
that the first words out of my mouth must be a request that you
give your greatest treasure into my keeping."

There was understanding in the doctor's dark eyes as he took
the measure of the man his daughter loved. There was nothing
to dislike in the earl's appearance and much to be grateful for
as he read intelligence and humor in the steady gaze that met
his forthrightly. With concealed relief he turned his eyes on
Chloe's glowing face, alight with love and confidence. Dr.
Norris gripped the hand extended to him and smiled at his
proposed son-in-law.

"Her mother and I have always placed a good deal of faith
in Chloe's good judgment," he allowed. "Welcome to the
family."